Endorsements

I can't wait to hear that your book is available and the details explaining how to purchase it. I plan to buy two, which I will bring to our next brunch, begging you to sign. I will keep one for me to read. You have so much wisdom and I can't wait to read more of it. The other, I'll keep as an investment. Then when you're rich and famous, with several books on the market, I can sell one first edition at market for a fortune. How's that for a plan? And, I'll still have my copy. Meanwhile, back at the ranch,

I'm so excited that your book is one step closer to being published. I can't wait to read it. You rock, Melba!

Paula Brenner

"I am the child of Boomers. All my life I held the delusional belief that life was easier for Boomers, because there was no global terrorism to fight, there were no complex life issues, everything was ideal. Melba has demonstrated to me that terrorism comes in all forms, even from those we are trying to work with. All life is complex and nothing is ideal. After reading 4/3 I wanted to apologize to my parents for being such a difficult child, and I can't honestly say I was any different in my youth than Melba was in hers. This book has been an eye opener. It is insightful, delightful, and an inspiration."

John W Partington

"I have always admired my mother's gift for being a memory keeper. She holds space for the experiences from which people learn and grow. Her ability to discover insight and wisdom within these many stories, voices, and experiences creates a remarkable Journey."

Lindsay S. McGee

"I'm glad to hear that Melba is ready to share her stories! Melba is not afraid to delve into her past and share stories with us that are heartwarming and relatable. Congratulations Melba for putting your treasured life stories in print."

Patricia E.

4
-
3

A Baby Boomer
Memoir

Melba McGee

BALBOA.
PRESS
A DIVISION OF HAY HOUSE

Balboa Press books may be ordered through booksellers or by contacting:

Balboa Press
A Division of Hay House
1663 Liberty Drive
Bloomington, IN 47403
www.balboapress.com
1 (877) 407-4847

Print information available on the last page.

ISBN: 978-1-5043-7381-4 (sc)
ISBN: 978-1-5043-7383-8 (hc)
ISBN: 978-1-5043-7382-1 (e)

Library of Congress Control Number: 2017901264

Balboa Press rev. date: 03/04/2017

Dedication

This book is dedicated to:

Melba,

who felt herself to be unheard and misunderstood; and who, though firmly established in her BabyBoomer time, was not connected to how that culture affected the way in which she saw herself and the way in which she reacted to everything around her. May she finally see that *She Is*, that *She is Good*, that *She is Enough*, that *She is Good Enough*.

All the Melbas,

who wanted to write, to find their voice, and to realize their dream.

My Amazing Family,

with whom I can share anything, who understand my idiosyncrasies, who ground me by holding my hand whenever I have spun off the earth, and who make me feel worthy.

Contents

An Invitation to Dance: Setting the Stage for Understanding this Book

Now There's a Story...

When trying to make sense of something, I thrash it about, I write about it, tell stories about my world, and share what I found out. The dialogue that ensues is so enlightening, is lightening the weight from heart and soul, is lighting my way forward, is righting my compass, and is filling my heart.

My friends and audiences say that they learn so much from my stories that I *must* write and share them so others can read and learn, too.

I have this idea for organizing my life's writings into a collection, with *Themes* from a lifetime of living, teaching, learning, helping, feeling, sparkling on command; of living a life in the culture of busy-ness and ADHD, cancer and wellness challenges; of being a *Workhorse; of* making sense of impossibilities; of being *Maiden* then *Mother* and then *Crone; of* being a bell-curved *BabyBoomer* forced to compete to stay within the top 10% of that bell curve; and finally, of living the *3rdThird*.

Living in the moment is a reminder about time and place; in this time and this place we live, we focus, and we make tomorrow's history. By living in the moment, we learn to make better time-and-place choices.

In the tradition of teaching through narrative, I offer you these stories.

Now There's Another Story.

See you in the dialogue,

WorkhorseMelba

Preamble

My brother and sister-in-law heard about my plans to formalize my writings beyond journal and blog, and they asked me what that was all about. Would it be a tell-all-secrets exposé about interactions with others in my life? Or a factual account of something? I answered back through an email message to them:

"Hi!

Yes, I did see an email from you earlier ... about my book ... about theme and tell-all potential.

I have reached a fork in my writing road: shall I continue to write for momentary satisfaction of getting it out of my head and onto paper, or publish beyond the blog?

I am putting together my stories to fit into the theme "*Thirds*". Have settled into the idea of life in *Thirds*; *1stThird* is about growing and learning; *2ndThird* about working, commitment, and keeping body and soul together; and *3rdThird* about retirement and reconnecting with self after career.

In the beginning, I put age numbers on the *Thirds*: 30, 60, 90. Then I decided that it is more about life style, commitment, and activity. Besides, when I beat the odds with cancer for the third time, I said

I would claim every second of the *3rdThird* ... and then invent the *4thThird*!

I now have a two inch thick collection of stories: some about children and young people; some about established adults; some about post menopausal and post workplace life. All are written in first person; all are inspired by bits and pieces that were experienced by me, or are flights of fancy arising from experiences of self or others, and all are a scramble depicting several of many inspirations. They sound biographical but they are fictional.

You have known me longer than anyone, and so you will surely recognize the kernel of inspiration for each story.

Writers write what they know, and they also use their imaginations to turn the mundane into a good story or lesson. The tag line on my blog is *'A Story Told is a Journey Enlightened*». I fancy myself telling stories that will commiserate; stories that will inspire; and stories that will grab attention taking people to similar circumstances in their own lives to revisit what was, what might have been, and what can still be.

So, it is not a tell-all about others, but is, rather, about a fictional, larger than life, freckled braided red-head, hyper, hair-on-fire, fancies-herself-smart (or perhaps she is too smart for her own good) main character whom the author has granted a do-over for some situations close to my own experiences, or to those of people close to me, or to people who passed close enough by my notice.

The decision to personify each story's main character by writing in the first person, by using the perspective of Melba, is meant to help readers to connect with Melba's experience and to enable readers to see themselves in just such an experience.

I may have just written the foreword for the book! So, now I move forward.

This project has been close to my heart ever since I first picked up a pencil and saw the 'majyk' come spilling out from its point, after I read *Emily of New Moon* by L. M. Montgomery about another little girl who dreamed of writing, and after hearing Mum's lifelong dreams about writing. Not all of those writing dreams were realized.

Now, I need to decide if I will make the publishing rounds, hat and manuscript in hand, with hopes of finding someone who thinks these flights of fancy might inspire or amuse others, with the hope that one will decide to publish and promote my work. Perhaps I will decide to self-publish beyond the blog.

I am researching possibilities, going back through my recent presentations at weekly Writing Group, speaking with published authors, and organizing my work into creditable sections, taking the Writer's Workshop from Hay House, and contacting publishers...

Thanks for asking ... this is what is in front of me now.
Thanks for being such a large part of my entire life.
(((Hugs)))"

Acknowledgements and Gratitudes

Thank you, *John W. Partington*.
My heart and mind are aquiver with excitement!
Tomorrow is the day. Someone I have trusted with my new-born is coming to visit tomorrow to give me some honest, post-inspection advice on my baby.

Have I...

- attended to every need?
- demonstrated the feelings I have for this baby?
- covered all the bases?
- given love on all fronts? All backs? All sides?
- been honest about what I'm doing?
- been true to this baby's potential?
- fed the baby with all the good and healthy things to help it grow appropriately and in its own right?
- understood and answered all questions that need to be addressed?
- considered how I can improve this baby's prospects for a healthy future?

How fortunate am I, a new author, to have found an editor who understands my baby, my writing, my need to maintain my own voice, my true intent's endeavour in writing this first book.

Thank you, John W Partington, for helping me to birth this baby, present it to the world in all its fullness, and for helping me to build a foundation that will allow this baby to grow to its fullest stature.

Thank you *Writing Family* for always being there for me even when I was AWOL.

These fellows are my Writing Family. They have welcomed me, listened to my first hesitant steps, and tolerated my arrival with a very rough copy spun together in inadequate time because I was working on blog or book. Still they encouraged me, shared our determinations to hold the pen and to see what majyk falls out of the tip. ("Majyk" is a gift from Spirit; "magic" is a clever trick that fools us into seeing what is not there.)

This is where this project was born and these people are my midwives.

Thank you, *Lindsay S McGee* for always being my sounding board, my staunch supporter, my one who reaches out to take my hand when Darkness befalls me, and who tells me when I need to rethink something. In this time, thank you for bringing that support to editing this labour of love, and to my voice.

With Gratitude.
Blessed be,

MelbaMcGee

Introduction - The Thirds of my Life

I find myself in this *3rdThird* of my life, and as is my way, I need to make sense of it, to study it, to plan it, to embrace it, and to be able to make the most of it.

I have seen other people who did not thrive in the *3rdThird*.

At some point in this next *Third*, I shall satisfy the biological imperative of dying, but not yet. First, I shall satisfy my personal imperative of living a fulfilling life every day of any *Third*.

My father spoke of the three phases of life in this way:

Our life is similar to the life of a tree.

The *1stThird* is about taking root, sprouting branches and

leaves, growing a supportive trunk, thriving, learning, and finally producing seeds;

The *2ndThird* is about working, fulfilling our purpose, committing to our family, making a living to support ourselves, and being the best branches that we can be to support family, and job, and all;

The *3rdThird* is described as the pruning years. Here, we are no longer valued as a family provider, or as a capable worker. We are devalued, pushed aside to make room for "more deserving", "more needy", or "younger" people. We prune away our lifelong affirmations, our teeth, our strength, our memory, our worth, our health, our independence, and our capacities. Then we wait to die.

This description had a profound effect on me. It was easily recognizable as all too true, but it was also depressing. It was an example of limiting and self-destructive thinking to prepare for death. I then decided to take a look at all three *Thirds* of my life, so that my *3rdThird* can be as exciting, as fulfilling, as successful, and as affirming as the other two.

It is, again, up to me to be determined to be happy, satisfied, successful, generous, and compassionate. And so, into the fray, my lovely, lovable, loving Melba.

Prologue - Route

A novel arena is prominently present in my life, and I'm finding myself conscious of where I am, which begs my attention to where I have been and where I am going with this ... (thinking) ...

My path has brought me to this place and I must review my route with an eye to gratitude for bringing me to such a world of wondrous possibilities.

In my *1stThird*, I had a connection with another spiritual place, with things no one else could see with their eyes, with things that I quit mentioning because I would receive admonishments not to say these comments again (because unfavourable judgement surely awaited me there, and uncertainty breeds contempt and distrust for anyone who opened the door that led away from the tried and true route, and led towards a path that only crazy people think that they can see).

My Mum used to have the ladies over for afternoon tea. Together we would host these occasions, spend the morning cleaning and then baking, greeting and welcoming the ladies in through the front door, inviting them to divest themselves of their coat (but never hat) and join us in the living room (never the family TV room!).

My first time, participating by actually hosting a tea-time event, was when I was, perhaps, 7. I had watched, listened, and learned from Mum; as usual I did not need any special invitation to jump right in. When the first lady arrived, I greeted her by name and invited her to allow me to hang up her coat. While waiting for her coat, I said to her (in my most ladylike hostess tones) that I admired her sparkly blues. The lady and my mother both looked askance at me, and Mum reminded me that Mrs. L's dress was most definitely brown.

Both women shared a glance that said, "Poor dolt of a child doesn't know her colours yet, even at 7 years of age!" I was a little put out that they refused to see the jewel-tone blue sparklies, each spinning on its own axis, all about this beautiful lady.

Next to arrive was Mrs. P. In a state of deja-vu, I did the coat-offer thing, and this time I asked my Mum why there was so much muddy brown sticking around Mrs. P. Mum stepped in and took over the welcoming tasks, and then asked me to "help her in the kitchen" using the tone that promised that the "help" was going to consist of a one-sided conversation, and that I probably wasn't going to be on that one side.

"What is wrong with you?! Mrs. P's coat is grey and her dress is blue. All right young lady, what are you up to?"

"Mum, Mrs. P is surrounded with muddy brown goo that is clinging to the air around her. And Mrs. L most definitely had blue

xx

sparklies spinning all around her. Why can't you see that? Are you sure you are even trying?"

"Oh my Dolly Dear, you must never mention this to anyone else but me, ever again. No one will ever believe that you can really see these things. And if you persist, then all will shun you from the social group. They will think that I told you about Mrs. L's new baby arriving next spring and about Mrs. P's devastating diagnosis when the rule at any social gathering is that no conversation ever escapes the room!"

From that point, I was completely quiet, for if I couldn't talk about what I clearly saw, then I probably shouldn't talk about what my brothers and I had been up to yesterday while playing in the park and building a fort on public property to match the one on our own private back lot using the rest of Dad's lumber stores. And I better not ask for a definition for a word that I had never heard before, but that an older boy had used on the school yard last week which made everyone gasp. And so talking about how the colours would shoot out, in all directions, from head and mouth around the minister or the teacher while they were giving the lesson was likely out of the question, too. They likely did not want a report of what the dog threw up on the back door mat after digging up and eating an old kill that he had brought home last week and left to ripen in the summer sun.

For many years, I only thought about the lights and colours while I was dancing at ballet, or playing classical music on the piano, or trying some new death-defying flip I had just learned at gymnastics. I had a teacher who tore up a piece of artwork on which I had included the colours and lights as part of my artistic interpretation and expression, so clearly art was only about drawing what everyone could see.

The colours were never mentioned again in my *1stThird*.

In my *2ndThird*, I would suddenly realize an insight about someone else, a family member, a child in my class, a friend, or a colleague. It would begin as a light or a colour and I would jump to a conclusion about what the other person was feeling that later proved right, more often than not. This ability helped me to understand that there were many occasions when someone else could not put thoughts or feelings to words, but the floodgates would open when I found a private moment to ask them how they were doing with … something. At some point in the conversation, they would give me a look that said, "Can you really read my mind all the time?"

But no, my earliest experience taught me that it was intrusive of me to go looking into the colours and lights of others. To the point where I would shield myself from consciously noticing. To the point where I would avoid and even think that I had destroyed the ability altogether.

Late in my *2ndThird*, I was having a conversation with my Indigo-Child. She had been doing some research and having some discussion about something called Reiki. Reiki is an Energy Work practice, that works with energies that are similar to lights, colours, tones, and sounds. One can attend seminars, right here in our town, and can take lessons and practice to learn how to 'give Reiki' on command.

We decided that she should start this journey first, and that I would join her after she had completed her first two levels of training. We would both complete our third or Master training together.

At our Reiki classes, demonstrations, and discussions, we would share our experiences around anything to do with Energy Work. So many years after my initial decision to avoid the energies that are within and that surround, I had finally come home to my comfortable place in the Reiki world of energy, colour, tones, sounds, and tingles. I would never again be shunned, would never again be heaped with admonishments and judgements, and would never again feel like there was something wrong with me. And there were more like me.

Yes, my path has brought me home!

My *3rdThird* path has, again, brought me to Reiki as a forefront in my focus. We are making plans to create a ReikiCommunity.

We are renewing and energizing our natural talents and opening our arms to embrace others who are ready to join us.

Welcome Home!

This Book, called *4/3*, is a collection of stories from the *Thirds* showing how the understandings from each *Third* affect, encourage, and limit us in the present moment. Perhaps my stories and lessons will lead you to inner understandings about your own path.

A Story Told is a Journey Enlightened.

Forward ... 57 and Stuck

57 years old ... (thinking) ... And here I sit, still at my desk, munching away at reducing the piles of work, papers to grade, daybook to be filled in, and lesson plans to prep so that the students may realize an enthusiasm for both concepts and lessons.

The buses collected the students two and a half hours ago; I have been teaching in some form for forty-five years, and professionally teaching grades 7 and 8 for thirty-five years. Yet, here I sit, ground to a halt, with no idea why I am so stuck. After all my enthusiasm, ideas, and encouragement in my work, after all the positive feedback from students, from their parents, and from colleagues, why am I just sitting here night after night?

And I consider the "R" word: Retirement!

The pull at home is great indeed and in this time there must be no deference elsewhere.

I have seen too many people who retired badly.

So I meditated on how to retire *TO* something rather than only retiring *FROM* something.

I found myself revisiting the *Thirds* of a tree's life philosophy. When we leave the *1stThird*, we use the experience and skills to move into the *2ndThird* with its unique needs and activity and demands and with excitement about moving forward.

I realized that this consideration and understanding are the essential core of the challenge of moving into the next *Third*!

We move forward to something ... and create an excitement about our life.

We do not move away from something ... because that would keep us stuck in a fearsome past.

Always.

The answer lies in embracing what we want to do, achieve, and succeed in the *3rdThird*. As with all things, it is all in the attitude, the direction, the effort, and the gratitude!

Despite all the head shaking that the medical community has done each time I fell so ill, I am insisting on claiming every second, minute, hour, year, and chuckling laugh of my *3rdThird*.

After that, I will invent the *4thThird*!

With gratitude, with happy-ness, with energy and enthusiasm, and with an attitude of sharing, may your journey be enlightened.

Welcome to the Narrative: Invitation to the Reader

This narrative will give you the opportunity to walk alongside Melba, who is a conglomerate of many BabyBoomers, as she grows, learns, experiences, concludes, and then *JUST IS*.

Perhaps, you will recognize your own life in some of these words, and you will be led, finally, to some conclusions of your own, in your own narrative.

1stThird - **Dancing and Sparkling**

Introduction: Meeting the Players; Learning the Skills

In this *1stThird*, Melba learns the skills and meets the players. Both will drive her roots deep into the ground, and will feed and nurture her throughout her life.

The *1stThird* is about growing, learning, and setting ourselves up.

In my father's discussion about our life as similar to the life of a tree, he described the *1stThird* as all about taking root, sprouting, growing, thriving, and learning.

In the Pagan and Wiccan consideration, the *1stThird* is refered to as *Life-as-Maiden*.

Labels were placed on me, and I wore and even sported those hats, every one of them. I was stepping up and stepping out ...

Born 1950, Deep River, Ontario

Being conceived and born in Deep River in 1950 meant that my father worked at Chalk River Atomic Energy. So, yes, my brother and I were the two glow-in-the-dark babies of the family.

The whole neighbourhood was populated with smart, curious kids born of clever, organized parents. We were independent and capable. We quickly organized ourselves into an activity without any politics-of-organization interferences. We got into things, like the teen who biked to the firing range and found a 'spent' tank shell and brought it home to the basement workshop with the intent to saw it open to take a look inside. His mother was in the tub; she was saved by riding the blast safely cupped inside that cast iron tub which landed in someone else's yard. No sign of son, shell, workshop, or house, though.

I always watched for Dad to get off the work bus at the end of the day, and then would run and jump into his arms to be carried into the house. Sometimes, Dad would come home from work wearing an orange jumpsuit and paper shoes. "Daddy, where are your clothes?"

"They are in a hole, deep deep under ground."

"Mummy is not going to like this!"

Hurricane Hazel was doing her best to blow us all down and over and under. As a four year old, I was fascinated by giant pine trees whipping and bending like blades of grass before the wind. Any toys and furniture left outside were pushed to and fro then up to crash down again. While I was aware of my parents herding our family to the below-ground safety of the basement, I was more interested in the exciting show beyond the front screen door while I stood between screen and inside doors.

"Where is Melba? Has anyone seen Melba?" Mum's frantic cries came into my head but did not outdo the the howls of the wind and the crashing outside.

My oldest brother was helping the efforts to secure family and property. "Who left this door open? Mum, I found Melba!"

I was scooped up amidst my protests about missing the show, and carried to the basement, after the heavy front door was closed and locked.

I remember the basement was creepy, cramped, and smelled of fresh cement and dark. I heard thuds and clunks from outside.

We emerged after the storm. We had some cleanup, but damage was not devastating. For a week, we worked together to right our home and property.

For me, making sense of the world and its happenings began

while living in a planned community environment in the middle of nowhere. This was a place where residents were told where they could live according to their pay grade and work assignment but without choice; where lived residents who were imbued with a love and appreciation for reason, curiosity, vocabulary, memory, calm, independence, and joyful mirth.

Learning to Sparkle on Command

My *1stThird* was about learning, and the part that was most useful was learning to Sparkle on Command.

Mum used to say to me, "Find out what the teacher / leader / boss wants and then give it to them! And give it to them with a smile and a cheerful demeanour."

"But what if I cannot do it, or if I do it wrong?"

"All the more reason to be of good cheer, at least!"

Where did the Light Go?

Another school day. My favourite green sweater is clean and I love wearing it. Next is going through my todo list, dutifully checking my backpack and then putting it by the door. Next is breakfast in the dining room, cereal, milk, fruit. My older sister is getting ready, too. My baby sister is making her usual demands for attention heard. Mummy and Daddy are up, and are preparing for their day. Everyone is busy and engaged in their own morning's demands.

I trudge to the bus stop. The hour-long bus ride to school is tedious but also fearsome, for that is where I have been punched and bitten and called bad names before. I sit quietly because I have been suspended in the past for fighting, yelling, punching, and biting. The school claims a zero-tolerance for fighting rule. When I try to tell what the others did at school, I become louder and louder in my insistence to tell and be heard in a class of thirty students, but I am told that I am "Too loud" and to "Be quiet!!"

I have tried to be friendly and engage with the other students, but I continue to be treated badly, hit, and called PoopieFace. They seem to be ganged up against me! Still, I persist in people-pleasing, hoping that making friends is the key.

The school staff has so vilified me that, when a supply teacher is coming in, the school principal calls my parents and asks that my parents keep me home because the supply teacher will not be able to handle me. My reputation at the school is set: I am trouble.

The school day is long for me. It is not uncommon for students to be sent to timeout for speaking out of turn or incorrectly. The lessons, and conversation are all in this new school language.

Over the course of time, my behaviour has strayed from my typically lively, happy and spritely engagement to angry, verbally aggressive, loud, unruly, physically aggressive, and refusing to join in. Everyone says it is because I am, for the first time, an older sibling of a new baby and I must learn my place. And that place is behind everyone else!

Today, things take a new and dark turn. I return my lunch kit to the cloakroom, part of the expected routine, and turn to find the mean boy from the older grade in the split-grade class. He confronts me, calls me PoopieFace and other words I don't know, has his hands inside my underwear, has his fingers inside me. I break free and return to the classroom but do not see the teacher and do not confide in the lunch monitor, because I have no words to describe what happened. But, I am proud of the fact that I did not fight, did not yell, and did not leave the classroom without permission. I followed all the rules!

Everyone is dismissed to go outside for a break: "No talking; just hurry up!"

When I finally tell my teacher ... nothing happens.

The boy is looking at me, pointing at me, while he whispers to other kids who then look at me and I can see they still believe that I am the bad one.

The afternoon drags by, and I am completely unable to focus, to participate, to understand what has just happened to me, to grasp what is happening when the boy points at me and calls me dirty names, and gets the other students to do the same.

The teacher admonishes me to, "Pay attention!"

Finally, I am on the hour-long bus ride home with the other kids, and I am starting to actually feel like a PoopieFace. I just want to go someplace by myself and hide. When I get home, Mummy does the daily check of schoolbag contents: lunch-kit to kitchen, coat and mitts hung up to dry for tomorrow, and papers handed over. There is a letter from the school, a short note saying what I had reported to the teacher this afternoon.

Daddy is called home from work. Mummy and Daddy talk with me, asking for details like when, where, who and what, and has this boy done anything else to me before today.

Mummy and Daddy show up at school next morning, without me.

An extra teacher is assigned to all-day every-day supervise the boy.

I "may" be removed to another school in the same school board at Mummy and Daddy's request, so I can still learn this curriculum, but the school says there will be no transportation provided for me to the new school.

I have to face the boy every day in class, remember the dark, nameless, and painful thing that was done to me, remember the names that I was called, and remember the year-long taunting which had been on-going even before the cloakroom incident.

It is just best if I go completely silent, rather than risk more bad treatment because of my previously energetic and spritely self of last year.

I am working every day at being a people pleaser, trying to please everyone all the time.

This is a hard job for me, while at the same time trying to get all my Junior Kindergarten work completed.

The special light in my world has gone out and I cannot find the switch to turn it back on.

Leaving

Melba from another time

"Please, Mother! Don't leave!" My five year old eyes are brimming with tears as I beseech Mother, tugging at Mother's hands, pulling them away from hatpin and boot buttons. "I'll behave! The others won't but I will!"

"No Melba, you children are so bad! I'm putting on my hat and coat and leaving!" With that, Mother jammed her hat down on her head, and jabbed in her hatpin with great emphasis. She reached for the doorknob.

"No! Please! Please, Mother! I'll be good, so good I'll be good enough for us all so you won't have to leave!"

Something about my sobbing pleas caused Mother to pause, to take a long slow breath, to turn, to remove hatpin then hat then coat, straighten her clothes and go to the kitchen where she rolled up her sleeves, donned her apron, and began the bustle of dinner preparations while the baby slept cozily in the warmth by the wood stove.

I crumpled, crawled into a corner behind Father's chair in the parlour, curled into a ball with Cat and cried myself to sleep, sobs giving way to hiccoughs, giving way to the soft shallow breaths of a young child's exhausted sleep.

From above stairs came the giggling laughter and boisterous noise of my three older siblings at play, completely unaware of the disaster narrowly averted downstairs by the door.

Mother, the Minister's wife, was caring for the families of the church during the great flu epidemic in 1918. Mere days after my pleas to keep Mother from walking out on them all, Mother was weakened by her sixth pregnancy and she died in that flu epidemic along with her unborn child. No amount of pleading from me could keep Mother from going out the door that last time.

The next week, we siblings were sent to live with different

relatives' families, spread across a thousand miles of Canada's towns and villages.

Melba went to live with an aunt, aged 65, and an uncle, aged 85, who taught her about doing what she was told.

Stealing

Sometimes stealing is ok, apparently!

Stealing home in the neighbourhood game of baseball is cheer-worthy.

Stealing an idea is fine because only a baby would complain; they are just words aren't they? No one can own words!

But then ...

I just have to have it. All the others have one, so why can't I?

I'm a good girl. I help out. At school, I work hard and achieve top marks (not THE top marks - that kind of achievement lines a kid up for extra-special attention from classmates and teachers and siblings).

I have dreams and wants and needs!

My allowance just does not give me everything I want. I have to make hard choices:

- to go to the movies with my friends or an after-lunch stop off at the candy store on my way back to school with the rest of the walk-along gang;
- to buy a hula hoop (*all* the other girls have a hula hoop, except me);
- to buy a new record for my record player only to find out at the checkout that it is $0.25 more than the others (because it is Elvis!) so I need to return it to the place where I found it or hand over another $0.25. I endure the walk of poverty-shame back to the shelf while the clerk tsk-tsk-tsk for the whole store to hear;

- to buy a scarf (all the girls are wearing scarves but I don't have one);
- to buy candy (I want more and more-more-more candy so if I cannot buy some at the candy store, and if putting molasses on the bread I am allowed between meals doesn't suffice, then I will just take Mum's guests-only sugar cubes each time that I pass by, or I will steal a whole jar of maraschino cherries, then eat all the cherries and then drink all the juice in one sitting so I can hide the evidence at the bottom of the garbage can)...

I begin to take more than my share, usually sweets.

These hard choices do not teach me the concept of reality or of making choices so one should make good ones. They teach me to steal. Sugar from the kitchen. Food from the carefully organized-according-to-our-budget grocery cupboard. Charging a candy bar whenever I am sent to the store to pick up a forgotten item. Today, I am entering the house after lifting a comic book from the drug store. Eagle Eye Mum notices and marches me right downtown to return it to the store owner so I could tell him I was sorry in front of everyone in the store who was listening, and I am forced to pay for it without being allowed to bring it home, and I have to promise I will not come back into his store for a month. Finally, I have to work off my debt to Mum who paid for the comic book herself.

Mum explains to me that by saving pennies every day, we get to go on our camping trips every year. We get to have enough food to eat at every meal, even between-meal snacks of peanut butter and molasses sandwiches. We have warm clothes in winter, attend Brownies and piano lessons...

Though all good points, I often hunger to make the choices for myself.

The Snake and the Rock (or, bringing up little brothers)

My appreciation for my younger brother was learned the hard way.

Youngest brother was the last of the clan, the last of the Juhs. Mum named all her sons with names that began with the "juh" sound: Jake, Jackson, Jeremy. In moments of great trial, of great challenge, of great emotion, Mum would simply say, "Juh ... Juh ... Juh ..." until she reached the one she wanted and the lesson would begin for the specified Juh. After all, we each had our own whistle blast so that Mum wouldn't have to shout our name through the neighbourhood as did the other mothers; we only responded to our own whistle series, and we only responded to our own name.

YoungerJuh and I are the babies together (though we had not quite the same three-ish years separating as did all of us siblings), sharing tub time, play time, story time. When it became obvious to me that he was riding on my coattails, I began the growing up process of declaring my elder-ness and independence from my shadow. No matter how he bangs on the locked door of tub-time, he will be given no entry; and this pretty much becomes our new normal.

I feel free-at-last; he feels rejected, and then he becomes a pest.

I remember an experience when I helped YoungerJuh through something awful.

Mum was having one of her summer tea parties in the living room and we were all dismissed from the house to play ball on the backlot diamond. "The boys must go to the bathroom outside; only Melba may silently enter the back door of the house and use the back stairs to tiptoe to the bathroom upstairs," Mum warned.

Playing ball is a passion of ours, with neighbourhood teams set up lending balance to the game. When the other kids see us come outside with mitts and ball and bat, they all come tumbling and whooping to the game. YoungerJuh has determined that he would like to catch. No protective gear in the 1950s; one was responsible for keeping their eye on their own safety, and everyone was on the line for playing fair and reasonably.

Up steps a strong, rough and tumble friend; when he had his hands on the bat, we all move out further into the field. His style is to hold bat up, swing back then forward with mighty force, which is what earns him the nickname 'Slugger'.

Only this time, Slugger's backswing nailed YoungerJuh right on the eyebrow with a brow-mashing, blood spurting thunk.

And YoungerJuh begins to bleed and then to howl, like he is mortally wounded! There certainly was enough blood to indicate the possibility of potential death, and the thunk was loud enough to give the actual indication of death, but really! We shush him, pick him up, and notice that one family-heirloom-gigantic-eyebrow is mashed across his forehead from hairline to eye socket, that blood dripping from his chin is coagulating in inch-long spikes. OlderJuh is for-certain worried that this incident would somehow be his fault and we should clean him up at the outside tap.

I was worried that if we don't get YoungerJuh into the house for mop-up and clean clothes, he will die before we can see if it is worth interrupting Mum's ladies' tea.

I start dragging YoungerJuh through the hedge when OlderJuh catches up and lends his assistance and greater strength. YoungerJuh is still blubbering and howling which I take to be a good sign that life is still contained in his skull. OlderJuh tells him to pipe down or he'll stuff his sock into his mouth.

I open the back door and stealthily scope out the occupation and lay of the land. No one in sight. We lay YoungerJuh out on the TV room couch which is, blessedly, the same colour as blood.

Suddenly, one of the ladies comes out to the adjoining kitchen to boil water for more tea and, having four boys of her own, recognizes the sounds of kids who need adult attention. She takes one look, and then starts shrieking for Mum who arrives with all the ladies posse-ed behind her. We are in trouble now!

Ladies queue up, forming a wet cloth brigade. Mum goes into raising too-smart-for-their-own-good kids mode, and falls into the rhythm of delegation, cleanup, and assessment. It is decided that stitches would do no good on a mash wound, and that letting the air at the wound would allow for quicker clotting and scabbing. The meagre supply of ice cubes in our 1950s fridge is dumped into one of the re-cleaned cleanup cloths, and YoungerJuh will remain under ice on the couch watching TV while OlderJuh and I go outside to send home the ball teams, and then just live with what happened on our watch until the ladies left. Gulp!

Mum wanted each and all of us to learn and demonstrate a commitment to a helping-hand-regard for each other.

My turn comes to start school and next OlderJuh keeps me in his sights on the mile-long hike, along town streets, through the huge park in the middle of town, across the creek swollen with spring and storm runoff, and trailing across town with neighbourhood kids (some of whom are trailing more than are the frontrunners who are after first pick on the monkey bars). Mum has told me that OlderJuh will keep me in his sights, just in case I need him, though I never remember a time when he was actually in plain sight, or hailing distance, or needed.

Yet, the assured knowledge that he is vigilant gives me great confidence.

After aforementioned wranglings over my independence, when YoungerJuh began school, it becomes my turn to offer that same confidence through vigilance, and safety in the form of someone to be there to watch over the trek to school, just in case.

YoungerJuh has taken to creeping into my room, with the intention of finding my diary no matter my efforts to secret it away from his prying eyes and big mouth ways. He waits until our parents are out of earshot, and then he quotes from my text, taking such inventive liberties which just make me sound bad, because it lacks the original intent of sharing private thoughts with my best magical friend, my keeper of ideas and outpourings.

This sets the stage for our walks to school 'together'.

YoungerJuh walks close to me and my neighbourhood age-group friends. He jeers and he speaks misquotes from my secrets making me and my friendships look bad, and he taunts me with his jabs and stabs between my shoulder blades.

Since our whole family lives with the idea that we are an inner circle together within the larger circles of our lives outside the clan (we move together, we help and support each other, and we seek help on each other's behalf) I am surprised and confused by this personal and public attack from YoungerJuh.

My jeering and maligning YoungerJuh is becoming too much for me to bear. We are walking through the long grass of a park that was never mowed. And there in the grass is a garter snake perhaps two feet long. I snatch it up and tie it around YoungerJuh's neck just so he can see that I mean business: no more trying to humiliate me out of any chance of a relaxed friendship with the other neighbourhood kids.

His howling rivals those of the eyebrow-mashing event. I leave him to untie the wriggling snake from around his own neck just to let him see the error of his ways and how his treatment makes me feel.

A sense of guilt makes me look back to ensure that he has successfully divested himself of snake and, indeed, I see him taking his great emotion out on said snake by whipping its head against the rocks. OK, he's relatively unscathed, now we'll see if he finally learned his lesson and will be more gentle with me in future.

YoungerJuh becomes quieter after that, walking in sight distance but no more taunting and jeering.

I fully come to appreciate him on the day of the rock.

Some older boy is picking up peach-sized stones and trying to see how far he can throw them into the air. Rocks, they go up nice and high, and then they come down ... Right onto

YoungerJuh's head. Another delivery of blood-clotted-on-chin though this-time-eerily-silent YoungerJuh unto the ministrations of Mum ... and then a run to school before I am late.

The Alice Effect

Stories are magical. Every story, large or small, transports me to another new place.

We live in a house where story time was as routine as mealtime, where we are surrounded by our own library of books on bookshelves on all walls in every room which become the insulation needed to keep out winter drafts and summer heat. The public library is one of the first places we visit after moving to each town. Thereafter, entering the embrace of the library is at least a weekly routine. Once inside the doors of that kingdom, the scent of old wood emanated from the generations-old stone town-hall, wafting and permeating every-pore every-corner, and the vision of colourful book jackets and so many shelves (some sagging under all that paper-weight), all those characters, and stories, and details beckon to me to simply open the cover and begin the adventure.

An early journey into a story has stayed with me since first resonating deep inside me. This story is read to me from The Junior Classics set residing in our home library, a go-to source whenever someone has time to read to this little girl who is working hard at learning to read so she doesn't have to wait on someone else's schedule. *Alice in Wonderland*, by Lewis Carroll, entices me into its magic from the first words.

> "*Alice was beginning to get very tired of sitting by her sister on the bank, and of having nothing to do; once or twice she had peeped into the book her sister was reading, but it had no pictures or conversations in it, 'and what is the use of a book,' thought Alice, 'without pictures or conversations?'*"

After white rabbit, fall-downs, puddling tears, and shelves, the next part lightning-bolts straight into my very core, ringing a bell deep inside me.

> "It'll be no use their putting their heads down and saying, "Come up again, dear!"
>
> I shall only look and say, "Who am I, then? Tell me that first, and then, if I like being that person, I'll come up; if not then I'll stay down here till I'm somebody else - but, oh dear!" cried Alice, with a sudden burst of tears, "I do wish they would put their heads down! I am so very tired of being all alone here!"

I am transported to every conversation, every experience, every feeling in my fulsome 2200 days. Some of these are happy and satisfying, and some are not.

And I realize the richness of this nugget for directing social interaction:

I have a choice!

The Librarian

Our small town library is named after our librarian. She is at least a thousand years old, wears rimless glasses and straight skirt with blouse and jacket. Her shoes have leather soles which means her travel across and within the library is silent. Her face is frozen in a permanently pinched and dour expression.

Thinking to entice young readers, she begins a book challenge. It is my first summer in town. She has made a list of eight books, one for each summer holiday week, each of which has a question the answer to which will be found while reading the book. Because I adore reading, I gobble up the challenge and the books and fill in each answer which shines out like a beacon from the page of the story, and I finish the entire challenge in two weeks.

Miss Jones is astounded, telling me that I couldn't possibly have read all those books, let alone found the answers, in a mere two weeks. I manage to crumple out that my library card shows that I have signed out each one of those books in the last two weeks. "Liar!" she rejoins for all to hear in the silent rooms and recesses of the library.

Completely devastated, I drag my red-cheeked and tear-stained self and my empty book bag home. Mum sees me come in the door uncharacteristically early on library day, after shortly before dancing out to the library full of bright shining joy and expectation.

Mum asks me how I got along at the library. "Fine...sigh..." I reply.

She notices that I never go to the library every day, or ever for a couple of weeks. She demands, "OK, what is up?"

I am hurt, and only said that I am on vacation from the library.

Mum is not easily fooled; she sets down her summer studies, puts on some earrings and lipstick, and walks to the library. She comes home and says that Miss Jones might be looking to speak with me. I resist going because I have suffered undeserved public humiliation for the first and last time. I simply ask Mum when we are going to move again.

Mum takes me by the hand, and we walk past the ice cream stand where we never went because ice cream for six people is just not in our budget, and arrive at the library. The dozen or so steps into the library seem to be longer and higher than ever before and yet not far enough to keep me from ever arriving at the library door, the scene of my unwarranted denouncement.

Mum prods me to the desk where Miss Jones keeps us waiting in plain sight for five whole minutes. Mum coughs gently, to which Miss Jones replies, "Oh, Mrs. McGee, I did not see you there." Fake smile. Brisk trot to the desk. "Melba, where did you ever get the idea that you would not come to the library any more?"

"Nowhere." Nudge from Mum. "I knew that you were angry with me," little voice.

"No such a thing!" Back-watering in an adult is a thing to behold. "Now what books would you like to sign out today? I have some new ones just pocketed and stamped and catalogued right over here. And I have a new library challenge for you," she says with what appears to me to be an evil glint in her eye.

We stop for an ice-cream cone on the way home: maple walnut, Mum's favourite, which becomes the taste of love and support and fair-won victory in my world with Mum.

I meet and win that new book-challenge ten days later (of course I am expected to not only answer the assigned questions, but, just for me, she asks ten extra questions for each book; Mum makes sure that she is always standing at my side). I begin a collection of my book prizes on a wooden shelf that I built for myself, with Dad, in the workshop.

Took Three in the Back

OlderJuh has saved up his paper route money and has bought himself a BB gun.

This is not an unusual achievement in that time of 1950s small town eastern Ontario / western Quebec.

We have done the Cowboys and Indians thing with cap pistols and gun belt as young kids, having assiduously been taught never to point the gun at another actual person, always to look after the equipment by cleaning and storing away in our own room, that in real life shooting things meant death and blood and gore and loss of life and, as well, meant food realized for family.

Now this BB gun takes us into the next stage: shooting at a target where we can check to determine our marksmanship, whether skilled or dud.

Having used up all his paper targets, the decision is made to dress someone up in one of our heavy raincoats and sou'westers of rubberized canvas. The original idea is to dress me up, but I refuse.

Then 4 year old YoungerJuh comes on the scene, wanting to participate, so OlderJuh dresses him up and instructs him to only look straight ahead (to protect his eyes and ears), to wait till he is told to jump, then jump across the doorway fast enough so as to serve as an excellent target, instead of an easy target which would be no test of skill! OlderJuh lies on the floor, shooting out the doorway so there is no damage done inside the house. And I find myself on the floor beside him.

OlderJuh yells, "Jump!", and YoungerJuh jumps across the doorway, shots are fired, a yelped "Ouch!"

I jumped onto my feet, running toward TargetJuh and yelling, "Stop!Stop!Stop!", to check out what had been hurt, and to assess the damage. Is it stop-crying-you-big-baby damage, or is it fess-up-to-Mum-for-certain-corporal-punishment-with-the-strap damage?

Simultaneously, OlderJuh, still firing, is yelling, "Get out of the way! You'll be hurt and you didn't put on your raincoat and sou'wester!"

"No! We have to check this out! Ouch!Ouch!Ouch!" Is my response.

OlderJuh comes rushing to me, prized BB gun dropped to the floor, and picks me up first to examine the welts on my back. He does the usual first aid, which is to spit on the wound and rub it in. After all, the prevailing wisdom of the age is that animals lick their wounds and we, after-all, are animals.

YoungerJuh has one smaller welt on his hand which was unprotected by coat and sou'wester. Same first aid.

That day I took three in the back in the name of learning the next lesson about how we treat others and use guns.

Cold War from the Perspective of a Child

"Mummy, my friends say their parents are voting for the Conservative Party in the election. What is a Conservative Party; what Party will you and Daddy vote for?"

"Never mind, Melba, we do not talk about such things."

"Why not? The other kids do."

"Because keeping our jobs depends on keeping private information and allegiances private."

They are installing an air-raid horn on the roof of the mill in the centre of town. Once a day, at various times of day or night, they sound the warning that our small town near the nation's capital is under attack so that we can practice our response. Our response is to close the windows, to get down under our desks at school, head for the basement at home, to huddle and wait for the all-clear horn or until our folks get home. Sometimes the horn sounds in the middle of the night and must be loud enough to wake even a sound sleeper like me. My light-sleeper father tells us it is enough to simply stay in bed or in place during these practices. When I say this at school, the teachers respond by more forcefully repeating the countering and original opinion of the air-raid drill instructions and make me get under my desk. This I report to Mummy and Daddy at home at supper that night. Daddy says, "The best thing to do at school is to do what the teacher says while you are there. The best thing to do during a nuclear attack this close to the target is to go outside to the top of a treeless hill and embrace the blast!"

"But why, Daddy? Won't I get blown up?"

"Better to be blown up in an instant than to survive a nuclear attack which will leave all local food and water and air so contaminated that everyone will die a miserable and painful death from fallout sickness, with our internal organs melting away and our skin peeling off."

"But if we save food and water in the basement, in an air-raid shelter, we will have enough to survive."

"Survive to what? Everything here will be radioactive; no one will come here to save us or bring supplies for fear of contamination themselves. Just embrace the blast."

Seemed logical enough. Later that week, they hold a drill while I am walking home through the park, for lunch. I find my six year old self alone with no other person in sight screaming, "Embrace the blast! Embrace the blast!" and frantically running from hilltop to hilltop searching for one with no trees or foliage, having peed my pants. When the all clear came, I made my way home, washed up, tried to eat my lunch, and then wondered if I should go back to school for the afternoon.

I tell Mummy and Daddy about the event at the supper table that night. A silent communication between my parents tells me that they heard me. A couple of weeks later, the drills stop. The sirens remain in place.

Busyness and Happyness

My parents come from humble and disapproving beginnings that teach them to give up any expectation of *finding* the life they wanted, and therefore to *make* the life they wanted to live, and that action started with pulling themselves up by their own bootstraps. Mum always says, "*The harder I work, the luckier I get, with realized goals just falling into my lap.*"

Like most parents, they want to satisfy two needs:

1 – give their children everything they themselves had coveted in childhood and never actualized;
2 – keeping busy a family of four children who, clearly, are exhibiting all the usual behaviours of those with extreme hyper-activity and the intellect to put it to any use: good, wise, or not.

With only one daughter in the bunch, to me falls the usual girlie things of the 1950s: housework, keeping the men happy and giving the larger portion to the men. Combined with that is the utmost requirement of allowing daughter all the same opportunities allowed to sons (with an added dose of protection, but not denial).

Combined with the extreme hyper-activity came a generous dose of OCD. *"Anything worth doing is worth doing right."* *"Anything worth doing must be better done than any of the other BabyBoomer inhabitants of the bell curve."* *"If anyone can do it, then I can do it."* "Just precisely follow your carefully developed recipe!"

As a four year old, I discover ballet. This is a beautiful art, full of evocative music, emotion, and graceful movement. It is intended to teach me confidence and grace of movement not available in the tomboy portion of my life.

The fact is that the teacher discovered my talent and always put me out in front as prima dancer, telling the other dancers, "Just follow Melba; she always knows what she is doing."

My head is full of music, art, rhythm; and my body is full of graceful, controlled moves. My heart is full of so much "easily won" affirmation. All I have to do was everything asked of me, and do it better than all the rest.

Ballet and I dance together for eight years, through many recitals, en pointe and off, dressing up in so many exciting and dramatic costumes.

During that time, someone from national ballet school came out, apparently to scout me. When they offered a position in that corps, my mother determined that would not be satisfying for me in the long run and the position was refused, without my ever hearing about it for years to come.

My dancing career morphs into baton twirling majorette activities, gymnastics, and cheerleading. So many of the same rewards are also found in their activity.

At the same time, I join in the rough and tumble lessons of kick the can, baseball, hockey, swinging on the jungle swing rope, firing rocks at dangerously located wasp nests then outrunning the angry swarm, playing truth dare consequences promise or repeat, working my way through all the swimming badges in halftime efficiency, tennis lessons and practice, riding a bicycle all over town including peddling all the way up our quarter-mile hill in front of our home without standing up - not even once, Brownies and Guides, CGIT, and Junior Choir.

Then high school arrives.

Time to get involved in high-school-specific skill-broadening activities like yearbook committee; curling; Student Council class rep and taking on extra responsibilities including dance committees, decorating committees, Secretary, and running for female co-president; being chosen as a Prefect; teaching Sunday school; being a cheerleader and staying in the top 10% of the bell curve to make myself acceptable to the university of my choice.

At age 14, I begin to work.

My first job is babysitting for two families; both experiences ending badly.

The one ends the night the parents arrive home two hours later than they had promised and find me asleep on the couch. They had made clear a strict rule about no sleeping while I was being paid to babysit. They also had lots of strict rules about no eating either their food or any food / caffeine / drink that I brought for myself, about no TV for me or their children, about having the children bedded down before I got there and I should be checking on them every fifteen minutes, about having their child home for a vacation from the developmental disabilities facility without notice or instruction for me, about no phone use, no allowances for supports that would keep me awake way past my habitually early bed time.

The other babysitting job ends when their eight-month-old woke up during the evening. When I check in on him during one of the fifteen-minute checks, I find him covered with his own excrement. He had filled his diaper, and then proceeded to smear it everywhere: on himself, in his hair and ears, on the wall, on the crib, on the bedding, *everywhere*! Not being used to babies (my younger brother was fewer than three years younger), I phoned my mother ... what else! Mother does give some sketchy instructions, but never offers to come and save me from the perils of the job. I go back upstairs, armed with cleaner and cloths, wrap the baby in the soiled bedding and place him on the floor of the bedroom, clean up the most foul mess of my lifetime and then head for the bathroom, clean linen and pjs in hand. I set the baby, soiled clothes and linens and all, into the tub. I run water into the tub, wash up the baby, and put him into clean pjs. We lullaby into the bedroom, I make the bed around and under the baby who is sweet-smelling and sleepy. About ten seconds later he is asleep. I determine that I have already earned my fifteen cents an hour and I leave the soiled laundry in the tub, soaking.

When the parents arrive home, they ask how the evening went. I start into a full report, and am bowled over by their headlong rush past me to check on the baby. They are very unhappy about the laundry not having been done. They suggest that they should not pay me at all, and then play magnanimous when they say that they will pay me anyway, even though my disappointing them is "egregious" in the extreme. I suggest that they keep their money since a simple thank you or Attagirl might have been expected, and since none was received the money is beside the point. I am affronted by them: I do not let them drive me home. I walk across town and through the dark park into the night, all by myself, just to teach them!

Summer teenager evenings are spent working at the soft ice-cream stand about two blocks from home. Yummm! Workers can eat whatever and as much as they want while working the booth single-handedly. The catch: one person working, no washroom, and soft ice cream just runs through me in lickety-split time. My second night on the job, I simply have to go to the bathroom; no customers are in sight; I lock up the stand and carry the cash box through the night as I dash home. Mother is sitting on the couch when I burst into the house, make short work of depositing the cash drawer on the chair, making it to the bathroom with mere seconds to spare.

When I return to work, I find a line-up of customers, indicating that the town's ball game of the night has just finished. I re-open, reinsert the cash drawer, and make delicious treats for everyone. I never again eat or drink anything during those work shifts again.

Persistence with swimming badges makes me eligible to work at the beach, as a lifeguard and swim instructor (at $29 per seven-day 70 hour week), eventually getting to the point of performing the duties of Supervisor of the beach (at $125 per weekday-mornings-only week). My first year at McMaster University finds me completing my Bronze, Leader Patrol, then Instructor / Examiner qualifications. It is a perfect job if you love kids, swimming, and being wet all day long no matter the weather. I would do it for free, I love it that much!

And the seed is sewn for what I wanted to do with my life: teaching.

Do You Love Me Enough to Save Me from This?

WooHoo! I'm in!

That thrill in the pit of my stomach is always there, keeping me distracted when teacher would rather I pay attention, but it gains strength manyfold when I dare to do what others would not. If they are afraid, then I am not.

Playing on the jungle swing rope by myself when no one wants to go there with me created a big event. We have fastened a thick rope with a knot at the end so we can jump off the roof of the chicken coop, sit on the knot, and swing back and forth, then climb even higher with each swing by pumping our legs. Just below the other end of the swing's arc is a foundation left behind from another outbuilding. Just below the arc's closest end is the chicken coop's roof.

One hot summer's day, when the saw flies were singing but all other life was still and panting in the heat, I decide to break the rule and go alone to swing in the breeze on the jungle rope. With each swoop, comes another line from a poem Mum used to say to me:

"*The Swing by Robert Louis Stevenson*

How do you like to go up in the swing,
Up in the air so blue?

...Up in the air I go flying again,
Up in the air and down!"

So enthralled am I that I lean far back so as to see below from past my eyebrows instead of past my feet. A swoosh of more air, empty hands, and ... thud. I land squarely on the old foundation where I lie until conscious thought re-enters my head and air re-enters my lungs. Looking up, I see OlderJuh and OldestJuh standing over me. "Mum and Dad are not going to like this, and I will surely be to blame! Stand up, no backing away from this! You were out cold so in you go for diagnosis by Mum," OldestJuh said.

Stand I do but walk I could not. I lie back down. This time Mum would have to come to me. After many can-you-feel-this, does-this-hurt, can-you-sit-up, can-you-stand, and can-you-walk, I am inside the house with Mum, while OldestJuh and OlderJuh take down the beloved jungle swing rope.

When Dad comes home and does his own examination, it is decided that the jungle rope can go back up after we all load up mud and pine needles, of which we had plenty, and leaves and weeds pulled from gardens into a pile over the exposed one-foot wall of the previous owner's shed until the cement could be taken away on the weekend.

I am cheered by the thought that the jungle rope's ride would continue to be part of our childhood culture.

Bent - Another Melba's Life

"No! Not that way! How many times do I have to tell you? Guess you are just too stupid to remember what I say!"

I review my actions while standing in the corner. I no longer have to be taken, or sent, or beaten to the corner; I simply have become in the habit of standing there while I review my shortcomings. That list is growing longer by the day:

- require too many reminders for the simplest things;
- even a smack doesn't wake me up.

My chores list is long, but I should be able to remember because each day it is the same:

- wake up without being called;
- wash and dress;
- put my sleep spot to rights so mother doesn't have to trip over it all day;
- get the baby up, cleaned and dressed and downstairs for breakfast;
- make breakfast for baby and feed him;
- clean up the kitchen and baby;
- make mother a coffee and take it to her bedroom without making a noise in case mother wants to sleep a little more;
- sweep off the front step so people won't think I am lazy;
- prepare for school in case mother got up to look after the baby and I get to go to school today;
- see if I can find some bread for myself to eat and if not then breakfast on water;
- if time for school comes and goes and no sign of mother, then put the baby in the corner with some play items to keep him from crying and waking up mother who will surely box my ears and remind me that I couldn't look after the simplest of things;

- start scrubbing floors, dust, sweep, make sure nothing was left lying around just because I am a sloven; and
- finally do laundry in the sink so I won't smell bad at school and be made fun of by the other kids, and then teacher will ask me if I just don't care about myself (and then the other kids laugh and bully me), and then teacher will get in touch with mother.

The essential trick is avoiding real injury once mother gets up. The broom and belt and hot iron are always within easy reach.

I am 6 years old, after-all. I should be able to remember a few simple things.

As the twig is bent, so grows the tree:

Once the school called after me every single time I am absent, mother insisted that I should get up earlier so I can do all my work before I "dance off for the day" leaving all the work for mother. Mother is angry that I purposely miss school so often that the school blames mother!

The best parts about school are: I can steal actual food for lunch from other lunch-kits; I get to sit down all day; and my bruises can heal before the new ones are handed out. Sometimes I can make money by meeting a boy outside on the school grounds behind the shed by the trees. I need money for granny rags and have no other means to get them. If I give in to what the boy wants to do, he pays me and usually doesn't hurt me.

I tried some drugs that I found in a lunch-kit which I had stolen. They made my feel funny for a while, but then nothing hurt for a while, either. While I am not on the rag, I can spend my shed-money to buy more drugs now that drugs no longer show up in my purloined lunch-kits.

I am surrounded by stupid teachers, stupid boys, stupid classmates. What a bunch of suckers they are, giving me what I want. Usually without me having to hurt them, again.

11 years old and not so stupid now, eh!

26

Bent and twisted, bent out of shape:

I am standing in the courtroom, 13, huge pregnant belly, my face bloody from the beating laid on me by cellmates because I called them names, and tried to bully them into giving up their seat.

A sucker of a woman is my lawyer, pleading with the judge:

About my inability to understand, at 13, why I couldn't get away with beating up my John for more money because I am hungry all the time now;

About my mother living in a filthy run-down shack full of vermin, sometimes with a truant bully of a younger son who leaves when mother doesn't provide for him and his hunger;

About my mother being pregnant again and so cannot make enough money from her Johns because her in-the-way belly is full with a term fetus; and

About my pimp trying to beat the growing baby out of my belly, though the fetus survived, so now no no one wants me either, so I cannot make money.

My lawyer is patient (a sucker) and points out my abilities (she is a moron) and talks about life choice options (she is also an idiot) for both me and my baby, but I can put up with her BS, because she brings in soap and shampoo, and other things I never had before, and I don't have to perform sexual favours to earn money to buy anything. The lawyer has arranged for me to have a real haircut, to meet with a tutor who works to find out why I cannot read yet so she can teach me to read so I can access information for myself.

My lawyer calls me by my name, Melba. Lawyer Jane and I talk, often.

I ask Jane to tell me another story about her life. Jane brings in items from her day to day life, and sometimes she lets me hold onto Jane's favourite stuffed teddy from her own childhood.

Jane showed me how to work on the computer, how to see pictures and read information about the big wide promising world outside the scope of my childhood.

We talk:

- about getting along with other people beyond suckering them in with the purpose of taking what I want from them;
- about jobs besides prostitution;
- about families with parents and children, and sometimes people choose to marry and become partners, and plan jobs and children and vacations, and what to buy next;
- about what choices I want to make, for myself, and if I want someone else to raise my baby in a world of choices, for a time, while I learn about standing tall in a world that I choose for myself; and
- about some things neither my mother nor I was raised to understand.

And I feel my bent, twisted self and world right themselves; I am bent into a better direction, so I can grow straight and tall towards the sunlight.

Bent but not broken!

Needle

Tonight's the night!

Now to put the plan into action. The summer's bright after-supper sky beckons me to the window and beyond, but first ...

"Dad, may I borrow the car, to go to Mary's house tonight?"

"What's happening at Mary's house?"

"Just some school plans."

And, off I go, driving through the summer's long evening light. Yes, I am going to Mary's house, and yes, we are off to some plans made earlier that day at school. I find it still works best if I lie using the truth; it is the artful dodge created when leaving out some information rather than adding untruthful and difficult-to-remember details.

My Dad has just purchased a new car, with a 326 engine, somewhat of a rarity in the small town where we live.

It's 1966, and at age 16, I am the holder of my own driving licence (something denied my brothers who must wait until they are at least 18 and have outgrown their male teenaged restlessness and recklessness).

My father always insists that either he drive me everywhere at night, or that I take the family car so he can be rest-assured that he knows the condition of the car driven and, as well, is assured that the driver is not some crazed hormoned-up teenager.

Off to Mary's, and then off to the unpopulated road by the Auld Kirk. Flat, straight, new pavement, and the residents won't mind because they are lying in the Auld Kirk's cemetery.

But this night the road is not unpopulated. Everyone is already there, lining both sides of the street, speaking in the hushed voices of teenagers who are in anticipation of the real deal!

Mary jumps out of my car with alacrity.

Her scarf is at the ready.

I am in position for the first challenge of the night.

To rush along the challenger, I press the brake and the gas at the same time, spinning the tires to warm them up just to the beginnings of the blue-black smoke of burning rubber (something that I heard to be a true and good idea for winning because hot tires grab the pavement better).

The back end of my car slews slightly to the side.

The challenger is a longtime success story from the impromptu drag races, and he is unfazed by my adrenaline and my 326 cubic inches of sure winner as he pulls up beside me, and gives one, long, considered look out his side window.

Mary's brightly coloured scarf is thrown high into the bright summer breeze and wafts ... gently ... down ... to ... reach ... pavement-WE'RE-OFF!

Through the deafening roar of engines, screeching tires, blood coursing in my ears, and the oh-my-gawd-what-am-I-doing looped-thought spinning in my head, I hold onto the steering wheel and try to acquit my own and my Dad's car's reputations and still not wet my pants! My focus is on the speedometer's needle and my intent is to bury that needle at its far end!

And then my opponent shifts gears and easily pulls ahead of my 326 sure thing!

There are other races that beautiful evening, lots of laughter and some thrills and near misses. Someone breaks out the beer. We all pretend that we like the taste of warm beer purloined from some parent's stash, sipping and cheering into the lavender hush of a night that promises many more of the same that summer.

After dropping Mary back at her home, after pulling over to throw up, twice, after chewing some gum to eliminate the taste of beer and vomit and pure adrenaline and core-deep blood-freezing fear, I turn the car towards home, following the line of golden pyramids' glow pooling down below each street lamp.

"How went the school plans?"

"No hitches."

"Car back in the garage?"

"Yes, thanks Dad."

Samhain and Hallowe'en

Setting alight a bag of carefully collected dog poop and then ringing the home owner's bell. Collecting candy by the pillowcase-full while trick-or-treating. Egging and toilet-papering the property of others. Setting a tire on fire and rolling it down the hill on the main street of town. Writing soapy (or worse, painted) messages on windows of private homes and businesses. Collecting the treats and then doing nasty tricks anyway. Dressing up in costumes that conceal the person's identity, and that demean and vilify homeless people, people who practice other religions, people who are generally well known because they are local or in media While all this is going on around me, and while all my friends are participating, I want to fit in with the crowd, so I stand close by as a by-standing enabler, and sometimes as a 'minor" participant enabler. And I think back to an earlier childhood Samhain (so called at our home) / Hallowe'en (so called in the community).

"Mum, can I please put on my lion costume now? Please! I want to be ready when the veils are lifted. I miss Grammum so much and I just know that she will come tonight, on Samhain, when the veils between living and dead are thinnest, and she will come with a special message for me."

"Mmmmmm ... Child, let's see if you are right:

Hmmmmmmmm...

The third and final harvest is behind us; the stores are laid by for winter; the air is chilling; the nights are longer; we focus no longer to the past and turn to the future; our dead will come with their final messages, beyond the lessons they taught us in life, and we will clear the air for the future.

Our preparations are finished by many hands working together:

- the laments of the past are done and so will not affect our future;
- the colours of orange, crimson, deep golds, brown, bronze abound in and around our home. White and black are both on our alter, along with silver bells and shimmery fine grey cloth;
- we have set out special stones gathered during our walk this afternoon;
- our home is cleaned and cleared of any and all that is unsightly or no longer useful;
- our table is laden with mulled cider, pumpkin bread, chicken soup to be served in pumpkin shells, roast pork with rosemary and mint, oven–roasted red potatoes and apples, Wheel of the Year Sabbat cakes;
- we have chosen who and what we want to be for this next year's turning of the Wheel and our costumes are ready;
- our preparation work is complete."

"I know, Mum! I've known this forever! Let's get ready to party!"

It is time to bathe away the labours of the past and then to don the clothes that best represent what we want to be in the coming year.

Through that evening,

- neighbourhood kids would come, invited, to our door Trick or Treating, gleefully reaching into our offerings;
- our Wiccan and Pagan friends would come and linger and share stories, and food, and drink;
- we would all scamper around the fires large and small, searching the flames for what the future will bring and for what we will make of the future;
- blessings would be called and received.

The majyk of that night so long ago was not the religion or ceremonies or the words or the food, but the majyk was our hearts filled with sharing and laughter and taking note of Wonder, Joy, Happyness, Success, the Promise all around us.

Late that night, as I basked in the delights of the evening while focusing on the dance of colours and lights around my bed, Grammum came to tell me a secret. I promised to carry that secret with me forever.

Dating: Project or Partner or Love

Once I am in high school, dating shows up on my list of activities that I am allowed to do, with a sliding scale of permitted participation.

First is my grade 8 graduation which includes dressing like a girl: in a dress, with upsweep hairdo, girl-shoes, and lipstick (pink, not red). After certificates, handshakes, and buffet, there is a dance.

If a boy wants to dance with me, he has to cross the floor,

and ask me to dance. My choices of response range from polite refusal of "Thanks but my feet hurt in my new shoes," to getting up to dance. Actually, that is the list; no range about it.

Our dancing looks like, we fancy, Saturday Date dance show on TV, which is our only access to learning how to dance for parent-protected members of my BabyBoomer generation. We only actually touch during waltzes, and the parent-dance-committee make sure there are no waltzes until the last dance. Waltzes are one hand clasped in hand of dance partner at straight armed shoulder height, my other hand on his shoulder whilst his other hand was on my back above my waist: no other touching, and no watching our feet. I am thrilled to go to my first grown up dance party. The boys seem to be all hot, sweaty, and clumsy; I'm not sure they are so thrilled.

That summer, the CYO (which I later found out to stand for Catholec Youth Organization) is holding dances in their school hall. The first one wafts wisps of music across the centre-of-town park to my window, enticing me to go, to move, to sway, to join in.

My parents tell me that the dance was only for the Catholec kids.

I have Catholec friends. We have to walk by the Catholec school on our way to public school, no matter whether we cut through the park on our summer route, or if we walk via the snowy roads on our winter route. They watch us walk by, and we watch them as we walk by. No devilish horns growing from their heads, no verbal barbs thrown in either direction, just kids who look like us but in uniforms.

My brothers and I are pretty tight-knit playing together when playing outside, but when it comes to having enough participants for an actual game of ball on our backyard diamond, or hockey on our own much-laboured rink, we are sensible enough and encouraged to invite the neighbourhood kids to come play on our acre of land to fill out the teams. My mother decides that if we are going to play sports and socialize amidst all that competitive energy and potential for physical injury, she wants it at our place.

That way, she knows the kids, she is present (in the house), and the money she spends on equipment can be protected by our hosting diligence after the game was over. The Catholec kids on the block show up, and bring their other Catholec friends to join in until we have enough for each team. There are no spectators; who would want to spectate; the thrill is in the play!

So I ask my Catholec friends if the CYO dances are only for Catholec kids. They ask the nuns. Then the nuns say I have to go meet them first. Permission might be granted if the nuns are properly impressed by me. So I meet these women of mystery, of long black flowing robes with stiff white garb covering chest, chin, and head, with a huge cross hanging around their neck and further jewelry tucked into belt.

I report back to Mum and Dad that I have passed the nun test.

The nuns have heard of us:

We have moved into the previous doctor's house;

Mum is the head of the Math department at the high school (town isn't big enough for a Catholec high school) and is known for her work with her students;

Dad is a "scientist" at NRC (National Research Council) at this point, and the word scientist is a word of whispers and respect in those days; and my brothers and I are hyper and into everything, and fearless in our approach to life and activities, yet respectful at the same time.

And the nuns review their rules:

Respectful behaviour;

Leave room for the Holy Ghost between dance partners;

No hyper raucousness;

No making messes;

Help cleanup.

I am in!

Mum and Dad are nonplussed that their 13 year old daughter has done all this on her own without their permission or help, but are gratified that their raising of us to be reasonable, intelligent, independent, and responsible for our own actions kind of people is duly noted and in evidence.

They tell me they can do naught but grant me permission.

These are Mum and Dad's rules:

Dad will drive me to the dance and pick me up:

Respectful behaviour (yes, the nuns covered that!);

No dancing too close (yes, the nuns covered that!);

No exuberant behaviour (yes, nun coverage!);

No making messes, either physical or emotional (yes, nuns!); and

Be a helper (yes, nuns!).

Mum and Dad, now impressed by the overlap in parenting and nunning, grant permission, which will be doled out one week at a time, for the next weekend's dance.

Mum and Dad come into the hall with me at the first dance, they meet the nuns who are impressed that the only parents to ever come in at the beginning of a dance are not Catholec.

By September of grade 9, I am an old hand at dances.

I have volunteered to be on Student Council as rep for class 9D; I hear about monthly dances at the high school and volunteer to "work at the door" as well as serving on decorating committee. This activity ensures that my parents would have no reasonable ability to deny my attendance at the dance. I participate at the dance for free (money is always an issue at our house because we were paper rich, meaning we had diplomas, but we were cash poor); and then I help with cleanup committee.

I still have to be driven to and from the dance by Dad.

This time, Mum is one of the Staff chaperones (but Mum, do you have to volunteer for every single dance?).

Also, at these dances, the lights are muted or the bulbs are changed to coloured bulbs. It is mood lighting, I am told. I like it.

Dates are activities like meeting up at a dance, or eating home-made bag lunch together in the caf, or walking from/to the bus together morning and afternoon.

In grade 11, I turn 16. I can get my licence and then I can drive myself to and from the dances, and I can accept a date picking me up in their car because I can drive if "something happened to prevent my date from reliably driving me home".

This is no small incentive to get my licence.

Now, dating is participating in commonly appreciated activities: let's go to the dance; let's drive to the river in another town at another beach for a swim; let's go to a movie; or perhaps, let's go to the local hangout for a chips and cherry coke.

My dates are as old as 20, still high school kids. One date actually asks me if my boyfriends got higher marks from my mother. (It is the kiss of death for that first, and only, date. "Take me home or let me out of the car!" I demand). Some boys have "backgrounds". They are on probation, or father beats mother and kids, or mother drinks, or "I won't tell you why but you cannot date that person" (which I think was code for: lax morals; cussing; sleeping around, wanted poster in the post office which contained same name; or a lot of other things I don't really understand). Mum says that these boys could be a friend, but can not be a boyfriend and I can not date them. When I put out my little chin in determination, Mum reminds me that putting out my chin in that way only makes it a better target for a fist or a hit, so it really isn't in my best interest!

And she says that she and Dad would be disappointed in me (yikes that one still has the ability to hurt!) and would cut back on my freedoms, and allowances. That really gets my attention, so I ask Mum what is really going on. She speaks of her psychology courses and mentions that kids grow up accepting their parents' behaviours as normal, and this would not be a satisfying way to live for someone like me who was brought up in a milieu of careful thought, one step at a time consideration, and keeping my eye on tripping hazards and on the goal at all times.

Mum says that these boys likely needed a friend, which I can surely offer, but when it comes to dating, I am better not to date a project and I should look for partnership potential rather than a project requiring me to change his behaviour or be his whipping girl.

By the time I leave the nest for out of town post secondary education at McMaster University which was 300 miles away, I was well versed on: where babies come from; what that means for my goals and plans and future with my parents and brothers; precipitous and promiscuous behaviours are never satisfying; there are men on campus who are looking for a green card or a strong woman on whom they can lean for the rest of their lives.

I must remember the partnership idea that we had discussed my whole life. Only spend time, away from classmates or friendship, with people who would be a worthy partner, who would agree to me being an equal partner, who would respect my own path and goals.

My dating career helps me to decide my thoughts on projects, on partnerships, on Love. As I teenaged in the 1960s, young adult-ed in the 1970s, I have all the confidence of a strong springboard or touchstone for relationships. And I learn, BabyBoomers had birth control. There is no getting confused by hormones, and lust. Just take the pill! Or abstain!

I find my mate, my partner, my Love. He was the guy my Mum held up as a example of good high school dating material back when I was in grade 9 (kiss of death for him in grade 9 was being Mum's bright shining example). [And by the way, Mum, he and I together prove to be a wild and crazy combination, wilder than any of my other on-probation "projects".]

He is the guy who stops the car on the way home, one summer dusk, after hearing I had never caught fireflies for the simple purpose of having them flying around me with their bright sparkle blinking around me in the darkness. He chases through the unpopulated property beside the car and catches fireflies, bringing them to release into the car and then darting off to catch another.

Though we had begun to date in high school, and we both had similar plans and commitments to family, and we were both

37

headed in same direction regarding post-secondary education, we decide to apply to our own choices of universities and careers and maintain a distance relationship. We decide that these big plans meant that we could be dates, and partners, and even lovers, but there would be no further commitment in terms of Life Partner, Spouse, or plans for Family of our Own until after graduation, until after my Mum died from her cancer, until after his father retired from the multi-generation farm, until we are ready.

Stay and Be My Research Assistant

Another essay to write for my third year university Psychology class. Another opportunity to speak my mind, to organize my own thoughts, and to earn top marks for my own ideas. So much more satisfying than Scantron multiple choice exams typical for us BabyBoomers still forced to exist on the bell curve. I am in my final year of my undergrad degree and looking to a fourth year which will be spent getting my teaching certificate at Teachers' College. It is my final step to realizing my dream of being a teacher.

I shoot out of the classroom and race to the library, before the others pull every book that has anything to do with the assignment topic then hiding the books elsewhere in the stacks under unrelated-topic-locations known only to them so they can come back after their day's classes are finished. I have played this game before. There is no way I can afford to purchase every single book required for research; there is no such thing as computer research or internet.

Twelve books on the topic; and another half dozen which might have a nugget or two. I lug my bounty over to one of the huge study tables and set about the task.

First, write down every book title, author, library number. Then peruse Table of Contents for likely details and jot down chapter titles. Then place un-useful books on the discard pile.

Then read-read-read, taking notes the whole time, roughing out main concepts of the essay, and writing each of those topics at the top of a page with jot notes added to each appropriate page.

During the entire hours spent at the library, classmates come to grab off my pile of library books for their own efforts; it is like there is no human being sitting there, only a pile of books useful to the cause of the other person. Ah, yes, BabyBoomers. These are the days when I am glad that I was raised with brothers and learned to stand up for myself rather than my natural reaction which is people-pleasing. A simple standup and barking, "I'm not finished with these books yet," seemed to suffice. "Come back after 7pm."

From rough notes, to setting topic concepts, to changing point form notes into prose. I am on a roll. Finally comes the condensing of the essay into the word limit (plus or minus 10% - usually plus 10%) and having a hard look at tone, content, and making my points.

At 7pm, the others show up, and all the books are already piled at the end of the table so they can help themselves without interrupting my train of thought. When the pile of books is depleted, some ask for help, for a perusal of my notes. I show them my organized point form outline. When they persist with their demands, another growl suffices to send them on their way to be responsible for their own learning and work.

The rest of the day and night I finish the essay, catch up my other classes, and hit the sack with hard-earned satisfaction. Next day I hand in my polished, jacketed, double-space typed, third year worthy essay.

The following day I receive back my work with a "D" mark. I take the prof's offer of explanation, and head to his office to ask how I had done so poorly. He complains that I had no bibliography. It is necessary to state where every single idea came from.

"Where did you get all these many ideas?"

"From books in the library, from textbooks, from a lifetime of taking an interest, and observation, and listening to lectures and to conversations."

"Well that won't do; you must have at least ten quotes in an essay this size."

"By when?"

"By end of week, three days."

I return next day with my essay which now boasts 105 direct quotes from fifteen different books, with a proper bibliography, and also quote references at bottom of each page.

He fans through my work, stops from time to time, then looks at me and says, "Well! I don't know whether to fail you or give you an A!"

"Then give me an A+!" I reply.

He tells me that he appreciated my treatment of the topic from the beginning, but that I had clearly ignored every bibliography lesson I ever had. When I tell him that the only teacher who had touched on essay writing was my inspiring grade 11 history teacher, but certainly no English class had every taught essay writing or bibliography, he is astounded!

He asks me where I had found the exact quote for each idea. I show him my initial notes which make it easy to find them again for the details required.

He sits down. He writes an A+ on my work and changes his mark on his sheet.

"I see that you are in third year. Where are you going next year?" he asks.

"Teachers' College."

"Please please please, stay here through your Honours degree and then to your Masters. I need you as my research assistant and you have so much to offer to academia."

Something twitches in the back recesses of my head: my research and work will be published in his name, not mine.

"Sorry, plans are made, and my parents are out of money. As it is, I am at Carleton because my Dad is here so my courses are 3% cost, and I am a ResFellow so room and board are free.

I have two brothers at university, currently, and one of those is in medical school at McGill. In order to finish a degree, which I am determined to do before Teachers College, I need to find a financial method.

Can you compete with that need within your offer?"

"No, I guess not, but I hope to convince you before year's end!" is his reply.

A Career Instead of a Job

Graduation from Carleton University finds hundreds of us graduates in black cap and black gown facing into the hot sun on the lawn outside the Registrar's Admin building where we had cavorted (innocently and with no disruptive intent - there were no signs saying we could not do this) in that same fountain on the hot days before summer recess and again at fall registration.

We all try to look like the cheap gowns and cardboard hats are a part of our regal-ness, maturity, and graduate-ness. Our heads are full of great and grand ideas of having achieved this goal, having stayed in the top 10% of the bell curve every year while others were rejected from registration their following year, having found time to participate in activities other than classroom, lecture, library research, or writing reports. Our focus is squarely centred on the Career we would follow, so unlike the Jobs we had taken to pay for shampoo, deodorant, late night pizzas, and more paper for class notes and assignments. This Career is to be our calling and our paycheque.

My parents join so many other parents who are there to celebrate this rite of passage into our chosen world. Mum had helped me sew a white shirt and skirt, and Mum and Dad had invited me out to lunch at the Chateau Laurier hotel, the grandest place in the city. They say their heads are full of their own graduation days, relating those to my generation-later experience.

When former Canadian Prime Minister and former Carleton University graduate Lester B Pearson steps up to the mic, I envision him joining the ranks of all who reminded us all how great we were, how far we would go with our newly honed skills, and how we would find our biggest problem to be deciding what to do with all our salary money and all our spare time in this new generation of leisure. Pearson steps up to the mic. We settle in to hot sun beating down on our black garb, pretending to be mature graduates who could take a little discomfort while listening to this world leader.

He begins to speak. He says he is not going to repeat the current suggestion that today is the end of our uncertainty, and the end of our impecunious days, and BabyBoomer status being responsible for crowding us out of success. He offers us his congratulations on our hard work paying off with this graduation diploma.

Then he begins telling us what no one had mentioned before. This diploma simply stated that we had successfully taken advantage of learning from and with some of the greatest minds on the planet, had successfully completed the study, reading, and writing required of these great minds, and had proved to ourselves and our teachers that we could keep up. This diploma is not a ticket to a great Career. (Gasp! Take that in! This is NOT as advertised!) He goes on to say that we have been a burden to our parents' pocketbooks long enough and now we must go out and get some training that will teach us how to do a Job in our chosen Career. And now we must continue our studies on our own, continue to grow in intellectual stature on our own, begin the rest of our lifelong learning on our own. "Keep your mind's wheels greased with new ideas, and old ideas, in a lifelong ceaseless flow."

I take off the heat-producing hairdo-flattening black garb, and let it slide to the back of my chair. If I am going to have to bake in this shocking new world, I will be comfortable so as not to distract me from the epiphany. After the presentation of diplomas and de rigueur mortar-board tossing, I fiind my way back to my parents. Though they are properly congratulatory, we are pretty much silent on the way to the Chateau Laurier.

Once there, we begin the first of many truly grownup conversations in our relationship. My parents congratulate me, present me with flowers, tell me how proud they are of my work and commitment, how appreciative they are that I had moved to Carleton where my Dad worked and therefore my courses were all but free, and that I had taken on a Job as ResFellow so my Res was free, too. (My move to Carleton from McMaster was precipitated by my younger brother, YoungerJuh, graduating high school and going to University putting my parents squarely on the hook for three kids in university simultaneously, one in Medical school at one of Dad's alma maters, McGill $$). They tell me that this achieved diploma puts me into a status that no one can ever take away from me; I am now a university graduate.

They gently segue into Pearson's comments, and Mum asks what I would like to do now, so that I could get a Job. I am still struck dumb. All this time, I had seen graduation as the goal, and now Pearson and Mum and Dad's words put me back at the starting blocks, not at the promised finish line ribbon.

I had sought and accepted another summer on the job at the local beach, and I would work there for two months as Supervisor, Head Instructor teaching kids to swim and pass tests and teaching older kids hired to teach classes how to do that work and touring the local beachfront swim schools to give swim examinations.

My parents bring up the Chateau Laurier conversation often enough to encourage me not to let go of the need to get this looked after before fall registration closed the door on me, but not often enough to make me feel pressured to move on or move out.

Mum arrives at the beach, armed with her ever-present movie camera, to take pictures of me working at the beach with students and staff, to record this part of my life. When she shows the family this film on movie night, she and I exchange an aha look. After movie night was over, she and I sit down, then she asks me to tell her which of all my jobs to date were the most satisfying to the point where I would do them anyway as a volunteer even if they didn't pay me: teaching Sunday School to wee'uns as a 12 year old, teaching and traveling the countryside examining swimming students, teaching others how to teach, teaching residents of my floor at Carleton Res how to be a successful student and how to leap hurdles that were proving too high. Off we go to Teachers' College to register Melba for fall session.

When I answer the Registrar's questions about why I wanted to teach, I speak of my precious experience and the *Joy* I felt when the light bulb of learning turns on. He reminds me that there are no teaching *Jobs*, anywhere; that he is pleased to accept my tuition money; and he is pleased to teach me how to teach anyway; and then he asks me to reconsider. I stand firm, Mum and Mum's cheque book standing behind me. I tell him that a good teacher education and my degree in Psych will take me to schools or to any workplace classroom where training occurred, that heading only to school board classrooms was short sighted in this teacher-flooded market. I was in!

A year at Teachers' College was a huge step backwards, back into the life as student, back into being under the thumb of "Masters" who were dogmatic, miserable, and unwilling to give anyone a top grade (even after evaluating me lone-teaching a double class of eighty grade 8 students, with no speed-bumps or hiccups in lesson, with no unhappy acting-out 13 year olds).

There was a time when school boards came to the Teachers' Colleges for hiring days. Following those halcyon days, the teachers' colleges had graduated double cohort classes and flooded the market. Now we are left to find a way to find a job where we want to teach.

Mum had just been diagnosed with cancer which was declared to take her from us in six months. I am desperate to be close to home, living and sharing and laughing and learning with Mum every day, while I can.

While on the Practice Teaching assignments, I ask my Associate Teacher if they would consider giving me a written recommendation beyond the evaluation form. As an added measure, I invite the Principal of the school to do the same.

A man whom my department-head mother had hired to teach Math at the high school (in the face of a bullying misogynistic principal who wanted another football jock on staff to help coach the team but not caring if he had a head for mathematics) takes an interest in my *Career.* He asks Mum how my *Job* search is going and suggests I phone his cousin who is looking for a grade 7&8 teacher at the school where the cousin is Principal. He has already spoken with the cousin who said that his conversation got me in the door to the interview but I would have to get the *Job* on my own merits.

The interview finds me sitting with two Principals, neither of whom is the cousin, with my handful of evaluations and written recommendations, with high hopes that the hyper anxiety would right itself for the duration, with fears that these men would be as destructively judgemental as my teaching Master had been. On my way in, I notice a set of headlights still on in the nearly deserted parking lot. I mispronounce the name of the Principal, ouch, but then he turns out to be the grateful owner of the still-lit car in the parking lot.

They merely peruse the many documents I present. They ask question after question but barely touch on education practices and theory. They ask me how I would teach a language class with no textbooks or with advanced-age textbooks in rough shape, how I would teach research in a school with no library and one depleted set of encyclopedia, what books I had read in the last year outside of the books demanded by my courses. I share my ideas in each case, and say I would ask my Principal for suggestions beyond that. And, I announce that I was the proud owner of an entire new collection of encyclopedias of my own.

They send me on my way, with the dictate that someone would call me about the outcome.

I beat myself up about my flounderings and my name mispronunciation and my lack of confidence about this one single, perfect job available close to home.

A week later, I receive a phone invitation to present myself at the school board with my diplomas, certificates, evaluation forms, written recommendations and my drivers licence. For two hours I sign forms, allow Gestetner copies, listen, ask questions about specifics, and am told that I have a job, way out in the country with no bus service so I need a car, starting in a portable with one of the interviewing Principals and then moving to the newly renovated school of the second Principal some time in the school year yet to be determined.

The *Job* in the *Career* of my choice, at location of my choice, is mine. Who says sparkling on command and keeping eye on prize doesn't pay off?

Moving Forward

Over the next five years, I achieve my permanent contract, travel the world at Mum's insistence, have many discussions with Mum (about Job, house building, raising kids, gardening, keeping body and soul together, maintaining my own moral code and perspectives, finding my own style, what makes a successful marriage, dealing with outcomes caused by witless others such as doctor misdiagnosis and big business shamelessness, etc) until we lose her from this plane five years later, four and a half years later than the doctor's predictions and after a lifetime of demonstrating that determination is what is required during any time in your life.

I am established in my *Career*; we are starting to build our house; we start planning our wedding which we would have IF we were still speaking after finishing the house to the point of habitation (you know ... enclosed and securable, bedroom ready for furniture, kitchen ready for cooking, at least one fully functioning bathroom). When Mum died, she knew all of the house colours, floor plan, function and furniture for each room, what my wedding dress would look like, how many people would be invited to the wedding, what names I was considering for my babies, and the value of family and relationship circles in my life.

I have learned much, and most of it inside the circles of family and friends and acquaintances.

Blame

I recently watched a movie again, and again I am struck by the line, "When something so horrible happens, someone must be to blame!"

The concept of blame came up during the 1950s childhood and again when I started my teaching career. When there is a problem with a child's learning, the child is studied, labeled, and the blame for the problem is laid, often at the feet of the parents.

Halting at the label does not help the student to find their way to a side door or a back entrance to learning.

Someone must be prepared take the student by the hand and teach them, make a difference in their life.

Starfish Story - adapted from that of Lorm Eiseley (or Why I Teach)

"Once upon a time, there was a wise man ...
... "I must ask, then, why are you throwing starfish into the ocean?" ...
... "The sun is up and the tide is going out. If I don't throw them in, they'll die." ...
... "there are starfish all along every mile? You can't possibly make a difference!"
... picked up yet another starfish, and threw it into the ocean. As it met the water, he said, "It made a difference for that one."

Advice from a Tree - adapted from that of Ilan Shamir

... Embrace with joy the changing seasons ...
... The Energy and Birth of Spring
The Growth and Contentment of Summer
The Wisdom to let go of leaves in the Fall
The Rest and Quiet Renewal of Winter ...

1stThird: Themes, Lessons Learned, and Wisdom

My father related our own life to that of a tree; the life of a tree is best understood in *Thirds*. In the *1stThird*, the tree establishes roots, and trunk, then branches and leaves; this is a time of growing and learning purpose so the tree can thrive into its future life.

In the Pagan understanding of life, we have three stages: *life as Maid, Mother, Crone*. In the stage known as *Maid*, many lessons are presented, some only once and many again and again until I recognized them, and then did away with the need for more repetition of hurt, shame, humiliation, and pain.

Hats and Labels:

My list of *1stThird* hats include:

girl, only daughter in a family of sons, sister, friend, girlfriend, piano player, ballet dancer, baton twirling majorette, gymnast, cooperative tennis player, swimmer, beach Supervisor / Instructor and Examiner / lifeguard, too smart for my own good, fanciful, energetic, lively, too hyper, talk-talk-talker, organizer, sick every winter, go-go-goer, always getting things done, happy all the time, generous, one of the boys, risk taker, Girl Guide, high school Student Council class rep and Secretary, high school Prefect, high achiever, resident of the top 10% of bell curve as definition of success, writer, choir member, sewer, laundress from age 8, performer, dutiful, the dependable one, sparkler, successful, sprite, water baby, keeper-upper, walker away, piano player and Royal Conservatory honours graduate, hula hooper, volunteer in community service, candy striper, excellent driver and teacher of friends who want to pass their driving test the first time, yoga teacher, hippy life-styler, health food researcher and advocate, hair-on-fire life-of-the-party, Centennial year Miss SmallTownOntario pageant invited participant, yearbook committee and organizer, university res-fellow, university graduate with honours, college diploma, teacher, friend, dater, lover, engaged woman, married woman ...

Alice Effect:

The Alice Effect slammed into my consciousness as a bright light that helped me to understand my free will, and it became a touchstone for me. I would ask the others what they expected of me and then I would automatically give them that.

Using the Alice Effect later helped me to understand what exactly were the expectations of others, then decide if I would love myself in that persona, or not. I used this in competitive experiences where I considered whether I had a chance in hell of winning; no chance to win in that arena means no participation; who needs another kick in the self-concept self-esteem pants?

Giving over control, determination, and affirmation to the other person had become a resonating theme, along with Melba as people pleaser.

And all that time, I thought I was in charge of me!

The "Alice Effect": When, in spite of my best sparkling and intention, I somehow do not measure up to the expectations of others, I shall simply make a choice. If the judgement of another does not lift me up, does not align with my own high expectations, deep judgement of self, and simple but strict moral code, then I shall simply smile, nod, and go my own way without them.

They just aren't ready for me. It is not that I don't measure up; we are simply on different paths.

The "Alice Effect" bell that was rung and resonated on that day long ago has never completely quieted. In my day-to-days, that bell may tinkle or may jangle in my deep recesses, but when I hear it ring I listen very carefully.

And I choose.

Self:

The Self is Selfish, is ego, negates all others and their needs; no one will want to hang around with me if I am selfish. Anything that serves me is to be avoided.

"Do You Love Me Enough to Save Me from This?":

I soon learned that others saw me as someone they liked to have around, at their parties, at recess, when they needed help. I was fearless:

- Play goalie without any protection on our backyard rink? I'm in!
- Take on the task of lifeguarding hundreds of kids at the beach as a 107 pound 17 year old? I'm in!
- Hitchhiking with my university roommate out to Jasper Park Lodge to be with a university friend on his summer time 21st birthday? I'm in!
- Let's go canoeing and camping through Algonquin Park, portaging with a 50-pound pack apiece and a 6 month baby, too? I'm in!
- Backpack around Europe in the 1970s? I'm in!
- We just bought a parasail. Wanna come try it out while we learn how to get it going? I'm in!
- Driving drunk (from my usual intake of a couple dozen servings of alcohol) as the DD after a party? I'm in!

- Teach grades 7&8 right out of teachers college? I'm in! And,
- Stare down school board superintendents and union bosses and principals on the job? I'm in!

In the beginning, I simply loved the thrill of it all and learned firsthand about exhilaration. I could handle this!

Then it became a people-pleasing ego-stroking gotta-have-Melba-with-us thing. Still handling this!

Until it became a risky-behaviour to help me soar past the deep-dark-hole thing, a do-you-love-me-enough-to-save-me-from-this thing. Nope, not handling this at all well.

"Needle":

Yep, lesson learned, luck appreciated. Never again would I risk it all for such an unsatisfying thrill. The risk of the loss of my Mum's and Dad's trust would continue to be a guiding principle on into adulthood and parenthood and through my whole life.

Though challenged again and again, I never again went to the drag races, not even to watch. I never again tried to bury the needle. I never again fed my ADHD adrenaline's need for speed, nor anyone's need to be the best, at such risk to drivers and spectators lining the road, and to vehicle or property.

Over the years, during any of the near misses that any person experiences, that same deafening roar and pulsating visceral fear popped up just to remind me how good it is to be alive, despite my own night of being the crazed adrenaline-ized teenager trying to bury the needle.

Yet, sometimes when I am driving home on a beautiful summer's evening, the radio is on and playing some nostalgic song, I harken back to my young, naive, freckled, braided, red headed, 16 year old, hair on fire self, and hear the old siren's call, "YeeHaw!"

And the car wants to turn towards the Auld Kirk, years and miles away...

"Stay and be my Research Assistant":

Though I did not take him up on his offer, I was complimented by his appreciation for my efforts, my abilities, and that confidence shone out from my intellect, from my voice, from my heart for the rest of my student and work life.

Teachers have such influence in everything they do and say, in every interaction with their students. I'll never forget that.

Happyness:

Why Happyness instead of Happiness?

In the *1stThird*, being happy seemed to be about getting a gift of some thing that I coveted or desired, or winning the game, or completing the task. And it became a hollow happiness, without deep meaning, satisfaction, or Joy. When the word Happyness crossed my radar, I chose to assign to this spelling the deeper meaning of Joy.

"Busyness and Happyness":

"You really have had lessons in everything!" This indictment led me to review all of my childhood activities. This examination turned up memories of trial and error and lesson, of being brave enough to try, of excavating a fearlessness that lived deep inside me, of meeting new people and learning about where trust lives, and where it does not.

Individuality:

In this *1stThird*, individuality was learned to mean which group you chose to belong to, such as club, team, neighbourhood, school, achievement group ... There were just too many BabyBoomers to allow any one of us to stray and take others to the anarchy created by splinter groups. We learned, often the hard way, that we worked to follow the rules and to fit in.

Education:

Education in the *1stThird* is all about being the student. There are lessons to be learned specific to the overcrowded BabyBoomer classroom, the family, the circle of friends, the job, the streets, the weather, the seasons, locations, activities, looking after needs such as food and cleanliness and sharing that with others.

Busyness, Work, Job, Career:

Once I started chores at home, some for free as a contributor to the family circle and some for allowance, started going to the homes of others in need to help, started teaching Sunday School, I realized that Work is satisfying, gratifying, and noble. To satisfy my perception of need for "things" I sought paid work, started babysitting for payment, started teaching swimming / lifeguarding / beach supervisor / Curly Cone maker of sweet dreams, started looking for paying Jobs so I could afford something I wanted, and finally sought a Job in teaching, the career of my choice.

Work was a means to an end; I could do something to earn my living and I could choose to treat it as a noble task determined by my moral code and befitting my need to please whomever judged my work or whomever needed my help.

Voice:

My Voice in the *1stThird* was whatever memorized piece I had been expected to say, was asked to say, appropriate and correct by the standards of others, and by standards that were not always as advertised.

Relationships, Family, Interactions, Influences:

Relationships were fleeting.

Our multiple moves from town to town should have helped

me to understand how to meet new people, but this sparkle on command forced extrovert only got to know her best friends who are the people in the house, the people who moved with me. That is where I learned about no place to hide, about the long run, about making amends, and apologies.

And I learned about enduring the rarely-altruistic day-to-day comments of others.

When, later, people ask me how we have managed to be married for all these years, and how they might find someone who could be a candidate for that success, I tell them to find the person who will catch fireflies for them for the simple unselfish bringing of that experience to the other. And to bring your own fireflies to him, unselfishly, willingly.

Teachers have such influence in everything they do and say, in every interaction with their students.

Just because someone exists alongside you every day on the job or in the neighbourhood, it doesn't necessarily mean that they are your friend, or that they have any mutual regard for you, or that they reciprocate your feelings, or that they really think about you at all, or that they don't carry a supply of back-stabbing blades.

(Note to older self: never name your children with names containing the same initial sound!)

When I point a finger of blame at someone else, I have three more fingers pointing back at me.

"Sparkling on Command":

Of course, as time went on, I matched my own moral code and compass to those demands, and followed their will to what they wanted as well as what was right as defined by what I could defend using my moral compass.

Mum also said that there was value in Sparkling on Command. Putting a smile on my face, a pleasant tone in my voice that said "I value you", invited interaction which I came to understand as my campfire. When I sat at night at my own campfire, my smile and sparkle and invitation drew others to my campfire, to share warmth, stories, circle, and belonging.

All of these *1stThird* experiences taught me that all I had to do in life was follow a few simple rules:

- Just do it! Do it right! Do it right now!
- Just find out what those in charge wanted and give it to them
- Just sparkle-on-command in all things personal and professional, foreseen and unforeseen, tasteful and distasteful

Thank goodness for a tremendous determination, for OCD, and for a generous dose of native ability. These would surely do me in good stead all my life. All I had to do was determine what they wanted of me, and then to deliver it in doses greater than any of the others could deliver.

And a forced-extrovert affirmation-dependent OCD was born!

"Leaving":
Through my entire lifetime, family was very important to me.

"Stealing":
I never stole anything again, and have always been careful not to borrow even when it is offered though I did not ask, to seek permission to enter or use someone else's things. I am fastidious about my stuff, more so the stuff of others.

Resentment wells up in me when someone else asks or takes or uses my things without my permission, when there is never enough money for things (like tires or furniture that need replacing if broken or worn out, or groceries, or gifts, or seasonal observances).

The net result seems to have been a looped message in my head: "You just don't get to have that, Melba!"

Oh, and that candy store? I later learned that it was a front for the town prostitute, who by the way was the friendliest woman I ever met. She served candy to the children out the front door and served the men out the back.

"A Snake and a Rock":

YoungerJuh and I developed a more mature regard and respect for each other after the snake and the rock incidents.

We morphed into our life-long ways of co-conspirators, fellow miscreants, justice-servers for our friends and neighbours, brother and sister confidants who helped each other through everything.

"The Librarian":

Over the years, Miss Jones would continue her erratic challenges of me, saying that Nancy Drew was just too old for me, claiming that the library could not afford to bring in more books in a series just because I had gobbled up every single one on file, or denying me the Hardy Boy books because those were just for boys.

My Mum was instrumental in arranging for a nurse to come to school to speak with the girls separately about the facts of life. The nurse recommended a reference book that could answer most of our questions as they came up, proudly stating that ten copies had been made available at the library. When I went to sign out one of those books, Miss Jones sniffed, she actually sniffed, and said she did not know what I was talking about.

Mum bought me my own copy, which I added to my self-made bookshelf.

Next year in high school, I was overjoyed that the school had its own library, and that a colleague friend of Mum's was the librarian, a real librarian who shared her love of the printed word and of all ideas.

Miss Jones in many forms has turned up in my life from time to time, any time that I am denied access to information or denied entry. I am not as shy or retiring about such treatment as

I was that summer in 1956. The timid wee kitten now has fangs and claws and a roar, fired in the heat of confrontation, denial, humiliation, and attempts to control.

"Cold War from the Perspective of a Child"
The ensuing years bring schoolyard discussions teaching me new words like commies, pinkos, Jews, Nazis, Ruskies, chemical warfare, nuclear fallout, anti-racial slanders, weapons of mass destruction, the need for secret agents like 007, the fact that there are persons and agencies that are trying to take over the world for their own ends. These were words that came up at the dinner table and we addressed them all, dispassionately, with historical perspective. I felt like I could trust no one outside the family circle. Each time a world event happens anywhere, when President Kennedy was shot, when the Vietnam War saw North American kids my age going off to fight the good fight, when people gathered to demonstrate, and for the rest of my life, I felt blood chilling visceral fear coursing through my body signalling that the nuclear blast and human life on the planet will soon be no more.

Health:

In the *1stThird*, my health challenged me at least annually: ulcers, nausea and vomiting, constipation, tonsillectomy, much dental work, HongKong flu, Mono, Hepatitis, miscarriage, very heavy menses that began at age 10, flipping end over end stuck in the carrier on the front of my brother's bike when being peddled fast down a long hill when my feet went into the spokes as I drew into myself in awe and fear, concussion when I fell off the jungle swing rope, and emotional trauma. In every case, my needs were looked after gently and dispassionately by loving family members or family doctor.

Achievement, Benchmarks, Milestones:

Achievement was measured in benchmarks, in school marks, in full allowance paid, in certificates and diplomas, in happy smiles of my judges and evaluators, in high scholastic averages, in getting access to the courses required to proceed toward my goal. Achievement was determined outside myself, and those judges could be whimsical, or fickle, or just plain mean.

Toolkit:

My toolkit was stocked with keen observation, hyper energy, quick wit, memorization, finding a way where others could not, surviving in the over-crowded world of the BabyBoomer where we were most often met with resentment and with fatigue-created burnout from others who were meant to teach or help us.

I was at the top of technology with a typewriter that my parents had given me as a high school graduation gift after spending my Latin spares in the Typing class learning to touch type. The typing teacher was diminutive in height and a giant in presence. "Why do you want to learn to type?"

"I hear it is a good idea for writing essays at university where no one will take the time to sort through anyone's handwriting."

"I hear you, I see you, you are gone-gone-gone!"

"Thank you, Mrs. Grace."

Wisdom: Making Sense of It All (from Reaction to Codes to Philosophies):

1. Sparkle on Command, first last and always.
2. Just do it, do it right, do it right now.
3. Not as advertised: beware of promises. Few are ever realized.

4. Fair is fair, and not fair is not fair. The Golden Rule reminds us to do unto others as you would have them do unto you... which means equal is equal.

Conclusion: And So the Stage is Set

And so the stage is set. The characters are introduced. For better or worse, both the setting and the cast will live in Melba's subconscious as though it were her very DNA, and affect her conscious decisions and what she lives with in her day-to-days.

Her boughs and leaves will shelter and nurture both herself and also those she invites or allows to take up residence.

This is her springboard.

2ndThird - Keeping Up With Success; Jobbing; Dancing as Fast as I Can

Introduction: Experience, Organizer, Facilitator

In the *2ndThird*, Melba experiences life in her home, with family, on the job, with the greater community. She applies her skills learned in the *1stThird*, and becomes the organizer and facilitator which will allow her to be of service to others.

2ndThird is about settling in and settling down, about keeping body and soul together.

It is about working, fulfilling our purpose, committing to family and to others, and making a living to support those dependent on me and then myself.

In my father's discussion about our life as similar to the life of a tree, he described the *2ndThird* as all about being the branches that support and sustain. Our branches become shelter for others, family, friends, neighbours, people at work, and the job itself.

In the Pagan and Wiccan consideration, the *2ndThird* is refered to as life-as-Mother, birthing and nurturing.

Job and Career: Education as Teacher

"Ms. McGee, please report to the school board office."
When I arrive, I am briskly shown to the office of someone

in personnel, who demonstrated the same new-to-the-job traits as did I.

After a lifetime of lineups, it is obvious to me that there are so few new teachers being hired that there is no wait time, no rush-rush, no push, no one else in the waiting room. This is looking promising.

"Congratulations on your new position and contract, Ms. McGee; welcome to our Board of Education. Please sit down. Did you bring the forms and documents requested?" Those forms are calmly explained and signed, with reminders about what this commitment would mean for me, and for the school board. Patience and kindness abound in the explanations, but there is no interference in my coming to my own conclusions about choices in the more personal documents such as insurance, next of kin.

After the school board meeting, I drive out to the school of the cousin-principal who had gotten me in the door of the interview. "Hello, Mr. White. I just signed my green contract for an Intermediate teaching position which will be located, eventually, in this school. Thank you for your support during the application process. Do you have time to give me a tour?"

"Of course, I have time. Are you on a schedule for the afternoon?"

"No schedule for me; I came to thank you and to get my bearings. And I have to admit that I would like to supply teach here for the the month of June. I must tell you that I signed up for Occasional Teacher work when I signed my contract."

We spend the afternoon touring the building, meeting some of the teachers and students, discussing teaching styles, philosophy, and getting acquainted.

One bright early June morning, the first day in the school as supply teacher, the cousin principal walks me to the classroom, with a bursting-at-the-seams grade 8 class, where most of the students are taller and stronger than am I. At 5'4" and 105 pounds, I was determined to prove more strong-willed than all of them together.

"This is Ms. McGee. She knows her stuff and is here to teach you today as a supply teacher. I shall be checking in through the day; there will be no nonsense; cooperation and learning are expected from each of you."

Whenever typical 14 year old energies built, someone at the back of the class would simply warn, "Door's open," much the same way that road-hockey kid-players on a residential street in front of their homes would warn, "Car!" I presume that the lookout has spotted the principal going down the hall; such is the influence of this principal.

As the students and I go through the routines and demands of the day, I begin to realize the rhythm of their needs, thoughts, and behaviours; I come to the understanding that though this is not the age group I was considering when I started Teacher's College, it is one that intrigues me. I am drawn to teach and to help them.

We just click. It helps that I am only nine years older than are they, that I am fresh from hippie lifestyle of Carleton University in the 1970s (One parent came in to meet me, saying, "I have heard so many good things about you; I just had to come in to meet you and see this paragon with hair down to here and heels up to here!"), and that I take myself and my commitment to them and their success very seriously. Though cautioned at teacher's college never to smile in the classroom in the first month, I smile often, sharing thought and enthusiasm for the lesson topic, for information, and for student success.

Come September, my green-contract begins in a portable at the neighbouring-school with one of the interviewing principals, with the understanding that I would later in the year continue at the newly-renovated intermediate wing of the school of the other interviewing principal. Phew! Three principals in six months.

When it comes time for me to set up my classroom for

September, I feel like I am acclimated to the culture of the rural hamlet neighbourhood and the people who live there.

"Wow! You interviewing principals weren't kidding!"

In the portable, I find textbooks, in poor shape; they are the same textbooks that I had studied ten years before, which were old even then. Uninspired, technical regard for the subject, they could demonstrate commitment to detail but certainly not to fun-based learning, sparking remembrance.

There is, indeed, no library in the school; the five-set encyclopedia, purchased with my own money, lives in my classroom and are used daily. "Knock, knock, knock!"

"My teacher heard about your library; she sent me to your classroom to borrow a book."

"Who is your teacher? I shall speak with her at recess. Meanwhile, just this once, you may look for your answers staying right here in our classroom and then off you go back to your classroom."

Nonplussed, I go and speak to the teacher. "Your student came to my classroom today, and asked to use my encyclopedia."

"Yes, I sent Joey. He heard about your encyclopedia sets from his older sister who is in your room."

"My books are used by my students minute by minute, which means they need to stay in my room. I also noticed that the school has a set of encyclopedia in the bookcase in the hall, that the school set is badly depleted and sadly abused. May I suggest you spend your own money to purchase for your students, same as did I?" Create a stir, I did.

The principal of the school comes to speak with me after school, "I hear that Mrs. Johnson sent a student to your classroom with a request to borrow from your library of encyclopedias."

"I received that request. I allowed the younger sibling to come into my classroom to complete his research, but I cannot interrupt my lessons for any continuing requests of this kind. It is just too disruptive. I make my case for protecting my investment which is scheduled to claim a portion of my paycheque for the next two years: why would I lend out my books to someone who was present when the single school-set of reference books was defaced and lost?"

The principal told me to stand my ground, and to continue to advocate for the learning of students in my charge.

"Whistle, whistle, whistle!" "Hey Cutie Pants!" "Come on out here, Teacher. I'll teach you something!"

There is construction going on in this school, as well: a new gym, and a new library, ready for Primary and Junior students once the Intermediates cleared out and cleared space.

Working conditions include construction workers, a tar pot outside our classroom windows, noise and sickening fumes, and unwelcome cat-calling aimed at the new young teacher inside. What to do?

I close the curtains and windows, with instructions that we will just ignore it all.

I am courteous and collegial with the workers when our paths cross outside the classroom, the rest of the day.

I bring my own home-baking for the construction workers' morning coffee break each day that week, and I introduce myself by name. "You know, Ms McGee, this is sure nice, but it is too much for you to bring this to us every day. How about once a week?" The catcalls evaporated.

One day, I am going into the staffroom to do some marking during my prep time while the French teacher is teaching my class. In the staffroom is the construction white-hatted lead. "Hello, little darlin'. Aren't you just the cutest little thing!" He advances towards me, backs me up against the door for unwelcome hands and mouth all over me while I struggle to break loose: what to do?

Another teacher, thankfully, arrives and is trying to get in; her calling and pushing on the blocked door makes the unwanted advances break off. When she gains entrance, (she was the teacher who wanted to borrow my encyclopedia books), she takes one look at me, at my armful of books-to-be-marked spilled to the floor, turned on her heel and then left.

I make my getaway, taking shelter in the Custodian's room for my marking period. When I return to my classroom, I find the principal waiting for me; he had been searching for me. "What happened in the staffroom? Yes, Mrs. Johnson came to report to me." The woman whom I thought hated me had reported her witness of the attack to the principal.

"Yes, it's true. I don't know how to get past this; certainly this is going to be more difficult than catcalls, and stinking tar-pot, and home baking!"

His jaw drops; he reminds me, "I am here for teachers as well as students, and for making the workplace a safe place for everyone. I will handle the situation!"

I express my gratitude.

That construction lead was replaced next day by someone new who came to me and apologized for his former colleague's treatment of me. There are no more catcalls. The tar-pot is moved away from any windows. My students and I can breathe again.

Because there is no gym, we have Phys-Ed outside in the huge yard. Again, no equipment, so I purchase a half dozen balls for that sport, and a giant bag to hold the equipment in a corner in my classroom. Again, the requests from other teachers to borrow; again, my refusal. "Way to win friends and influence others!" Nope, I was protecting my property so I wouldn't waste my considerable investment taken from meagre funds.

My students and I were in a portable outside the school. It is a self-contained unit with blackboards, shelves, desks and chairs, cloakroom, and two doors.

When a student needs to collect their thoughts, a euphemism for "get out till you settle down to learn, and let the rest of us learn", they are sent to sit on the steps of the portable. I remember a time when a student was dismissed to the step on a day blustering with the first flakes of winter's windy promise. After some time, I notice the early wintry weather outside the windows, find the student's coat, hat, and mitts in the cloakroom, open the door, and then hand over proffered protection from frostbite.

"M-M-M-Ms. McGee, thanks for my hat and coat and mitts. It's soooo coooold! If I promise to pay attention to classroom and learning tasks, to be quiet, may I please come back in?" I never had much need for steps-time for any student after that.

My students respond positively to the idea of square dancing, in the portable, as an active class in movement, dance, and socializing. Within eight minutes of mention of the activity, the students carry every desk and chair outside leaving space for three "squares", or maybe lopsided ovals, one of which loops around the wall separating classroom from cloakroom. My newly purchased portable record player and records are in place and turned on. Thirty minutes later, every desk and chair is carried back in and placed in correct position, without mishap, and without desk contents being jostled out of order. We enjoy that activity beyond Phys-Ed classes when it becomes a reward for finishing work early. This activity demonstrates cooperation, and commitment to helping others; not one single student is left out of the calm, spontaneous, joyful, and active participation.

It is a fall of making do, of finding a way, together.

Before we go home for winter Holydays, we have to pack up that portable's contents so all could be moved to the new school where we would report first day in January, now that the construction over there was (more or less) completed. Decisions are made about what goes with us and what would become trash. Nothing would be left behind; all the Intermediates are leaving the school.

We invite Principal and Office staff and Custodian to our last day pot luck (yes, the students created their own food contributions) farewell. We square-dance, unsquare dance, chat and munch our way through the day, telling tall tales about meeting each other for the first time, how we wonder about the influence of our new location and new rotary timetable in January, and discuss our plans for successful completion of grade seven.

Good thing we invited the Custodian to lunch; by the end of day, the garbage pile of trash bags fill an entire corner of the portable, floor to ceiling! But the floor is clean as are desks and chairs. Years later, I met Custodian Mrs. Kennedy and apologized for the condition of our departure. She reassured me, "Every single classroom is always piled up with trash before any vacation! But none was ever as clean and well organized as was yours!" Phew! One bridge not burned.

In January, in the new wing of the other school, my students and I have to find our way in a new building, with another principal (the second of the interviewing principals) and a new timetable which find me teaching my own class students Math and English, and all the Intermediate girls (6 classes) Phys-Ed along with grade 1 Phys-Ed. There are many more students to meet and serve, without the small number ease of the Autumn setup. More consideration will be required to determine how to offer the same level of personalized service to eight times the number of students, in a school where the principal was similarly busy.

Every morning, the principal makes the rounds before the buses arrive, again during first period, and again at end of day. He rides one bus each morning and another at night as he learns where each student lives, and what their body language while walking their laneway says about home. Though the principal makes sharp comments to me about my self and my personal life, he teaches me about dedication to understanding where the students are coming from, both geographically and emotionally.

New School - New Atmosphere - New Leadership Style

For the first time in my Jobbing Life my local boss is not supportive of me, is not interested in me finding my own way and pressures me to follow his way. It is his way or the highway. I choose the high road rather than the low road! He has a lovely wife who is kind and giggly with me; they have a strict religious life. He points out to me, "Without an active Christian-based religious affiliation, you are never going to measure up!" My response is to purchase for him Kahlil Gibran's text, *The*

Prophet, which I present to him for his consideration. Though he sometimes teases me and laughs with me, he has a hard and uncompromising edginess that often feels more like meanness and judgement, that leaves me thinking that I am meant to feel incomplete and inadequate.

I certainly have much to keep me busy: this chosen Career, this Job now with scores instead of dozens of students to teach, guide, and encourage toward independence. That busyness keeps me from dwelling on my many inadequacies and shortcomings, which are never clearly defined, and with no clear method for overcoming them.

There are two intermediate teachers, whom the students acknowledged as leader of their class, who are well regarded by staff, students, and admin. I speak with one about my determination to continue to develop as a teacher, and ask if I could take my prep times sitting in the back of his class just so I can soak up the culture, and every aspect of his teaching style which is based on encouragement. Throughout my career, whenever I was nonplussed, I would ask myself what Terry would do.

Everyone of this new Intermediate staff is lively, energetic, and completely involved in the tasks at hand, forming the foundation of the importance of teamwork. Though I am the youngest and newest, they treat me as an equal, accept that I would be a good team member, and make teaching and work and responsibility fun, and trust me to do my part well.

Environmental Studies is a curriculum topic; it involves each and all of us in making our surroundings better for us having been there. Our school yard is devoid of trees. Though we have a huge school yard, certainly room for two soccer / football fields, two ball diamonds, teeter totters and climbing apparatus, tether ball poles, and basketball nets, there is no shade for those recesses when the relentless sun beats down on us all, during clear and hot summer days.

My class determines that we should improve the yard by

planting a shade tree, a deciduous tree that would leaf out for those days when we most need sunblock protection. "If we plant a tree a year, by the time our future kids come to the school as students, there will stretch a wall of shade trees! We should do this!" Enthusiasm bubbles over.

One student spoke at home about our discussions; the next day he and his father arrive on a tractor with a fifteen foot Canadian maple tree with its roots still in a ball of earth, along with a couple of cubic yards of manure from their pile on their farm, all contained in the bucket of the tractor. This farmer, a former local school board member, looks over the yard, and the activities housed there, and finds a spot where even a large tree would not interfere with any sport or activity. He releases the tree and manure from the tractor's bucket, and then begins to dig. Once he and the tractor have removed the most difficult part of the hole, he pulls out several shovels and the gleeful classmates take their turns digging until sufficient space is created and ready for manure, and then roots, and then earth. The custodian attaches the hose and we soak the planted tree roots, smack the earth with shovel-back to jiggle out the worst of the air bubbles. Then the father gathers into the tractor bucket what used to be in the hole, and goes home. Though many students and staff come to see what we are doing, the principal does not.

A cousin of one of my students has come for a visit from Italy. He attended our classes hoping to strengthen his English language skills, does the same work as the rest of the students, possesses a quick mind and a strong work ethic, and he completes superior work. Claudio speaks on his last day in our Canadian school about coming back for a visit as a grown man when he would look for our tree which represented his feelings about being in this Canadian class as a fully accepted member of a very special group.

When we leave for the summer holidays, our tree stands straight and fully leafed out. When I return in the middle of August to set up my next year's class, the tree is gone. I run to the custodian who said I needed to speak with the principal. The principal says, "No one consulted with either me or the school board about planting a tree, about a good location on the yard, about an appropriate tree species, and so the tree was taken down and away." I ask the principal why he did not come to speak to me, the morning the tree showed up unannounced, while we were measuring and determining location, why he did not allow the class or the teacher to hear and participate in this destructive part of the process. I am dismissed to go back to my place.

The treatment is unfair, immature, and disrespectful. It affects my relationship with this community leader on into the future.

Still he is my boss and I have a duty to him.

One day I go to his office, on his open door policy, to seek advice about a boy in my class who never does any homework, ever. I review homework expectations in place in my class, and compare them to those of our school in general. I review the student's overall achievement of fairly good grades that would be dragged down by noncompliance in the matter of homework completion. "Do you have any suggestions for what I could try next to help this student?"

The principal tells me to go back to the classroom, and then bring the student down to the office. When we return, the principal is on his feet, jacket off, and two straps on his desk. Startled, I look at the principal who glares back at me. The student is asked which strap he chooses for the beating; he chooses the biggest one; he holds out his hand. The principal tells me to stay when I try to intervene and then to leave; he covers the student's wrist with his other hand, gets a crazy-fierce look on his face and straps the student's hand, hard. My agony and my tears erupt. Second stroke, I start to cry profusely. Third stroke I bawl like a baby right out loud. There are neither tears nor outburst from the student. The principal tells the student to do his homework from now on, and to go back to class. I turn to leave with the student, hoping to apologize for somehow making this horrifying thing happen to him.

But, oh no: "No, no, you stay here Ms McGee!" After the student left, he tells me that would have been a lot easier and would have had better effect had I not bawled like a baby the whole time. I am dismissed, too, with a "Now get back to class, yourself!"

Once back in the classroom, the rest of the students notice my tear-stained face and ask if I was ok, to which the receiver of the strap said to classmates, "Mind your own fucking business!"

He and I have a chance, later in the hall, for me to apologize to him for somehow precipitating something unintended, and not necessary. The student says, "Some principals are just crazy and mean, like some dogs! It is not your fault. I should have told you sooner that I get off the bus and straight into the truck to go help my Dad at our business. We don't return until fall-into-bed-time leaving no time for a real supper or any clear-thinking homework."

Though I do as I am told as a dutiful employee, I never again seek advice, eventually quit attending staff functions at the principal's home, and I certainly never initiate any contact or conversation with that principal. I feel like I have been forced to witness something immoral leaving me with the feeling it was all my fault.

When Woman / Women Became Womyn

As a child growing up, I learned about conventions of language. When seeking a singular pronoun for a mixed-gender group, one defaults to the male pronoun. Makes sense because it is easy. And this demonstrated the unrest that grew all around us.

Though I grew up in a house full of boys, I was never subjugated below them or by them. I didn't have more or fewer chores than they did. My mother had as much say as did my father. Both parents shouldered the responsibility for discipline and punishment; they both could wield a strap, in fact they each had their own strap from their teaching-to-pay-their-way-through-university days. No matter which parent was present, there was no deferring discipline by using the "Just wait til your father gets home!" style as my friends said was the case in their home. My mother eventually sought and became the head of the Math department, a job that she loved, at the high school where she taught. My father eventually became a glassblower, a job that he loved. My brothers would complete some post-secondary education as would I; this statement was the same as "everyone eats breakfast before heading out for their day". My brothers took swimming lessons, and so did I.

I begin to notice a shift in the respect paid to others.

The news is full of stories about discrimination between races and genders, and about demonstrations for equality, and about the price some pay to win equal treatment.

The homes of my friends have mothers who work at home instead of outside the home. When we visit after school, my friend's mother might be found ironing, making supper, hair in pin-curls so her fresh hairdo would be ready when her husband comes home from a "long and hard day's work" to a quiet and well kept house and wife. The brothers of my girlfriends would push aside their sister even when the sister gets there first.

Books and songs show up in my world: *The Female Eunich* and *I Am Woman Hear Me Roar* and so many more.

I begin to mouth and mimic slogans and buzzwords and song lyrics.

I refuse to use the phrase man and wife, and replaced it with wife and husband.

I dress and act and speak to suit myself not my partner.

I learn that it is important that I know my 'place'; however, my place is no higher or lower that that of anyone else.

I give deference to others when they earn it; I give respect to others always.

When a form had "Sex" beside a box, I fill in either "Not today thanks" or "Yes please", and fill in a suggestion that they use the word Gender for their purposes in future.

I present to the world a person named Melba, no better or worse than any other, not a girl or teacher or daughter or sister or mother or girlfriend or dancer or artist or piano player or swimmer or deferrer or subjugater of self or teacher or wife...

I choose to wear a lot of titles and hats because it makes clear the job that I come to do and my legal position.

I am me!

Mum sees my response to the unrest which held society in its grip. "Mum, we make no claim to gripe or rip at society. We simply choose to make changes so that no woman will ever need to see the word man in woman. I am a womyn!"

"Do you embrace Affirmative Action? Because I will never let Affirmative Action be thrown in my face as the reason for my achievements. Every single one of my achievements comes from my own determination and dedicated work. Never did I allow anyone else to claim my achievement as theirs." Mum speaks her point of view.

"We need to set an action in place that will punish anyone who keeps another down, who subjugates another, who holds others in their control, who takes away their freedoms and rights as a human being.

We eschew any action that somehow makes someone else the one in charge, turns the tables but still leaves someone in charge of someone else, as does affirmative action.

Everyone, no matter their gender or race or age or religion or origin or economic status or intellectual endowment or any other determination gets an equal shot.

This is what we 'roar' for!"

"You know that the powers that be, the rich, the politically powerful, the industrialists will not go gently into that good night?" she counters.

"Well, I'm going to stand for trying, for outlasting the wrong side in any fight!"

"And who are you to decide which side is the wrong side?" she asks.

"I am the side of the moral right. The side of correct, and fair, and equal, and able."

"Then be prepared to be shot down, destroyed, eschewed, shunned, fired, lonely."

"I just need to be able to look myself in the mirror every night and say that I didn't put myself first every time, that I didn't put myself last every time. I shall let my moral compass point due north to the Golden Rule (Do Unto Others as You Would Have Them Do Unto You); it shall guide my way. I shall continue to serve others. I shall be my best me."

"And I shall support you all the way!"

Building a House - Making a Home

Ten years after our first date, after traveling to see the world from different perspectives, after meeting people outside our small communities, we decide that we should make some definite plans for the future. After all, we still happily gravitate towards each other for weekends, for special occasions, for family events and local events, or travel, and our friends are "our" friends.

We decide to build our own house on a corner of the property to which his family arrived many generations and a hundred and fifty years ago. If we are still speaking when the house is habitable - enclosed with lockable doors and windows, bedroom ready for furniture, one working bathroom, usable kitchen - then we will get married. Some of our friends are "living together" without getting married; though we have an appreciation for that lifestyle, we live and work in a small rural community, and we are planning to have kids. The community and my job are not ready to see me having children out of wedlock. They barely tolerate pregnant womyn teaching or any womyn wearing pants unless it is a pantsuit!

We pour over house and floor plans, with an eye to what we

had watched our friends build, and in what way they said that they would have changed their plans after living in the place for some years. We also consider lifestyle, and parenting from the perspective of their experiences.

I show Mum each plan; she asks questions; we make adjustments or we are galvanized into understanding that ours was a good choice. We talk about furniture, colours, windows and window coverings to keep out the Canadian winters and summer heat, gardens, timelines, the one year plan, the five year plan, and the ten year plan.

In April, Mum lost her battle with cancer, after living ten times longer than any doctor had pronounced, after losing weight down to her final 65 pounds, after putting out her own determined chin even up to the last two weeks of her life; we break ground in May with a feeling that Mum is with us when we put each plan into action. Dig we did, right down to bedrock; we decide not to break into that bedrock floor because we did not want to create a wet unusable lower floor which would have been more swamp than floor; I sweep it off, we bring in the crushed stone, and up we build. Our ranch style bungalow becomes a higher structure back-filled to look like a house with a basement rather than the split entry which had become the bane of the existence of some friends who had chosen that style. Already, we are proving to be open to plan adjustments.

We make a plan that requires no mortgage. We hire a contractor who is amenable to our doing some of the work; he and his crew would frame the house, enclose the house, roof it, side it, lay the flooring we bought, install the giant heat-liner fireplace, drywall, and assign what we would need to complete before the next piece of work on the to-do list. We do plumbing ourselves after firing the plumber because he wanted to do it to suit him not us (why should I give up a baby-changing counter for a second sink in the family bathroom; why give up a larger single bathroom for a tiny shower complete bathroom off the master bedroom back to back with a tiny tub family complete bathroom off the hall?). We also do our own wiring and insulation and finishing. We confer with the pros, telling them our ideas and wishes and listening to what their experience has taught them. We refer to our Readers Digest book about how to build a house step by step, every single day.

Though we each report to work every day, we go straight to the house site after work to put in several hours of work before sun goes down, which is when we go home to late supper, and I to my marking. Sleep came so easily in those days.

We decided to build the first of three phases:

First is a simple bungalow, easily finished preserved-wood basement where the bedrooms would be in a later plan, upstairs / ground level with a big open country kitchen incorporating dining and sitting areas with no walls, so whomever is working in the kitchen could still be part of the conversation, three bedrooms with only one full family bathroom and a powder room inside the back door for those quick-quick-quick moments in any family.

The infrastructure is based on technologies of the time, looking at environmental impact:

- We position ourselves with the living area big windows facing the sun for three-season much-valued solar heat.
- Our huge fireplace would dominate the living area and have a heat-liner so we can fan in outside air which would circulate around the firebox and be into the house.
- One wall in the living room accommodates our sound and light entertainment system which includes giant tv, sound system with eight foot long "paragon" speaker-system home-built from red oak, recording equipment, and enough correctly balanced speakers to make us feel like we were sitting right there in the middle of movie action or music.
- Our appliance list adds a dishwasher to take advantage of water and electricity saving technologies. And we buy the biggest freezer we could find to accommodate our

growing, harvesting, preserving, and setting-by for winter needs.

- Our R-value insulation is double the current standard to guard us from cold and heat. -Our windows and doors similarly meet our security and environmental needs. Ceiling fans in every room would reverse so we can enjoy a breeze or gently waft the heated air at the ceiling back down onto us.
- Solid 3/4 inch oak floors, ebony stained, built to last any lifetime, are installed in the living area.
- Our forced-air, combination electric and wood-burning furnace just makes sense. Future plan calls for a heat pump adding air conditioning in summer, and releasing us from all that tree cutting, sawing into lengths, and splitting required each summer. The decision to move away from the wood burning portion of the system came when my husband later had knee surgery at same time as the difficult birth of our first child, both of which dictates no exertion for either of us for months. When it comes time to lug in wood, bend over to heave a giant block of wood into furnace for another six hours of heat, we both look at each other, and then flip the switch to the expensive electric furnace.

All of our decisions are based on money on hand at the time, the list of sequenced tasks to be done, our determination to use our resources of time, our ability to learn, our consideration of purposing our land, our back-to-the-land instead of easy-but-expensive lifestyle choice. We are living the dream of doing for ourselves.

We finish up the first phase, and while still at the house one evening, we realize we have reached habitable stage. We look at each other to assess whether we are still speaking, and find that in this moment we are indeed.

"Well, what do you think?"

Next step...

Well, the House is Habitable, and We *Are* Still Speaking ...

Still speaking?

After all that hot, sticky, heavy, itchy, heretofore unfamiliar steep-learning-curved work? After all the compromises to each wish-list which felt to each of us like the compromising was all in one direction? We are starting to relax into the idea of inhabiting the results of all our labours.

We begin to revisit updated opinions and feelings around the rest of the agreement: if we have created a habitable living space, and if we are planning to live together, if we are planning to have kids, then we must consider marriage in the climate of this locale and culture.

"I suppose you want an engagement ring?"

"I'd prefer toilets and sinks for same cost."

When friends later ask to see my engagement ring, I take them to the bathrooms and point to my "ring".

In some ways, we are feeling like there has been enough compromise and neither one of us has the energy or will to toggle the concept.

Off I go, to phone our most recent and much beloved minister at my family's church, the church of most of my childhood, where I was baptized at 12 as was my mother's family way, joined the church, attended and later taught Sunday School, participated in the Junior Choir, attended and helped at the Christmas Bazaar, and knew every nook and cranny of the building. This was the church where my mother had served on UCW (UnitedChurchWomen), had helped prepare and and serve at funerals and weddings, had helped and taken Lead on the Christmas Bazaar, had attended services after first polishing up her often-truculent and resisting family.

"Hello?"

"May I speak to the Minister, Reverend Wylie, please?"

"Reverend Wylie is away for some months. In the meantime, you will have to speak to me as interim minister."

"The reason for my call is to make arrangements for my wedding."

"You deserve no wedding here in this church because you are unaware that Reverend Wylie is absent for six months. You are not a loyal supporter of this church!"

There is no moving the grump; he is from another branch of the Christian church where, clearly, ministering unto the flock in their time of need was not as high on the list as was judgement. Feeling the tears well up, I sign off from speaking with the brick wall on the other end of the phone line.

Six months before, Mum had died and was funeral-ed in this same church. She would have preferred me to be married before living together and before having children. She would have preferred me to be married in our church.

Dad hears my conversation, and my tears. He is as dumbfounded as am I.

Next call is to my fiancé.

Dad had been taking the bus to work, having given up the three hour commute time while driving himself; each day he would board, at our corner, the bus that served people in our small town who went to the city to work, again gathering them up at end of the work day to bring them home. When he comes home the next night, he says, "You should call the minister again." That was not what I wanted to do after the last night's conversation. When I say as much to Dad, I hear that Dad had sat with one of the church elders on the bus that day. The elder is furious that I had been spurned by our church, and has made contact with the minister, who is told how we do things in our church to serve our congregation members.

Making that call is like stepping back into the whupping of the precious night. The man makes me wait for fifteen rings until he picks up. "How dare you run behind my back! That is not a very Christian thing to do!

I will only marry you if you agree to attend my marriage course, a series of four evenings, offered only because I am being forced to marry you."

Next call is to my fiancé who is not as church committed as am I. "What is the time commitment required of me?"

"The time commitment is being required of us both!"

Silence. We set our calendars.

Off we go on our first class. The faith practiced and ministered by this man was more fundamental than our United Church. I can't tell if his hellfire and damnation oration is a product of his sulk, or of his training. We are asked to respond in unison at certain moments. The closed-door room was getting hotter by the moment, due to the closed door or maybe the hellfire? This is when my fiancé leans over, and in his whisper (actually, he never did master the technique of whispering), he says, "If he makes me get down on my knees on the floor, I'm out of here!" My gasp and head-spin turn to the minister. His hard glare response speaks volumes of disdain, but there is no getting on our knees.

The minister refuses to say "declare you husband and wife", but insisted on "man and wife" instead. He refuses to tolerate *Here Comes the Bride* and I say I want Pachelbel's Canon instead. I insist on my favourite *1 Corinthians 13: 4-7* verse as the reading.

I must have worn him down, because there is no discussion at all about the *Wedding March.*

This minister grudgingly agrees to a rehearsal the night before the wedding, but insists on attending the dinner in the Ladies Parlour, following the wedding, where all Mum's friends prepare and serve the meal. I notice that they serve the minister last; word gets round in a small town.

I feel Mum at my shoulder through the entire wedding, from planning, to sewing my dress, to fine crocheting my lace shawl, to cooking the wedding cake, to sending out invitations to our small wedding (Mum had so recently died that I had no will to hold a big event. She had always wanted me to have a big wedding, something that she was denied herself). Mum is saying, "Well done, Melba!" She isn't just talking about details; I imagine her pride is also in how I take the whole minister thing like a womyn and a lady - rare for me!

After the ceremony, we all twenty of us go back to Mum and Dad's where we toast with champagne, throw copious amounts of confetti, and open gifts.

Groom and bride then leave to spend our first night in our new home as husband and wife, and the vacuum comes out to clean up all that confetti that is actually rectangles punched from punch cards at OldestJuh's work. Of course, this is small town Ontario, so many of the revellers shivaree us there in our home; that is to say the party continued until the wee hours of the morning.

Our wedding day had started at 4am when one of the pipes-in-progress let go with a blast of water exploding down onto the basement floor. We dash to solve the problem, me jumping up on the sawhorse to crimp the make-do hose thus feeling like a hero, him going to the shut off valve and with a simple twist of his hand proving himself to actually be the hero. Our wedding day seems to be over nineteen hours later so I retire to a lovely soak in a tub with my peignoir set, a gift from Mum, hanging and ready for wear. Suddenly, the best-man, a friend since forever, opens the door and tells me to get dressed and join the party. Good thing that I had chosen bubbles instead of oil for my bath, eh! Out I go in my wedding night finery thinking I could shame them into leaving. Nope, stay they did, even beyond my excusing myself an hour later for some much needed sleep for tomorrow's continuing festivities: 250 relatives and friends and coworkers invited to an Open House at our new home.

I Put Butter on my Plate Five Times yet I Still Cannot Find Any Butter for my Bread!

I love entertaining. From the decision to invite: to the planning and listing; to the shopping, cleaning, and preparations; to the conversations, laughter, and sharing; and finally to the cleanup while I smile over each sliver of light remembered from the event. We finally had finished actual flooring, furniture, deck and picnic table at our new home. We love spending time with people. It is the social-nicety thing to do: invite people to come to dinner in response to a gift or an invitation to their home.

It is full summer and we have family in town. We have just built the deck and a giant picnic table. WooHoo! Let's have a dinner and party.

After menu planning, having found the perfect pewter plates, grocery shopping, cleaning, food prep, make fresh bread, and set up for our barbecue cooking, our guests begin to arrive.

Hosting duties include appetizers and drinks in every hand. Conversations begin, leaving the hostess in the kitchen glad of the decision to leave out the living area walls so she can hear and participate in conversations. Call to table has everyone lining up to load their plates with all the yummies they have enjoyed as scent-only to this point.

I love cooking for people who love to eat my cooking!

We serve our plates at the high kitchen counter cum buffet serving table and head out to the west side of our chocolate brown bungalow in the full sun of late afternoon, eastern Ontario summer. We begin to notice the ice supply in our glasses is melting before our eyes. My Dad is turning redder by the second (my freckled, red-headed, receding-haired-Dad always claimed that he was losing hair because "you cannot grow grass on a runway"; or that his lack of hair put him "one step further from the apes".) I fashion a towel with a headband over his head and neck, a la desert-style. People are calling for drink refills. Still we remain out on the deck, in a following-the-plan sort of way.

Until Dad says, "I have put butter my fine pewter plate five times, and still I can find no butter for my bread!" Inside we go, plate and drinks in hand, amidst much jocularity and willingness to eat standing rather than remain under that unrelenting solar power. Though we consider it, the large picnic table on the deck simply will not fit through the patio doors.

Babies ... Mmmm-Hmmm

"He loves me, he loves me not!" After post-wedding playing of the child's game of loves me loves me not" with my birth control pills, we anticipate the imminent pitter-patter of little feet. After all the money that we spent on birth control, after insisting that we would take no chances because we weren't ready or prepared yet, after all the visits to Planned Parenthood clinics and doctor's office, we are close to 30 and don't want to wait too much longer for strong and able children.

We thought that all I had to do was stop taking the pill and start planning the layette!

Ah yes, the best laid plans!

After six months of "Why did we bother spending all that time and money and effort on birth control when apparently we could have avoided all those resulting side effects," we come to realize that we really are indeed capable of conceiving a child.

I feel amazingly well. I put on a little weight. We start planning a nursery full of the needs of a baby. I start buying fatter clothes when I see that I now weigh in at 115 pounds after my usual 105 pounds of 15 years. This is easy! Late in summer vacation, I visit the gynaecologist / obstetrician for a conference to hook up within the obstetrics side of his practice. He is happy for me that things are going well, and that I had finally made our dream of parenting come true.

Plans are in place:

- pregnancy plan;
- career working outside the home plan (uh, also named quit teaching and play my flute in beautiful meadows plan);
- house rearrangement plan;

- letting family and friends know plan (a child can survive in an incubator after five months of mummy's tummy - so no need to alert anyone until that time - our own private secret);
- birthing plan;
- breast feeding plan;
- child rearing plan;
- homeschooling plan;
- stay/work at home plan.

The end of August finds me setting up in my classroom with a secret smile on my face. I will teach through the first term then go on maternity leave with a consideration for resigning after the leave was up to become a full time parent.

Then ... All that cramping and all that blood! I phone the obstetrician who tells me to get across the city to the hospital Emergency RIGHT NOW, where he will meet me. When I get there, the doctor is tied up in another delivery, and triage is unsympathetic, telling me, "Sit down on one of the plastic waiting room chairs and wait your turn!" Being a good little people pleaser, I follow orders. I mean they are caring professionals, right? They wouldn't harm my baby by doing the wrong thing, right? After more than an hour, someone comes out, and calls my name. When I stand another gush of blood runs down my legs causing consternation about cleanup from triage nurse.

She says, "Just look at all that blood!"

To which I reply, pointing to the puddle in the chair, "You mean that? Accumulating for the last hour after you told me to sit down and be quiet?"

No sign of baby; I am passing giant clots, and having to collect everything every time I go to the bathroom, which means some immature student nurses and some impatient nurses had to come paw through it all searching for fetus body parts. There were lots and lots of tears. I remain in hospital, and am given a D&C to give me a fresh start. Still I had lots and lots of tears, and no one to speak to about this unspeakable loss of baby and loss of confidence in my womyn-ness and mother-ness .

Then I have to tell everyone:

- family would not be enlarged by one more come winter;
- school would have to start without me. I am required to be present the first day of school or my contract would be voided. I am feeling pressured to show up at the beginning of first day, five days after the D&C, but I have to let the school know because the doc said I might not be able to stay on deck for a whole day after so much blood loss, and
- friends who wonder why this party girl wasn't participating in Labour Day partying demand an answer.

My loss and shame at being unable to do such a normal thing as bearing a child weighs heavily on me.

First day of school, I greet my new students, follow through the usual physical and collegial setup with my students until 11:30am when the bottom falls out of my world, again leaving me completely drained physically. I turn grey, sit down on the floor, and ask a student to go get the principal immediately. When the principal and vice-principal show up, the students are taken to the library, and I am driven home amidst my reminders about our just-in-case plan in place making sure the on-deck supply teacher is coming in and reminders about where the detailed daybook is.

I choose not to go to the hospital again. There is just not enough blood in my estimation, and certainly not in the mood for another plastic-chair-in-the-waiting-room episode. I just go to bed, and wait for my husband to come home from work.

I stay in bed as doctor orders, for the rest of the week. Back to work comes the following Monday.

I have never felt so alone in all my life.

School Board and Teacher - Seven Years Later

Apparently, my "episode" of Sick Leave has left a distaste in the mouth of School Board decision makers.

Finding myself pregnant again, after spontaneously aborting our previous pregnancy at the four month mark, I begin to plan my leave which means that I am forced to share my news earlier than I would have preferred. I apply for, and receive a letter stating that my return to the classroom in September would be half time teaching and half time Sick Leave; my maternity leave would commence first of November. I have certainly saved up enough Sick Leave. I had a letter from the doctor describing the threat of another spontaneous-aborting termination of pregnancy, and describing the high risk aspects of my pregnancy, my complications, and symptoms. The letter granting school board approval of the plan arrived into my hands by mid-June.

Come the end of August, I have spent two weeks setting up my new assignment in an unfamiliar grade, sharing the teaching with a teacher who wants me to do all the heavy lifting and marking like: Math, English, History, Geography, and Science, and leaving her to teach what? I receive a call to report to the board office in the city next day, Friday afternoon before Labour Day weekend, with school start the following Tuesday; and they insist that I bring my documentation. Off I go with contract and letter of agreement for the school year.

I walk into an office with three men in three piece suits. And me. One of those men is the polite, kind, helpful, and professional man who had helped me on contract-signing day all those years ago. They start right in: "We have asked you to come in to speak with us about your inappropriate use of Sick Leave. We cannot grant you Sick Leave when you are not sick. Complications of pregnancy are not sick; they are pregnancy / maternity," one says.

"But I have given you a copy of my doctor's letter indicating that I must teach only half time for September and October, listing my complications, symptoms, and risk, and I have my original right here. Also I have the letter that you sent to me last June giving me the permission to return to the classroom half time teaching and half time Sick Leave for September and October, after which I would be on Maternity Leave beginning of November," I answer.

"May we see your originals?" When I hand over to them, they trash the pages right in front of me; I begin to cry; I could feel the familiar and frightening gush of blood between my legs.

They offer to call my husband, my doctor, but not my Federation representative from my pre-union federation.

"I feel threatened after seeing my documentation trashed in my face."

They continue to defend their actions.

I declare that I would have to displace Stella whats-her-name from my familiar full time grade 7 assignment because if I had to risk losing another baby, I would do it in a familiar job assignment and curriculum. They say I could not do that.

"You leave me only one choice which is to resign to half time." At that time they each, and all, lift their arms up and point out that I was the one who suggested a resignation to half time.

I lose it! I call them all a bunch of unprofessional fuckers and inhumane subhumans. "When you go home after work today, and kiss your wife and family hello, you should remember someone else's wife and baby that you have put at risk today."

I ask for the return of the pieces of my paperwork. They say they can't find them. I sign the previously-readied contract papers and leave.

There are no technologies available so I drive to the school, tell the principal there what had transpired at the board office. He is astounded and concerned about me, but he too offers to drive me home or call my husband to come get me, but still, no mention of Federation involvement.

I go home, to bed, and to pray for divine intervention on behalf of our unborn baby.

When did the field of education and seeing to the needs of children in our care become so chilled with aggressive lack of concern for the needs of the workers?

Late that year, our first born arrives:

- after an 80 pound pregnancy,
- after bleeding every single day during the pregnancy,
- after morning / afternoon / evening / night sickness,
- after a breech delivery that ultimately required an hour and a half of intense stitching ("more three oh silk, more..."),
- after his, and my heart stopping during delivery meaning that there were eight people in the room besides the baby and me ... Four to save baby and four to save me, and
- after only four hours of labour.

After all this, I hold my baby-boy in my arms and realize the greatest joy, the greatest prize, and greatest responsibility of all: parenthood.

When he, and I, are finally released from hospital, we bring him home and place him in his wee bed, turn to each other and say, "Oh my god! What have we done?"

An hour later, he is changed ... again; fed ... again; rocked ... again; and yet still crying. I put him back in his bed, lie down on the hardwood floor outside his room and start that exhausted crying one knows after complete shutdown. I look up to see baby-daddy heading out the door.

Tearfully, "Where are you going?"

He responds, "Going to plant trees around the driveway; either that or take to drink!" More tears...

BabyMumma - Hitting my Stride

"Just remember this: I raised my babies, and I am NOT going to raise yours! I am sick of your new generation of womyn who whine about a little labour." These womyn who visit me in hospital after the birth don't notice that I have a blood transfusion dripping into me, also an intravenous, and a catheter, and the sides were up on my bed for a reason.

When I cry, they sniff and demand to be taken to the window of the nursery to see the baby without me there to introduce my baby-boy to them.

"God, I miss you, Mum!"

In the hospital, in late 1970s, no staff is apparently interested in helping me to learn about breastfeeding. I figure I would just put my baby to breast and nature would look after the rest. Reality is that I am sitting on an hour and a half worth of stitches, I have inverted nipples, and there is no comfortable way of relaxing and letting the milk down.

Even a nine pound baby hungrily looks forward to the next meal and latches onto whatever he can find; sometimes finding skin which breaks open and feeds him blood instead of colostrum and milk.

In the middle of the night, the feeding nurse marches to my door, arms across her chest, "I hope that you are happy with all this breastfeeding nonsense! Your hungry baby is crying in the nursery because you refused to have rooming in..."

Mentally: "(uh, check the sides up on my bed!)"

"...and you refused bottle feeding support, and you insisted on a four hour feeding schedule. You are going to have to live with what your decisions are doing to your baby. There is only one baby crying in the nursery and it is yours so when you hear the cries you can just think about that!"

Lonely tears ...

When, next day, I ask the feeding time delivery nurse for some help, I'm told that breast feeding is a natural thing so I should just let nature guide the way.

When the Obstetrician comes in to see me, I show him my bleeding breasts, and cry, and ask for some support. He suggests a bottle feeding at 10pm, change the baby to on-demand bottle from me until 6 am and then back onto the four hour nursing schedule through the day. Though this means that I bring home a baby that is reliably sleeping more than six hours at night, I hold that bottle of factory generated poison to my baby's eager mouth, and asked God and Baby-Boy both to forgive me.

At some point, the Scottish accented paediatrician assigned to Baby-Boy comes to the room and asked, "Do you have any questions?"

"What about his circumcision?"

She becomes agitated, "That is unnecessary and antiquated butchery! If you insist on going forward with that, I am off his case!" That would be leaving my apgar-first-scored-at-3 Baby-Boy without the continuing vigilance of a paediatrician with experience treating at-risk babies.

She storms out; I start to cry with no one to support me, or even hold me in my aloneness; my roommate hardly broke breath while whining about how she just couldn't do anything with her freshly showered hair here in the hospital with ho hair-blowers allowed.

My roommate is engaged in going on-and-on about her three stitches; "Unheard of!" had said her midwife grandmother. She doesn't much like getting up and going to hear the demonstrations on bathing, swaddling, and how to flip over and whack a choking baby.

The day I am relieved of catheter, IV, transfusion tubes, and railings, I get up and walk to the lesson room where are assembled a half dozen new mothers for the day's lesson, among them my roomie. When the nurse comes in and tut-tuts about why didn't I ask for a wheelchair, and I have to sit down right away, roomie whines, "I never got that care and I had three stitches after all."

After a lengthy stay at hospital. Baby-Boy and I are each cleared by our doctors and we go home, he nestles in my arms in the front passenger seat with no seat belt for either of us. Baby-Daddy, like our generation did, figures that it was his job as the driver to take the responsibility for avoiding any and all accidents, and to protect us.

At home, I break my doctor's admonishments about not walking beyond bathroom breaks, not lifting even baby, when I have to take over my own care, making meals for the household, cleaning up, and looking after Baby-Boy every four hours. After the first week, I even have to do the grocery shopping, all by myself, and quickly so I didn't interfere with anyone else's schedule. I don't even ask other family womyn for help after the dictate thrown down by them at the hospital; there is to be no help there.

The questions about what diapers to use, where to buy them, how to dispose of them, what formula to use, ("Well the lactose free one, of course!"), I realize that the formula's labelled ingredients always begin with cow's milk, and finish with a long list of chemical names which I couldn't even pronounce.

One day I answer the door and there stands a public health nurse who visits all new mothers and babies to answer questions, and check the baby and me. I hug her and bring her into the house, strip down Baby-Boy and start into a list of concerns and questions. After reminding me to follow doctors' orders at checkout time from hospital, after giving me advice about BB's rashes and how to care for umbilicus and uncircumcised penis, she examines me. When she leaves, I had visions of hanging onto her rather than letting her go.

My psychology degree doesn't begin to help me to understand, or to get past weighty thoughts like no one to help me, like minute by minute need for decision, like diapers, laundry, housework and all the while feeling that I am about to drop out of myself between my legs, sore cracking nipples, feeling useless because I am no longer bringing home a paycheque, the loneliness of being a country womyn far from others, wondering if I would ever lose eighty pounds to get back to my pre-pregnancy recognizable-body weight of 105 pounds, continuing to sparkle on command just so someone would smile at me, autism, ADHD, housework and heavy lifting, after a lifetime of walking away from people who didn't like me or didn't want me as a friend or made me feel bad about myself causing me no choice but the Girlfriends-Forever syndrome, This high functioning sensitive depressive is forced back to work because baby needed a paycheque, groceries, health benefits, and snowsuit and...

Maybe it makes me "better" because it forces me out of the deep dark hole! "Hey, Alice!"

When anyone asks me how the pregnancy and labour went, I simply say it was bad, the doctors and nurses said so; then I change the subject.

School Board and Teacher - Return to Work after Maternity Leave

After our first child and I are home from the hospital, we are assigned, by the doctor, a full year of maternity leave, meaning that I can not go back to teaching until the next November. Six months after birth of our son, I apply for the rest of a year's Maternity Leave, and include my doctor's orders (after carefully making a copy and keeping it to myself) which states that I required a full year of Maternity Leave.

In 1970s, Maternity Leaves were often two years in length. If a mother does not return after four months, her job is available but her location is not assured. The new 1980s thinking is that a return to work must take place four months from the first day of Maternity Leave to ensure a return to same assignment and location. Otherwise, a job is assured for only one year.

Here we go again: sounds familiar! I mail in my request, having no taste for another ugly scene with the scoundrels of last time. Back comes the letter saying that I must return September 1, after ten months of Leave, or resign from my now part-time job at the school board.

Having no choice, given my continuing health challenges, I resign completely.

At end of the year's medically prescribed time off, I drive out to the school and meet with the principal and vice-principal (who is my former colleague whom I observed during my first year preps), to ask if they have a job, either supply teaching or contract. I am back as a supply teacher.

Two years later, when returning from my second Maternity Leave, I meet again with a new principal and same vice-principal, looking for a job. They give me a contract teaching job of teaching one forty-minute class a day, five days a week. I mention that the baby-sitting costs and transportation costs of that contract would negate my income, and ask if I could do it all on one single day a week. They agree. After a year of wondering where money would come from, I would have some income.

One week before that job was finished, I am called into the school office where they ask me if I would consider getting hired back on full-time contract. Imagine, I didn't have to beg or cry or fret; they want me! I leapt at the chance and sign the papers that they had already prepared for me.

We talk about crowd control in the classroom, intimating this had previously been a problem in this assignment, and what ideas do I have to offer. We talk about the good ole days at the school and they give me carte blanche in curriculum decisions so Family Studies could be fun for the kids again. And finally they ask if I cooked and sewed; I reply that I do. After much handshaking and smiling, off I go to plan and prep.

Community Commitment (or, Serving Needs of Others)

The thrill of serving others, of helping someone else to realize a goal or a dream or an understanding that they are not alone, not worthless, not incapable, is an immeasurable joy. This is the thrill that has nothing to do with momentary adrenaline of burying the needle, but rather this is a joy that is sustainable forever moving me forward in a positive emotional and spiritual direction.

When I have, I give. When I don't have, I find a way to give. How can I be happy when there are others who are not? This is the idea of Ubuntu.

Communities in my life include family, greater family, neighbours, colleagues, fellow travellers on this plane, hometown, global village, nature, Mother Earth, Energies, finances, troubles, cures, and healing solutions.

Skills that I bring to the table have been created in the foundry of life, of hell, of survival, and of success. I get through the challenges, take note and take notes, review for improvement possibility, and rework alternative methods.

When someone mentions my success, compares mine to theirs, I offer an open door to help.

Some latch on as if I am a lifeline, honour and value my gift, and tell others, "Melba just showed up to help me! She is amazing!" I blush - after all, all I did was share my observations and work.

Some latch on to me personally, greedily taking all I have to offer with no respect for leaving me with my plans and notes complete and intact, starting a whisper campaign against me about who do I think I am and challenge me publicly on some twisted version of a story or comment that I made, and then start in on my personal time, my family, and my community.

Some just want to talk and talk and talk-talk-talk but do not want to do the work required to make any changes, to achieve any improvements, or healings. Energy and time thieves they are. And, they want me to carry their burdens so they can dance off unencumbered.

Some just don't want my help. All I can do is offer. If they decline my offer, it generally means that they are not yet ready, or capable of doing the work to heal, to stride forward, to learn.

All of my service experience leads me to the habit of signing up or volunteering for only a year at a time, most often leaving after fulfilling my own self imposed mandate. Sometimes I realize that I'm never going to be what they demand me to be: immoral, mean-spirited, selfish at the expense of others, and needing to hide because their moral code has been lost.

Sometimes the experience is so profound, I allow them to convince me to stay. Rarely but sometimes.

When I Got Up This Morning, I Had One Nerve Left

... and now you are getting on it! What happened to my nerves of steel? In the day to days of parenting, I find myself dealing with the typical yet terrifying usual issues. Do I breastfeed or bottle feed? Cloth diapers or disposable? Back to work and hire a babysitter or be a work at home Mum? What age is best time to start the child at the dentist? Vaccinations, yes or no? Discipline, punishment or redirection? Simple whole foods prepared at home or fun processed foods easily acquired at the grocery store? Chores, at what age do they start?

Despite my continuing study, and search for knowledge, I am limited by what I find in the library and by what experienced parents in my world are willing to share with me. Many great, supportive, and encouraging ideas come along.

Some events are not even on my radar, until I am solidly in the middle of one.

Our child's allergies turn to anaphylactic shock to anakits to epipens to allergy shots to considerable lifestyle changes for home and school and everyone in the child's environment.

Our child decides to cut her hair to the scalp instead of watching the kids channel on satellite tv while I prepped food. Moreover, those sharp and long scissors are housed in the basement which meant transporting the scissors up the stairs by the two year old.

Our child decides to go swimming, as a three year old, and I say that we would swim later after my chores are finished. When the clothes come off anyway, I figure some naked play was not an unusual choice at our remote country home. When I go out to check on her whereabouts, I find my child (one of a very short list of people I would die for or kill for) floating face down in the pool, blue, and not breathing. Someone never quite made it out to close the gate last night when they meant to. I jump from the deck, over a four foot railing, across five feet of space, and over the six foot fence around the pool, turn the baby over and begin artificial respiration. Our trip to the closest hospital and then to the children's hospital once the critical hours had passed is filled with my demands to the heavens, "Give me back my baby; I'm not finished with this one yet!" Hospital staff, once they have a drowning victim brought in, line up to beat up the parent, threatening her with children's aid coming and taking my baby away, all the while she is standing in front of them in a wet dress that smells of chlorine and puke because I blow too hard in my frantic attempts to apply every ounce of my will and of my lifeguard and first aid training.

Not every school and every teacher has my child's best interests and learning in mind, when they deny my child's significant capabilities, and their basic needs like free access to drinking water in a portable classroom sweatbox on the hottest days of the year. When they say that my child is not smart, and I have to move my child to another school, and I delight in delivering the next year's report card from the other school with straight As.

When we are parents, we face scraped knees, hurt feelings, disappointments, unfinished chores, the challenges that come from typical bright kids, bullying, unfairness, refusal, and independence rearing its head all too soon.

And we survive, as does our child, their independence, their health, and their achievement in the face of great challenge.

Keeping Your Straps Tied Tight - Lessons in Parenting

As I grow through the various stages of parenting and our children grew through their years and sizes, I often harken back to my role models, my own parents and the parents of our friends.

My parents taught me, in vivid display, the realities of day to day parenting ...

My Dad was like Farley Mowat. Each summer, he would pack up the station wagon with mother, three sons, one daughter, one cocker spaniel, and himself, the whole family, except for cat because no one would take an independent puss on a seven day road trip!

We would head to some place new, somewhere in North America, camping at sites with a beach and rarely, but occasionally, staying in a motel with a pool. While my Dad attended an American Glassblowers Association symposium, sharing his knowledge, techniques, and learning new ideas as well, we five would scout about the area looking for knowledge and experience, the kind that you cannot find at home.

Like the Griswolds and the Mowats, our station wagon was packed to the gills! This list included:

- a canvas tent that my Mum had sewn on her black Singer sewing machine,
- the fold-away cots and air mattresses;
- towels, sleeping bags, sheets, pillows (what delight the Juhs would have farting into the pillow of the other, until they discovered, years later, that neither of them had slept on their own pillow because they each artfully exchanged pillows with the other at bedtime unbeknownst to the other. You should have seen the looks on their faces when realization dawned many years later);
- clothes;
- camp stove;
- pots, pans, dishes, utensils, cutlery, implements, and tools;
- leash for the dog, and
- expandable water pail for hauling water to the campsite.

All were stored in cloth or canvas bags, tied closed with a

one-inch or two-inch canvas woven strap. Though every item was carefully planned and catalogued, some had double duty. Among those were the canvas straps which guy-wired the tent upright by night and strapped belongings into their carry-bags and onto the roof-rack by day. No straps meant no tent by night, a mean feat in deepest, darkest, mosquito country in 1950s backwoods North American campgrounds, and stowed gear typically lashed on top of the car moved inside the car by day, the result of which dominoed YoungerJuh and me into the leg-room-less back recesses of the station wagon, while OlderJuh, who considered his stretched-across-the-seat legroom to be his domain, took up the back bench and OldestJuh in front between Dad and Mum.

We never even thought about suitcases; we certainly did not have the money to purchase a suitcase for everyone, and my mother's honeymoon suitcase would not carry six people's clothing needs for a week. Mum made cloth bags, much like pillowcases, which they became after the trip. Rather than one sack apiece, one bag carried everyone's pyjamas, another the bathing suits, or sweaters, or long pants, or short pants, etc. Each bag was labeled with Mum's oldest lipstick so we could quickly find the one we wanted at any time of need. The year came when it was my turn to label the bags. I was proud of the trust placed in my ability to do such an important task, and I was anxious to put my newfound spelling and abbreviation-ing skills to work. I hunted up the sweaters, and printed "SW" on the bag. Next the pyjamas with "PJ". Following was the bathing suits; yup you guessed it, "BS" printed with large prominent letters on the white cloth in Passionate Red lipstick. I was humming and getting the job done when in came OlderJuh, whose previous job had been bag labeling. I guess he just had to check that I was doing the job according to the superior standard he had used when he did it, up until last year. He was shocked to see my last label.

"Melba, you cannot write "BS" on that bag!" he exclaimed.

"Yes, I got it right! I am using abbreviations so I don't use up all of Mum's lipstick. PJ for pyjamas, and SW for sweaters, and BS for bathing suits, and next up is LP for long pants!" The whole time I was reviewing my brilliance and eptitude, I was sounding out the words just to double check.

"Don't you know what "BS" stands for?"

"Yes, bathing suits. Just like I told you!"

"No, it stands for bull shit!"

As an indication of how good was the job my parents and the Juhs had done keeping me innocent, and using a large formal vocabulary rather than falling into colloquialisms and inappropriate emotional, or bedroom, or bathroom language, I had never heard the phrase "bullshit" before in my seven long years. Imagine the innocence in 1957 that a small town girl who ran with her brothers and their friends and played outside with every kid on the block and in town, yet had never heard that phrase before!

"Juh!" I replied. "With all the B words and all the S words in the world, who would ever see the two letters together and arrive at the conclusion that they stood for bullshit! Really, grow up!"

OlderJuh left to summon Mum who arrived with another sack, helped me to print BSuits on it, then loaded the bathing suits into it. Then she and I went to the laundry in the basement for my first lesson in advanced laundry: how to remove lipstick from cloth.

The back of the station wagon was first fitted with two cot mattresses on the floor at the back, then the bags of clothing and pillows, the picnic hamper which was our food storage locker, and the dog. In would go the two youngest children, YoungerJuh and I. The floor in the back bench seat was packed to seat level, leaving no leg room. It was no wonder YoungerJuh and I preferred seeing the trip backwards out the rear window, sometimes making the pulling signal to upcoming long-hauler trucks in the hopes that they would blow their air horns to our delight and to my driving Dad's distraction at the sudden noise. "Dagblastit!" Dad would shout. "What does he want? To get by? I'll just pull over and let him go!" We would be hard pressed to say which delighted us more, Dad's sudden and exciting departure from pavement or the generosity of the truck driver as he blew his horn to thrill two young kids in the back of a station wagon from Canada.

My first time using a diving board found me atop a ten foot board at a travel motel pool. I clambered to the top of the ladder fearlessly. I stepped gingerly out to the end of the long board. I tentatively bounced on the board to get the feel of the spring. Imagining the ridicule if I did not go ahead and dive but rather chose to back down the ladder instead. I attempted this feat with roaring in my ears. In fear, I pulled up at the last minute which left me flat on the surface of the water, wind knocked out of me, with rising welts on stomach, thighs, chest, and arms, and rendering me completely unable to move and just as helpless as a newborn puppy. Both OlderJuh and OldestJuh leapt to rescue me and towed me to the side where Dad pulled me up, and lay me in a semi prone position until the wind started to re-inflate my lungs. In the background was Mum, talking to OldestJuh and OlderJuh about how they needed to be careful about what they inspired me to try.

Those welts persisted for the next twenty four hours.

Dad was always trying to get in a few more hours and a few more miles before stopping for overnight. This left us cranky, hungry, and misbehaving in our cramped quarters. These were the hours when we learned important life lessons, such as: Dad could reach out and cuff any one of us, no matter in which seat we sat and still keep his other hand on the steering wheel; we kids could successfully pee in a can in the car, but the dog could not and our parents would not; in a pinch, we could stop by the side of the road, open both right side doors to block the view from passersby giving us some privacy for bladder and bowel relief; we did not go into the bushes for bathroom breaks for that is the place where bugs, snakes, poison ivy, and other bothersome experiences lived; we could make a passable lunch from the picnic basket while covering a mile a minute in the car.

We were driving through the Adirondack mountains and our later afternoon of delaying our camping stop had put us solidly into deep dark, and solidly into cranky sleepiness or outright sleep. We slowed to read each sign, and we hoped for a campground. All were marked "No Vacancy". Then up from the horizon and into our headlights rose the perfect place, bringing into our sights the sign; "Chuck's Cabins" sang out in the golden light pooled down onto the sign. "Vacancy" invited us into a campground that had everything we needed: picnic table at each site, sandy beach for a quick swim to wash up after a long day of many miles, parking space beside our site, and the whole place to ourselves which meant children's suddenly-released exuberance would bother no one. I dove for the "BSuits" and "T" and "PJ" bags, Dad and the boys dove for the tent and sleeping gear, Mum dove for the picnic basket, stove, and utensils. Mum sent us to the beach to wash up (and to get us out of her hair, and her ears, for a half hour).

After our swim and our energy-releasing exuberance, we came back to the picnic table for hot food; the pyjamas were donned; and lights went out. No pillow farting fights that night; snores were immediate.

Come morning, we awoke to early morning sun warming the mist over the glassy water. These are the kind of mornings about which poets wax poetic. Out we went to start breakfast, thinking about another swim before breaking camp. Ah, the perfect sun over the perfect beach, and the golden rays reaching whispering fingers into the trees behind us, revealing a solid carpet of poison ivy ... which was everywhere!

Each one of us fell suddenly silent, and started to itch in anticipation of the ivy's revenge. "Do NOT scratch! Not a single swipe!" Mum's admonition was delivered along with every bar of green soap brought on the trip, all the while giving directions: "Pull the entire campsite; take everything from tent to straps, to sleeping bags, to selves, to dog, down to the water; and scrub everything along with every part of yourself and the dog with green soap!" Dad pulled the car up to the water's edge. We took our soggy selves and soggy belongings to the local laundromat to dry everything (except the canvas tent, because that much canvas will not fit into any dryer, anywhere!). Next stop was for a gallon of calamine lotion which we applied liberally, even though no rash bubbles had begun to rise.

We found our way to another symposium in the south-eastern United States. Our family had settled into a motel on the outskirts of town and Dad had settled into the symposium with the other glassblower members. Mum and we would go on walking tours around town, stretching our legs, looking at the sights, and seeing how people lived in this new place.

One hot and humid day, we were trudging back to the motel along with the beautiful southern lady with the drawling accent who was wife to another glassblower. We saw the husband of the other womyn in their car, driving with Dad and another passenger in the car. Thinking to save herself the rest of the walk, the womyn waved her handkerchief to flag down her husband. Her husband sailed on by. Umph...looked like there will be no reprieve for us from this relentlessly hot trek.

The other womyn broke from her usual genteel manners to say, "No wonder he didn't pick me up. He would never expect me to get into a car with a nigger! He will have to clean that car inside and out before I'll get into it again!"

"Mum, what's a nig..."

"Never mind, Melba! Quickly, let's go!"

Another trip found us walking wide eyed with heads swivelling through Times Square in New York City. Bright lights flashed all around us. The sidewalks teemed with people of all ages, colours, clothings, and accents. And they all were friendly and they all wanted to talk to 10 year old me! Some of them smelled of something that made them slur their words. My parents held mine and YoungerJuh's hands and steered us along the throngs of people and away from some who were just a little too friendly with a side of creepy.

Our hotel room in the city's downtown was inexpensive

("affordable"). The door to our room rattled in the wind all night long. In the morning, we found cigarette butts and spent matches in the hallway outside our door. We packed in a hurry that morning!

In Boston, on another trip, we attended the glassblowing displays. A huge room overflowed with glass examples of every flower that I had ever seen. I saw such vivid colours; the flowers looked entirely detailed and real and were finely attention-ed with every separate floret. I had often heard Dad speaking about his glass crafting, and he had brought little offerings home to offer as a tribute of affection to his wife, but until this moment, I never really paid attention to his talent for details.

Between the trials and demands of travel, there were sights and experiences that gave me a lifelong grounding in the meaning of Joy, dependability, beauty, mutuality, single-mindedness of purpose, and what is important in life. This was the experience I hoped to bring to my own children. No matter the trip, I always tried to keep my own straps tied tight, straps both on the car and in life.

The Whole Ceegar!

"There he is! I KNEW I could smell a cigar! Here – on hospital property! Even if it is the smoking section, really? A cigar? Stinking up the place! I'm going over to him to straighten him out. Tell him what's what; tell him about himself; tell him why he cannot impose his behaviour on the rest of us!

I found you!" she ranted.

"Thank you for looking for me," Melba's friend responded

"It wasn't that hard; I simply followed the stink of your cigar!"

"Congratulations on your success. Have a cigar?" He proffered a cigar.

"How dare you! Have you no consideration for the people around you? This is a hospital, after all. You should show more respect for what people are going through here at the hospital!

Put that cigar out right this minute and let the stink be blown away from the smoking section!"

"Afraid I cannot do that. You see I promised my wife."

"You promised her that you would smoke a cigar, here? What kind of a womyn is she!"

"YOU WILL NOT SPEAK ABOUT MY WIFE!" he said each word deliberately.

"I do not care anything about your wife. Just put that cigar out right now! It is a matter of common respect."

"Since you persist, let me tell you about my wife.

When we met, I enjoyed a cigar every now and then. My father smoked cigars back in the days when a simple pleasure was just that.

My mother said she liked the smell of a good cigar; it reminded her that her most precious husband was close at hand, that he had put down the cares of the moment, that he was relaxing in his easy chair. After his cigar, he would come find her and they would share precious moments together, moments generally involving laughter, hand-holding and touching, completing a task together.

Sometimes, my father would give me a cigar and we would light up together; it was a bonding moment, a sharing moment, a letting-go-of-woes moment. I remember every one of those cigars with my Dad."

"So where does this wife of yours come into this?"

"You confronted me, remember! Now I shall share with you, without interruption!

I met my wife on a sunny cloudless day, yet I was struck by lightning! She bumped into me in the bookstore while she was backing along a stack searching for, oddly enough, the same book as was I. I was thrown back by the force of her sparkling eyes, her quick smile, and her elbow. That was it! I knew that I was struck by the force of the realization that this is the one for me. I fell down in amazement.

She helped me up. We found the book together and made

our purchases. Then we went for coffee and talked and laughed through the day and into the night.

Home later, my Dad asked me to join him in a cigar. I couldn't wait to tell him about my great abide for this womyn. As we puffed on our cigars, we spoke a little in between long gaps of silence that spoke volumes, as always during our cigar times.

Dad and Mum asked me to bring home this Wonder of the Universe. Invite her for supper. I realized that I did not know her name or her address despite our long conversation together.

After camping out at the bookstore, missing classes and sleep, I finally found her again, in the stacks where we had first met. We both rushed to speak about the what-is-your-names and how-do-I-contact-yous, then laughed then took out papers and pens to share digits. And yes, she accepted our invitation to dinner, that very day.

After dinner, when she and my Mum were having womyn-chatter over another cup of coffee, Dad and I spoke over our cigars. "This one's a keeper," Dad said. "You are so smitten you can barely speak; she rarely takes her smile or her eyes off you. Make sure that you include her in your plans, somehow, because if she leaves she takes a piece of you with her!"

Some time, chats, laughters, and cigars later, she and I married. She always said I was more myself after my cigars with Dad, and even though we invited her to join us, she said she and Mum were in the middle of something of their own. Somehow not being attached at the hip felt right and fair with us both.

During our wedding, our pregnancy, and our may occasions, plans and thoughts were shared over a cigar with Dad.

Until one evening, we chewed on a cheroot in silence. Dad finally told me about his appointments, treatments, and his final diagnosis. He said he had wanted to wait until the baby was born, but he was afraid he'd run out of time. And every cigar time was even more precious after that.

We got together even more often, talked about the state of the world at large and about our own little corner of it. We planned our next home because the apartment was barely big enough for two and certainly would not contain our growing family and our needs. We talked about renovations, baby cribs, painting, heating, and being forward looking rather than backward looking. And all of this over our cigar after dinner.

Baby grew, was evidenced in ultra sound pictures, but Baby did not care to show enough to let us know if boy or girl.

Dad shrank, became more frail, but always became more robust at cigar time. He talked about continuing the tradition with my family; he said it didn't have to be cigars, but a ritual must be determined and continued. He handed me a box of cigars to hand out to mark the baby's birth, a long tradition in his generation and family.

I wondered why he didn't just wait until the baby's birth to give me the box; I wondered no more the night my wife's contractions began.

Cigars were tucked into the hospital bag we had prepared; my wife had insisted. Off we went with all the same thoughts every parent has when the birth is nigh.

The beepers that had been hooked to my wife began in a reassuring rhythm, but all too soon turned into insistent demands for attention. The room filled with hospital personnel. I held my wife's hand and her gaze, and poured every ounce of strength through our clasped contact and into her and Baby. And then the activity of the room became less frantic, more measured, but the beepers did not slow down.

At my wife's insistence, they took the baby by Cesarian in the midst of all that chaos. And my wife became so calm, peaceful and serene that I thought all threat to her was over in the midst of Baby's squalls. I only took my eyes off my wife for a few seconds to welcome our daughter into the world, and the family. But that was all it took. My wife was gone.

After the chaos came the calm, and then the chaos started again; BabyGirl was letting go of her tenuous grip on her life and my finger. Despite my willing her not to go, BabyGirl joined her mother in the next realm.

I could not weep, for it was good that they would be together for eternity, right? Every BabyGirl needs her mother, right? Who am I to question that!

I called Mum and Dad to let them know the outcome of the night, but could not get through to them. I called the neighbour and was told that Mum had rushed Dad to the hospital during a more than usual frightening health event. She drove herself rather than wait for the ambulance, so urgently was care needed. At the end of their street, at the same stop sign where they had stopped every time for 60 years, she drove through the stop, and they were killed instantly, together. They were holding hands just like they always did when in the car.

So here I stand, smoking my 'stinking' cigar, the whole 'ceegar', without regard for the rest of you standing here in the hospital smoking zone. And I'll be damned if I am breaking with tradition to keep an insensitive person from chewing on me.

Here, have a cigar!"

We finished our cigars, left the box for others to enjoy and went our separate ways. Because we had shared contact information, a lesson learned all that time ago in a bookstore, we found ourselves drifting together regularly, over a cigar. My new cigar friend had lost her cigar-smoking husband that night, from lung cancer, because he inhaled every puff of his cigars.

Neither of us inhaled even a whiff of smoke; we just were, together, each lost in our own thoughts. Over time, we began to chat about politics, and the world, and everything but ourselves and the trials of the night we met.

I think that sharing the tradition was always going to be as intimate as we would ever be. It's just easier talking only about the outside things rather than the inside things.

Wash

There, just beyond the corner of my house, red and orange, green and white, blue and yellow, even purple, all fluttering in the breeze, all asking to be let back in.

I sit over my afternoon tea, munching on a scrumptious piece of friend Melba's gift of blueberry pie with whipped cream, savouring, while reviewing my day.

Though it started usually enough, with the noble tasks of the day to days, the day stretched behind me, now crammed plug full of so many of the unusuals.

Dawn had earlier peeped over the trees, lighting my way to the coffee press and kettle, the bubbles carrying the aroma of fresh new start, and fresh new coffee. Today was my first day in so long that dawned with the promise of completion of tasks that had beckoned, then called, then demanded doing. Clean and vac, then dust and tidy, dishwasher full and started, laundry sorted, begun, and drying, and the delicious feeling of being in charge of my own domain.

I came up the basement stairs and was yanked back from my reveries of satisfaction from task completion, and checkmarks added to my ToDo list.

What was that?

A shift in the shadows of my home, shading my bright colours of the day, calling me back to the moment. Yes, there, not a shifting shadow but an actual person, inside my home.

Yyyyoink! I was thrown back into the past:

After all the warnings about continuing to live in this neighbourhood;

After the guy next door had flipped out, all that yelling and pounding and then the crack-sound, again, again, and one more time, after the reclusive womyn next door had fled her own home and come running to beg entry at my door, after all that blood on my clothes.

And after all that, the authorities had come to remove the

bodies, to arrest the neighbour, to confiscate his gun, to take the reclusive lady next door to the hospital and then to her sister's in a neighbouring city.

The real estate agent had arrived to see to the cleaning of that horrifying day's debris, to stage the home, perfect for another young family, with the fresh paint and the new windows, with the basement already sound-proofed for a music studio or a children's play area with reinforced walls solid enough to use existing brackets to support or secure heavy fitness equipment or maybe a Murphy bed. After the new and brightly chirping young family moved in, the sounds from next door revealed the simple and natural rhythm of family normalcy.

And now, after all this time, someone is in my home, slowly, stealthily, going room to room, searching for I know not what!

How did he get in?

I had studiously kept my new heavy doors locked ever since. And yet there he was, hulking over my hiding place in the hall closet.

"Come on, Little Girlie-Girl. You shouldn't make this so hard for me. You know that always makes me even madder!

Now, how about you make your old man some supper, now that I finally found you again. Don't make me wait, now!"

And I was back, to an even earlier time, to my childhood, to my basement dungeon, to the chains that kept me in a part of the basement with no window, with complete soundproofing and a mean dirty mattress on the floor.

But by this time, I had installed panic buttons, escape routes, and I had girded up my fearful mind so I could escape from his psychological influence. Panic bells ringing, outside following an alley to the next street over, cell phone in my hand connected to 911 where I had registered so long ago.

It all seemed like some kind of too graphically-hauntingly-real, nightmarish dream.

Later, police and emergency vehicles were gone. Paperwork completed. My father back to prison. And here I sit, again reclaiming my right to my own life, place, and decisions about where I shall live and go.

The wash catches my eye, colourfully fluttering like butterflies in the late setting sun. One more task to complete: bring in the dry clothing and linens, fold, iron, hangers, put away. Then back to Melba's gift of pie.

That blueberry pie was the best I had ever tasted! It had washed the taste of the day's terrors out of my mouth, and the friendship with the baker had washed my heart clean, ready to trust and interact again.

Heavy doors are locked again. Curtains are drawn. Windows are closed and locked. Windowless basement, once my childhood hellhole, now my safe panic room cum bed-sitting room, where maybe I will read that new romance novel. Or maybe some spiritual Sunday TV. Or maybe to sleep innocently, deeply, and dreamlessly.

"Ms. McGee, You Have Cancer"

Those words were offered gently, clearly, in a tone that I later called the cancer voice. Those words forever changed my thinking, my emotions, my stability, my ability to take anything for granted, and my habit of deferring any gratification or plans.

I had gained even more weight beyond my pregnancy weight. I found myself given to deeper and darker bouts in the deep dark hole of clinical depression. Throwing up, nausea, constipation, and diarrhea were more facts of life that had to be reckoned with. My emotional responses to events overtook my ability to examine the facts and find my way back onto the path of my day to day needs and successes with and for others. I began to think more about me than about others. There was a lump in my side that felt the same as my breech baby's head under my ribs. When I pushed against that lump, I could not palpate the lump but could feel it grinding against my ribs as though it was a stone. When I indulged in my usual binge eating or drinking,

I could no longer tolerate what had become my usual level of imbibe-ment. I was tired all the time; though I would fall into bed exhausted at midnight after all of the day's duties were finished, and though I would be instantly asleep, I would awake as early as 1am and there would be no sleep for me after that. I tried to lie there and watch old movies, to get up and fix hot milk, I just decided to get up and do something on the ever present not-yet-completed list. My floors and house were never so clean. My daybook was never so detailed. My journals were overflowing with the majyk that flowed from my pen. I upped my research into healthy whole living and eating, into anything that could guide me in understanding what good health should look for me.

I went to my doctor with my complaints. She tried to palpate the lump and said she could feel nothing, and asked me how I knew there was a lump there. When I reminded her that I had had a breach pregnancy, and when I took her fingers and pushed the lump so she could feel the grinding against the ribs, she simply sniffed and said, "This is just the phantom memory of a breach pregnancy. Now stop this imagining. You are too quick to take your imaginings to medical attention, and too demanding of immediate medical response. Just like when you insisted that your daughter's tonsils had to come out just because her throat was swollen completely closed for the fourth time that year, and you sought another doctor's opinion and he agreed with you. Just like you brought your son in for imagined appendix attack which turned into a surgery at the hospital just as his appendix was rupturing. This isn't a restaurant where you come and order up what you want when you want it!"

Up I stood and began to dress.

"What are you doing? We aren't finished yet!"

"Oh yes, we are finished. I am finished with you. And you finished your long winded tirade. We are finished!"

"You'll be back. We are the only clinic in town!"

I found a new doctor in the city. At the intake exam, I presented my list of concerns and I helped her to palpate the grinding lump.

"Well, I cannot feel what you do. But if you can feel it, then I will order the tests that I am allowed to order and we will go from there. We will start with an X-ray."

A week later, "Ms. McGee, you have cancer." This phrase was repeated again by lab and test technicians, oncologist, surgeons, nurses, PSWs. After the first initial shock that took me back to Mum's battle with cancer, the phrase came to have the same effect as though they had commented on me having blue eyes.

Three days after the first test had turned up a tumour the size of a peach, on my liver, I was sitting in the surgeon's office while they ordered further tests. Days later, the results were reviewed and the same comment, "Ms. McGee, you have cancer," was uttered. I had a peach sized metastatic tumour on my liver.

Everyone was so solemn that I tried to lighten the mood. "So, how long will be the incision for the surgery?"

"It will be considerable."

"Yes but how long? Will it be this long? Or this long?" (finger gesturing).

"Your request for this information is a first for me. Most people don't want these details, and would prefer not to hear them. If you don't mind, why do you ask?"

"Well, my husband just had a gall bladder surgery that left him with an eight inch scar across his abdomen. We have gotten into a discussion about who has the most linear feet of scarring. We were closely matched, but his surgery put him out ahead by five inches. So how long will it be? Will I be out on top with this one?"

Smile. "Yes, you will be on top! Thanks for your humour. And congratulations."

The surgeon asked me if I would allow an epidural anaesthesia. I responded in the negative. Nonplussed, the doctor asked me why I was so dead set against this one thing.

"Because I don't want to be awake and aware during the surgery. You know how, when you purchase something, take it out of its box, decide that it doesn't suit you and try to fit it back into the box for return? How it never goes back into the box after much frustrated effort? Well, I don't want to be awake and hearing all the hauling of all my guts out while looking for the primary and then hearing the frustration of trying to get all those guts back into such a tightly packed space!" He smiled and said that I would be unconsciously but lightly sedated during the surgery and would not hear anything. That the epidural would be applied before surgery and would stay in for some days after surgery.

I asked him if he would get rid of any lumps of fat he found in there, much the same as one hauls out lumps of fat from inside a turkey before stuffing it. He said he would see what he could do. We were laughing at this point.

Surgery was scheduled a week later, and in that time I had to get my affairs in order meaning update my will, my living will, establish my estate executor, tell my family, tell my principal, make up a detailed daybook for the next six weeks and a general curriculum for the next eight months, complete a set of report cards for the first term, and generally gird up my loins. I satisfied myself that if I had to have cancer, it was good that I had persisted in finding appropriate action, and I was lucky enough to have liver cancer because one can lose as much as 75% of the liver and the liver will regenerate itself.

The surgery was masterfully completed, successful in finding and removing the "primary". I had a cadaver cut, a twelve inch incision. Part of my liver was removed to make a good margin around the tumour. The bottom of my stomach and top of my small intestine were removed then re-sectioned after the primary tumour was removed. I was confined to bed with seven tubes running in and out of me, including epidural, nasal gastric suction tube, oxygen, two intravenous, catheter, suction drain, blood transfusion. I could lift my arms and I could turn my head. The epidural was left in for some days after surgery so I would be spared the after effects of a lengthy gut incision. The nurses, technicians, and PSW were gentle angels of mercy and compassion, who stepping into my world the size of a hospital bed.

My surgeon, the lead at the Liver and Pancreas Cancer unit, was gentle, thorough, reassuring and found sitting beside my bed when I woke up. He talked about what he had found, what he had done and why, and what that would mean for me. He came back every morning at the crack of dawn with his student entourage to talk with me and update me, always acting as though it was a simple conversation between just him and me. Because it was a rare cancer and surgery, there were many following my case and observing how my treatment was affecting me.

When they sent me home, the surgeon gave me his office number and the name of a person there who answered the phone every time I called. And he gave me his personal cell phone number in case I needed it. I did not call him, but did feel considerable confidence that I had those numbers. He called me the next morning, just to see how I was doing. A good and gentle human being, and a medicare system that had enough workers to get the job done right.

Chemistry Lesson

This drug, known as oxycodone, is an opiate, a reliever of severe-pain, and addictive. Most of us have heard about it in media and movies. Because of its high street value, drug dealers find and steal it wherever they can. A single pill can cost many dollars on the street. This is the stuff of lost lives, of prostitution-of-every-ilk as a way to earn enough money for the next fix, and of lost futures.

This chemical crossed my path, again, after my kidney surgery. My golf-ball sized kidney stone was too large to remove the new way (without an incision) so I was to be relieved of the constant grinding pain by cutting into my back, cutting into the kidney, removing the stone, and then restitching everything back together.

The internal pain caused by the stone was gone when I woke up, and the surgery pain was livable…duh, they had me high on anaesthesia! They added more of the good stuff to keep me ahead of the coming pain. I also had some naturopathic chemistry to help with recovery, and pain.

When I was discharged, I was given some scripts which I tucked into my purse for consideration. The discharge nurse reviewed the need for me to keep ahead of the pain, which was likely to be considerable in the first days. If the kidney pain got ahead of me, I would be crippled by it. Most people are. She talked to me about using the oxycodone, one of the scrips, which had me set up for more than a dozen pills.

So there I am, much relieved to finally, after a year, be free of grinding, can't-straighten-up pain. So, who needs Oxy? Nevertheless, I decided to swing round the pharmacy anyway, for the other scrips.

Once at the pharmacy, I handed over the prescriptions, including the one for Oxy, and asked for only one pill of Oxy, just to have it in-case. The pharmacist was astounded, even stupefied. I'm guessing that most people want it, want it all, want to take the first one right now. He asked what I was thinking, not to take the full script, that no one ever asked for only one pill.

I told him, "This chemical is much in the news! The potential for addiction is, apparently, great. I have decided fifty years ago to live the life of real food, natural remedies, living consciously." (Aside: sort of begs the question of how I then got that kidney stone, and got cancer, eh!) "I don't want that kind of potential abuse to be in my home where I babysit the GrandKidlettes, where other adults come to visit, and where live my husband and I (I am a recovered but still wary alcoholic)."

The pharmacist reminded me about the keeping-ahead-of-the-pain thing. I acknowledged the rightness of his advice, and I asked for my single pill. I asked him to keep the rest on file and someone would certainly come by for another pill if and when needed.

He excused himself for a moment, and returned (I think he was reading his pharmacist's manual, or maybe he was giving me a minute for sober second thought) to mention that I would be paying the dispensing fee each time I accessed the chemistry / script. This fee was in the neighbourhood of $6. Added to the astoundingly low cost of the Oxy, I figured I could afford it.

I went home, with my single pill of Oxy, and did continue the naturopathic homeopathic options.

In the night, the pain arrived and I could see what they were talking about. In the morning I called the discharge nurse to ask her if this was normal, and she calmly, and politely, and professionally reminded me about our conversation of the day before. She asked if I had taken the pain med. I said, "You mean the oxycodone?" She said, "Yes." She, too, was astounded at my reasoning, and suggested that I take that one pill and send someone to pick up more Oxy.

I asked her if this was likely to be the top of the pain curve, timing-wise. She said likely, yes.

So I emptied my incision drain bag, drank the required giant glass of water, lay down, watched some mind numbing TV (at my house that is old movies) until I fell asleep. I always prefer to sleep away any pain that I cannot ignore by living beside the pain instead of through it.

The next day I had, indeed improved. The following day I flushed the single pill, called and asked the pharmacist to put the script into my file history.

School Board and Teacher - When Teacher is Sent Blindly into the Middle of the Frey

Our colleague used to teach here but now she has "climbed the ladder" to become a principal, "as any smart teacher should do". She is flirty with young male teachers. She admonishes us to step up on yard duty or hall duty, giving us particular behaviours or students to watch out for, to make sure we get the student to do what is demanded. She brags about being a bully as a child. I am cautious.

At a staff meeting, she spoke about a student who would be attempting to leave the Junior yard and come onto the Intermediate yard. She insisted that we make him stay off the Intermediate yard and return to the Junior yard. There was no background about condition or possible reasons, or learning and social styles.

One recess I reported for duty and found a delivery truck parked outside the music room making a delivery while his truck was in the middle of the basketball area preventing a hundred students from playing a much-loved game. I went into the music room and mentioned that moving the truck right now was impossible with so many kids standing around. He told me that I had to keep the kids away from his truck, and its contents; I told him to go out and lock up the truck. I went back outside after saying that going forward, making sure the truck was not parked in the middle of the intermediate yard at any recess time would make the yard duty job easier, and his truck free from curious fingers.

Outside, there was a student I did not know, picking at the driver side mirror. When I asked him not to touch the truck, he turned a deaf ear. More energy now in my voice, I repeated the order. Again no change. I introduced myself; he was silent. Out from behind the mirror came a folded piece of cardboard obviously placed there to keep the mirror from falling out of place. One of the other students called the student by name.

Ah, this is the child mentioned in the principal's orders. I told the student to leave this yard, and return to his Junior yard. I scanned the throng of students. No response to my order. Louder repeat of order. I scanned the throng of students (it is the nature of the observant yard duty teacher's job). The student, who received the order, strolled away from the truck, and headed for the skateboard area where he set down his board and prepared to roll. I repeated my instruction to head back to his own yard. He prepared to skateboard and began to strap on his helmet. I bent over and picked up his skateboard and directed him to the vice-principal's office because of non-compliance. He held his helmet by dangling strap, and assaulted me with his helmet aiming at my head but hitting me on my upraised defensive arm. My rotator cuff was damaged while fending off blows to my head. I turned to go into the office and suggested that he should do likewise.

Workplace Climate - Middle Management - Corruption of Autonomy in the Workplace

The busyness part of my career is upon me.

Selling chips and pop to make money for Phys-Ed and Family Studies equipment and supplies, that is until my project was taken over by another teacher when a new principal came in. Did she ask me if she could participate in the work and the funds earned? No; she went running to the Boss who flexed his power muscles, and didn't even come to speak with me first.

"Find your own damned project to earn money for your own classroom," was my thought.

My class developed a Community Service Project. We found that it was impossible to enrich the classroom experience with the plethora of multimedia options becoming available, recordings, taped music, movies, and documentaries, because there were only three VCRs in the entire school. There was a signup sheet, and we could only sign up at the end of Friday for the next week's time-slots. Movies sanctioned by the school board were ordered a month in advance. VCR tapes were purchased with a teacher's own money, not a classroom budget. The atmosphere around this new technology was so grim that I felt like I had toenail gouges up my back from other teachers climbing over me, erasing my signups and entering their own. We taught on a rotary timetable, which meant that if I offered the film to each class, several signup times were required. The afternoon before special occasions and HolyDays found the equipment in high demand.

Our classrooms were not air-conditioned. With thirty-five students being the average class size in intermediate, with teaching on the west side of a dark brick building under a black flat roof, with no trees around the school, with a kindergarten sandbox play-yard outside our windows leaving sand blowing around and in windows, with only three 40cm by 120cm openable sections of window in the classroom, and with blinds that let in light being put up into the classrooms to replace the blackout curtains, we found ourselves unable to keep up with the heat. Most teachers purchased fans and fridges with their own money, and these went missing from vacant classrooms over the summer. Some teachers had master keys while others did not.

New elementary schools were air conditioned; all secondary schools were air conditioned.

My home-room class and I determined that if we sold pizza once a month, we could afford to buy TVs, VCRs, tape recorders, and fans for every classroom and portable in the school. We developed a plan:

-two students from our class would be responsible for one other class. They would pick up the orders, open the envelopes, count the money and double-check against the order to make sure it was correct. If not correct, they would go back to the students and ask them to bring in the rest of the money tomorrow, or they would return the order over payment with a note (if the student was a primary student) to the parents;

-Once finished, the class order would be taken to the two Master Accountants for the final tally;

-Two students would take the master tally and phone the pizza place saying how many pizzas and how many drinks were required for delivery on Friday. When the delivery guy heard what we were doing, he dropped his usual delivery charge;

-two students would roll coins into rollers, would stack up

folding money by denomination, fill in a tally and take it to the Office Staff in charge of moneys; and

-On Friday, the classroom masters would pickup and deliver the pizza orders, handing them out to the children, bringing empty pizza boxes to the recycling bins, then back to the classroom for their own lunch.

Once the routine was practiced, we found that accounting day took us about eighty minutes and delivery day took us about forty minutes. We learned the skills of visioning, accounting, accepting responsibility for others, handling food for other people, community service with no reward, meaning there was no free pizza for our class, because one slice for each of 37 students = $46.25, and that would mean that no new fan for another classroom each month.

We purchased eight of Walmart's best VCRs the first year, and a fan for every portable.

We became proud of what we were doing and some students who had been told all their lives that they were useless, worthless, and trouble, suddenly had curly-haired primary kids who called them by name and waved at them in the hall and on the bus, rather that being afraid of them. "Hi Sam!" Giggle, wave. "Hi Sonya! Hi Tara!" "Fans of yours, Sam?" "Oh yah!" Smiles that lasted all week.

We learned that we were capable, likeable, community citizens.

Giving back; becoming the helpers in the community; over the years, my class became proud of what we collectively had contributed to the school and we learned that community service is its own reward.

The principal, after seeing our accounting sheets, wanted my project, making up excuses that there were more important things that the school needed than fans and VCRs. She would have seen our gains dumped into the big black hole of the school budget, perhaps going to only one grade level or into consumables. I refused. She threatened. I refused.

Furious about my backbone and lack of respect for her position of authority, she began to concert an effort to negatively influence how other staff and parents see me and my work. She was a whisper-campaign bully.

She told me that she wanted me to get out of the school, this school where parents fought for their child to be in my classroom, where I had built a reputation of hard work and fairness and sensitivity to the needs of those in my care. Nope, no leg to stand on there.

She would skulk around behind our backs trying to get something on staff members; she found out how to get into the server and she read our private work emails on the interactive network; she created a climate of fear and uncertainty. Hardly conducive to finding a way to make things better and more supportive of student needs, as well as maintaining a collaborative workspace. Hers is an abuse of authority.

Another new principal.

I introduced myself, as is expected, as a Union steward and Union executive member / general Secretary. She heard about my work at the Union, and reminded me that she had once run for president (unsuccessfully), before she decided to become a principal. She chatted with me and told me things about her unsatisfying home and family life.

She confessed to me that she had never taught grades seven and eight. I mentioned that if I could be of service, to just let me know. She came several times to my door during a lesson to seek answer to a question such as teacher so-and-so just sent student so-and-so to the office for such-and-such reason. Any thoughts?

When she asked later in the year if I was going to the Union AGM, I affirmed my attendance. Her comment, "Just you wait and see; it's going to be the craziest greatest party every!" My response, "With the weight of 2500 Union members on my shoulders, with their concerns urging me forward, why would I think the AGM would be party time?"

Our Pizza Days and community service project continued.

Though I had invited the principal to come see our Accounting Day in action, she did not come. Until the day she came to tell me that she had received complaints and we would have to shut down.

I pushed to learn how many complaints, what were the complaints, who complained. After re-explaining what were were doing, and after some digging, she gave up the complaint (why can't we offer more than one pizza flavour choice), and the names of two parents, two out of five hundred, sisters, both with their oldest kids now in the school. I called the first parent. I reiterated the blurb we had sent home in the end-of-first-day-newsletter and again in the pizza order form. I invited her and her sister to come in on next accounting day and pizza day to see us in action, which they did.

They were astounded: every kid in the class had a job, every kid getting a piece of pizza was happy, the custodian was glad that we did not leave extra mess for him to clean up, the Office staff was glad that they did not have to count, roll, and prep all those pennies, coins, and dollar bills for delivery to the bank, the parents reported their gladness that one lunch a month, they could order on the pizza order making one less lunch to prep, and the kids in my class were proud of their work. The two parents asked if all their kids could be in my class in grade eight. They agreed that ordering more toppings choices would only complicate a well-oiled activity.

Now, why couldn't the principal have just sent the parents straight to me instead of caving and cancelling a worthy project out of hand? What had happened to the previous idea of principals who were in the school every day, spending some time visiting each class every day, instead of attending meetings at the board office or hanging out in the office every day? Why has middle management stopped being facilitators and become power-hungry ladder-climbing office dwellers?

From coming down to my room and asking what I thought

that she, the principal, should do because Teacher A has sent Student B to the office for infraction C to being on her hit-list took no time at all.

She talked to the former detracting middle manager principal and together they hatched ways to take me down.

Two whisper campaigns back to back, encouraging staff to turn me in, to shun me, and to vet me.

I continued to battle for staff members who were viciously disregarded during times of professional and personal need, and of great human weakness or loss.

Principal middle manager became unhinged. Her face would contort and spittle would hang on her lips when I would not give up the moral high ground. She would threaten, and lean across the table between us to menace me. I began to involve the union, because I was afraid she would add physical aggression to her list of emotional aggressions against staff. The union demanded a public apology to me (something I did not want, did not think would be helpful):

-after she tried to send me to teach grade 5, a junior class where I had no experience, close to my retirement age and while I was loaded up with added voluntary responsibilities at union;

-after she had verbally assaulted me and physically threatened me during a conversation in front of a union rep; and

-after she had threatened me with career annihilation and public denouncement.

Her behaviour became even more the behaviour of one who is completely unhinged, replacing that of an active professional, after this apology that I never asked for.

One day she left the school during the day, went to the school board then to the union office. She told everyone in both places that Melba McGee had ruined her career, a very successful career, and she was quitting. No one in either building contacted me for a chance of rebuttal.

When I asked my union what they had done to support me, a union member, an executive member of five years, they side stepped and told me that I would never be able to run for released executive member position after this denouncement.

I finished my tenure at the union by writing a New Teacher's Planner, full of calendar and month-specific information that proved useful to both new and established teachers. The union did not note or recognize my work, and tried to keep it from being mailed out to new teachers. I guess that the unhinged principal had some kind of something on even the union exec.

Next election, I retired from union volunteerism by not running for a fifth term, and never again encouraged anyone to think that the union actually had their back.

School Board and Teacher - When the Teacher is Sick

Over the years, my body was showing wear and tear.

There was now twice of me inside my skin. I was tired and I ached, and I was laid low by hot humid weather. Irritable Bowel Syndrome was a challenge to someone who worked at a job where bathroom breaks came every three hours. A hysterectomy had relieved me of periods so heavy that I missed three or four days of work each month because I could not get to the washroom every hour, and this was gobbling up my Sick Leave. I didn't do sleep; oh I fell into bed exhausted after finishing my job's homework at midnight only to zing awake as early as 1:00am; sleep was over for the night so I would get up to do housework, or more marking. I took no pleasure in activities in my personal life that once gave me great joy or satisfaction. I was living in The Deep Black Hole.

I was diagnosed with Clinical Depression. This diagnosis was never shared with my employer or their representatives at the school; this diagnosis was stigmatized by caregiver professionals who hold the tender lives of fragile children in their care; there was a culture of whispering, backstabbing and doubt; some principals used this knowledge to push a teacher over the edge.

Superintendents would not support a teacher in any dispute when the teacher was known to be mentally ill.

I tried prescriptions that seem to work for a while then end up making me too fuzzy to work at my usual effectiveness level. Talk therapy and journaling helped, for a while.

Over time, I completely lost sight of Melba and her sparkle and her energy. And since I had lost sight of myself, I heard what others said about me and was crushed by it. The perils of people pleasing.

I came to realize that I could and must do my own research by using a computer, and speaking with an enlightened Naturopathic doctor who knew other healing methods, and speaking with dedicated, knowledgeable medical doctors who are on my "healing team".

After some time living with this constant companion, another darkness challenges me: "Ms. McGee, you have neuro endocrine cancer. We will do your surgery in one week; go home and put your affairs I order." The first surgery involved a fifteen inch incision, called the cadaver cut, and seven months before being able to return to work full time. Long Term Disability insurance coverage was dutifully paid each month by the employee, but collecting it left me feeling like I was judged to be stealing. Unknown vehicles parked down the road from my gate, and when my husband took me on a little outing, the car followed. I soon started pulling over beside their car each time to tell them where we were going and for what reason, just in case they got lost in traffic.

I fought my way back to work, starting with a half day a week as a volunteer in my own classroom, adding more time each week, then teaching in my own classroom for longer times week by week. This drove the LTD people crazy. They liked me off work or back at work; no working up to the level of energy required to be on deck with a room full of thirteen year olds. People who work at a desk don't get it.

And neither does middle management get it.

I was informed that the cancer will come back; it is metastatic by nature. And back it came nine years later and again three years after that. And then we realized after more careful and regular study that all these tumours were growing in number and size.

Living under the cloud of cancer should be easier than the deep dark hole of depression. At least cancer has gained the understanding of society that it is not a choice so much as an affliction. However, an employer still looks at claims for Leave and days missed as somehow LMF or Low Moral Fibre. And the people who should be my colleagues become resentful.

The Decision to Retire arrived, whether it seemed like my choice or not. Always dependent on my pay cheque and benefits made me hang in as long as the students in my care seemed to be thriving from my care, until my 85 factor kicked in, before my Sick Leave ran out leaving me without the negotiated and promised retirement gratuity. The gratuity was based on how much Sick Leave still remained in one's account. Healthy teachers get a retirement gratuity; the rest of us get a portion or none at all. Oddly, other employees do not have retirement gratuity based on Sick Leave accumulation.

What-To-Do-What-To-Do?

Another story from another twist Melba's life could have taken:
Faster … faster … FASTER!
Gotta get there …
Now …
Urgent …
Because …
Nope, not here at the track … there should be lots of people here at the track today?
Wait! What day is this?
Why am I driving from the front right seat?
Why am I driving on left side of the road?
Where am I going?

Why is this urgent?

I know:

I am not the kind of person who panics, because after all I am, ... ummmm?

I usually don't drive on the left side of street in a car with right side steering wheel.

Yet I know how to do this.

I know when the track is open.

I found my way to the parade grounds track so I must know about this place.

Looking down I realize that I am completely dressed including coat, but in dress clothes, but without my skirt. My shoes are muddy.

Ayyyyyyy!

STOP! Pull over, ... breathe, ... THINK, my mind screams!

Eyes closed ... search mind's eye ... see the people of my life ... partner ... children ... coworkers ... my head hurts ... Gotta sleep. But when I lie across the seat, my head throbs even more. Is that blood on my fingers? I hit my head?

My daughter flashes into my mind ... her name is ... Sirena! Yes. That's it. Follow the first clue to the next ...

I was rushing to go to Sirena ... special occasion ... at the track ... yes! her graduation at the school field house.

And I slipped down the stairs when my heel caught in the unfamiliar stairway carpet,. ... we have't lived here long because ... I changed jobs to England because Sirena was here and we have always been a close-knit family. Yes! It is just Sirena and me now, after the car crash that killed Carl and young Frankie, that gave me a head injury, and yet miraculously left Sirena untouched, except for the nightmares and panic attacks.

In my headlong tilt to arrive on time, as the only family to be present at Sirena's big day, I fell into the grandfather clock at the bottom of the stairs, which explains my bloody and strangely empty head. The docs said I must avoid head injuries after the major damage left by the car accident.

The rest of it?

-skirt not yet donned before rushing to answer the phone's incessant ringing … maybe Sirena calling?

-I must have been passed out for some time because the graduation location was completely deserted when I finally came to;

-muddy shoes because I stumbled around in the front yard until I made my way to the car;

-panic because I didn't want to fail Sirena like I did when I was driving the family in our car when we were intersection T-boned by a car that drove through a stop sign.

I dialled 999 and said I was a medical emergency and needed police assistance. When they arrived, they helped me find Sirena who had been at the police station trying to find me instead of participating in her graduation.

Really, I am a clever and capable person.

The real me is not given to panic, to flights of fancy.

I can land a job tomorrow in any of several countries with my track record and qualifications.

I don't want to be this helpless person, especially when my daughter needs me.

I cannot work if I take my head meds. No one will hire someone who demonstrates fuzzy thinking.

What-to-do … what-to-do!

I have it!

Sell the car.

Hire a driver.

Move to a new place where no one knows me as this miserable incapable foolish womyn.

Go figure, if only I could.

Poor Sirena. Stuck with me as her entire and only family.

Memories

At our home, we have recently celebrated the Celtic New Year, called Samhain, when we clean away the last year and celebrate in the new.

Also, yesterday was Remembrance Day which is the essence of memories and memorializing and remembering.

Today I find myself engaged in a conversation about events that are remembered very differently by each person involved. This takes me more deeply into the concept of memories.

On the morning of our first frost, I awoke early enough to capture the sunrise's foggy mist wending its way through the trees, hinting at both past and future sunrises that found us intending on those days, as well as hinting at other first frosts and their portent of the season to come, and the indicator that season-past is fleeting.

On any day of remembrance, we cast about in our experiences like the meandering mist, reaching into our minds and scooping up first one then another and another memory, like hauling marbles out of our marble bag.

As with the marbles, some memories are bright, colourful, full of notice and delight. Some, conversely, are dark, and cracked by the emotion attached to them. Some are highly prized for their appearance or because of the battle waged to win that marble. Some are gifts from someone special to mark a special occasion.

Marbles had various names based on their appearance: aggie, alley, butterfly, ade, catseye, beachball, devil's eye, oxblood, pearl, Clearie, galaxy, princess, mica, steely….

Long before I carried a purse or even a pencil case, I carried carried a cloth bag of marbles. Sometimes the marble bag was satisfyingly full. Sometimes, the nearly empty marble bag was a graphic reminder about the paucity of my gaming fates and the wisdom of my decisions over the last while.

Similarly, memories have various names, based on emotions

evoked by remembering: joy, happyness, grief, sadness, darkness, anger, rage, fear, FUD (fear, uncertainty, doubt), satisfaction, achievement, belonging, longing, jealousy, disappointment, cup runneth over.

A poignant song, always considered by me to have the title "*Memories*", came from Barbara Streisand, *The Way We Were*. She sings of memories "lighting the corners of the mind", of "leaving smiles behind", asking "if we would do it all again".

And so, as I pass through these days of remembrance, I cast about in my memories, naming the memories, assigning each a place of importance because of the feeling aroused by the acquisition. Some are crystals, sparkly and bright and worthy of repeat. Some are oxblood because of the wounds so obviously demarcated reminding us to avoid any repeats.

Some are solid, heavy, huge, reliably capable, and dependable. These are definitely keepers.

Holding onto, cataloging, donning those old memories like an old coat threatens us with reliving all the emotions as though the experiences still are ongoing, trapping us forever and denying us any possibility of moving forward further into our future's possibilities.

Revisiting all these memories invites us to revisit the lessons in life learned during that experience. We give gratitude for the lesson and the people who came to teach us that lesson; we release any hold it has on us thereby trapping us in the past.

Let's lift our glasses to remembrance, lessons, joys, celebrations, moving on past, and journeying forward. Letting them guide us then letting them go. After all, they are in the past.

Time really has rewritten and should rewrite every line...

Driving Home

I'm in my car, driving home from a job of work taken on after retirement.

Though most often attentive to the details of driving and the drive,

today I notice:

high and low;

left and right;

In front and behind;

colours and textures;

activity and stillness.

I am detached from all but physical detail.

Emotional detachment means that I have backburner-opportunity to deal with the final outcome of the day: my job has suddenly finished, suddenly cut short.

It was a good job:

satisfying;

doing something that I can do well that uses skills honed over my many work years;

receiving compliments that praise my commitment and abilities;

working in a peaceful environment;

getting paid;

working on my own schedule; and

spending time with enlightened and peaceful others.

When the emotion breaks through my self-induced fog, I realize that I am

grateful,

happy to now get done things left undone during this work period,

complimented by the praise heaped on me before my departure.

Though I did not choose for this job to be finished, I choose to embrace the finality. After all, I had completed most of the first list of tasks. And the employer said that she needed to catch up to me.

It was a good drive,

one that will be archived in the museum of workday memories, with the title "Satisfied Gratitude" ... or perhaps "Test for Gratitude" ... or even "Gratitude for the Understanding that working for a Boss who gives that person the Right to do her Job as She Decides".

Glass Menagerie

In my own life, I have many associations with the idea of Glass:

Glass Ceiling:

Having heard this phrase in my lifetime, I have assigned the following conclusions: the glass ceiling is glass, perhaps, to intend that others below can see what is up above but there is, nevertheless, an obstacle to getting there. I simply choose to understand it as an-easy-enough-to-shatter-my-way-through kind of boundary between where I am going and where others have made their own way but now want to prevent anyone else in an effort to assure their own position is not threatened.

Never having accepted selfishly motivated boundaries, I generally double check my motives, and the thickness of the glass, and just crash my way through.

Works for me.

Glass Half Full:

The glass half full idea is a statement about the impact of Gratitude on our lives. If we persist in jealous and negative perception, then we will never be satisfied with the outcome. A glass half full is a high achievement or perhaps a great jumping off point for reaching a goal.

Glass of Courage / Cup of Courage:

Where do we find courage? Often, when we find ourselves lacking in stamina and determination and courage, we turn to an outside influence. This influence might be alcohol, drugs, food, sex, or the attention of others. In the moment, we may escape our pain, but as any alcoholic or binger will attest, the next day the pain is so much worse having been exacerbated by the binge influence.

It is better to find courage deep inside ourselves, forged from difficult situations and baby steps of success.

Stained Glass:

We had stained glass windows in our home when I was a child. The sun would shine through, making the colours brilliant and sparkling, seeming to dance on the rays of the sun, calling me to fanciful and vivacious play. Whenever a difficult time settled over me, I turned to the colours and light to re-energize me...

As children we were admonished to keep fingerprints and stains off the stained glass windows, indeed off all windows and mirrors. Having raised a couple of kids and enjoying the company of GrandKidlettes, I now clearly see that handprints of children are not stains! They take us back to the moment of delicious play when the child was so enthralled with their play that they reached out to touch the colours and light, or perhaps to steady their faltering initial steps.

Turns out that we need not be distracted from the sparkles and colours by a few handprints or stains.

Glassblower:

My Dad settled into glassblowing as his final career choice. Though he worked over open flame, six of them on his lathe, which sent him home with burns, and with glass dust or shards that cut him and gave him nosebleeds, he delighted in fashioning some unique piece of equipment to match what a graduate student of chemistry or physics needed to prove the developing thesis, and as well in making some delightful piece of artwork such as a sailing ship complete with rigging, a buck in mid-leap, or a ballet dancer balanced precariously on a single toe. All were fashioned and detailed completely from glass rods and tubes.

When we married, I made the fruit cake, my mother-in-law iced, then decorated it, and my Dad fashioned the adornment for the top of the cake: a clear glass rod fashioned into a heart, with a bar across the lower third. On that bar sat two birds made from blue glass. One bird was sitting and confidently trilling with head slightly back. The other bird leaned forward and was bellowing insistently. Dad would never say his intent, but I told everyone who would listen that the demure and sweetly singing bird was I … and the the leaned-into-it-bird was the groom. I left the decision about agreeing with me up to the listener.

Dad was wise enough not to actually get the standard glassblower joke: Did you hear about the Glassblower who forgot to blow and breathed in instead? He got a "pane" in his stomach! I think Dad got a "pane" in his stomach every time someone told him that joke.

Here's to your own glass menagerie, even if your glass is only half full!

2ndThird: Themes, Lessons Learned, and Wisdom

In the life of a tree in thirds consideration, the 2ndThird is about providing shelter for others in the branches and foliage grown during the 1stThird. It is a time of great strength and ability.

In this stage known as Mother, a whole new range of responsibilities came into play. This is the time when I actually became a mother, nurturing my children at home, the children at my job, my relationships with partners, home, house, gardens, colleagues, and friends.

Hats and Labels:

2ndThird included many labels for me and I gloried in my habit of living in the top 10% of each; I wore each and all of these 'hats' proudly and consciously.

Hats of the 2ndThird are numerous. The list includes:

- wife, mother, Mum, housewife, gardener, housekeeper, chef, helping my kids to see a world of possibilities in their future;
- Founder and Chair of Parent Council where my children go to school, Parent Council Secretary at Cubs, Sweet Owl at Brownies;
- church volunteer serving as Elder and Sunday School Superintendent and Board of Elders member / secretary (as well as befriending minister - against whom some congregation members launched a vicious attack - then ending up serving as Secretary on the Pastoral Relations Committee to choose a new minister;
- teaching yoga classes and crochet (both skills gleaned and learned to help myself and then offered to others);
- school teacher (and intermediate team leader and filling in as Vice Principal while the original was off on sick leave, organizer of events such as Graduation / Career Days / Ski Days / Track & Field sales to fund bussing to the next levels of competition, colleague, guidance counsellor to students and their parents, practical psychologist, Union Steward and Executive Member and general Secretary;
- Activist, Volunteer on community committees serving usually as Secretary whilst serving on more than one committee at a time;
- meeting demands of adult generation members of the family after my mother's last words to me saying, "This family will never stay together unless you do it, Melba!";
- dancing to stay on my feet in the face of brutal and aggressive mental health manifestations hurled at me from adults in family and at work;
- entertaining by inviting 150 people to an annual Hallowe'en party for which I did all the decorating and all the cooking and all the cleaning, hostessing parties for kids and for adults, keeping up social contacts and responsibilities for family members;

- student of anything that would help me to do a better job under any of my labels;
- party girl, doer, doing it all, taking it on, home-maker, housekeeper, temptress, positions of added responsibility, entertainer, community participant and willing volunteer, dweller in the deep black hole, insecure, sad, depressed, cancer warrior, making personal concessions so I could keep up to the needs and demands of others, standing up to bullies, and still self-imposed Sparkling on Command.

To me much ability was given; I use it to serve others before myself.

Alice Effect:

Alice Effect has now grown into Dancing as Fast as I Can. If I only dance a little faster, longer, and more often, then I can do it all and have it all. I gave up waiting for someone to ask me to come out of the hole, waiting for someone to notice me, my needs, or my silent cries for help.

After all, if it is to be, it is up to ... Me!

Self:

Party Girl is my private life. The Job is my public life.

In my private life, I assigned myself the role of story teller, heavy drinker, try anything, laughing and sparkling and never quitting. Alcoholism was 'just my party persona' and it never troubled me. Until it did. What I learned was that other heavy drinkers and stoners do not like having a reformed person in their midst.

Self can sit and wait. There is a long list of people who must be served before Self even shows up on the sheet. Though I have a psychology degree, and teacher training, Self still comes in those shallowing breaths between falling into bed exhausted and allowing sleep to quiet the hamster on the wheel inside my head. When Self is not being heard, she wakes me up in the night, making me sleepless yet lost in the need for enough sleep to keep up to the todo list of next day. Self becomes health.

Happyness:

How can I be happy if the other person is not? Ubuntu.

Individuality:

Having spent most of my life, through to the final years of the *2ndThird*, I began to realize that there was nothing but hollowness in such great effort to fit in and to follow rules, and I questioned why I was working so hard to fit in. I quickly snatched up the idea, why am I working so hard to fit in when, clearly, I was meant to stand out. Every one person is meant to stand out.

Education:

Education as Teacher was the new perspective for me. I did continue to study so I would learn how to meet the needs of family, friends, students, colleagues, and job. All so that I could be better at serving the needs of others. The real focus was on education from the other side of the desk. Issues that had come up during my tenure as student resurfaced and clamoured for sober second thought, requiring a better way than I had received, better than methods that had failed students in their quest for finding their place in the world. Minute notes were kept, including what worked and what did not work, and filed away in my head for retrieval in the moment when need popped up or reared its head.

I learned how things worked by getting involved, by volunteering, by taking on tasks that involved added responsibilities, and by asking questions again and again until I put together the big picture and the back story.

Busyness, Work, Job, Career:

I stayed at the same school my entire career. When people heard that, they said I was lazy or stupid because any wise ladder-climbing teacher would move every five years just to network for when they decided to climb that ladder to principal (they obviously and demonstrably thought being a principal meant power and relaxing rather than meant being a facilitator for every student and teacher and staff member in their charge). I told them that every year was a new school; everything changed each year except me and the building, though both the building and I had undergone considerable physical changes over time.

Work became the Job. When people asked me what I did, I responded with the tasks that brought home the healthcare benefits for the kids, the reliable paycheque that I could count on every month, and a pension.

Housework, craftwork, cooking, preserving and putting by for winter, growing food, maintaining social responsibilities and etiquettes, teaching the kids how to be the kind of people that other people wanted to have around; all became add-ons shouldered willingly because they were needed.

Building a House, Making a Home: Over the years, we added a deck on the west side which soon proved to be unusable in any season. It was buggy in spring, hot in summer, cold in winter, and fall found us back to school and work and too busy to sit out much. We later enclosed the deck to make a solarium with beautiful wooden arches and windows on all three sides with blinds that could block the hot sun in summer, and allow solar heat during cold seasons.

We put in a patio at the back taking advantage of the shade of established trees so we could barbecue and sit outside without getting fried ourselves.

We gave up the idea of finishing the basement bedrooms when our first born developed allergies that took him to anaphylactic shock and asthmatic reactions. No basement, even carefully finished, could give him what he needed.

We gave up the idea of formal dining room and living room with bay windows where the garage doors were originally placed, when our work fortunes reversed.

We gave up the study for a second bedroom for our second child.

Best laid plans to enlarge became better-improvements-to-existing actions.

School Board and Teacher - When Teacher is Sent Blindly into the Middle of the Frey:

How did a teacher of twenty years find herself in such a mess?

I knew better than to come onto an unknown student like a bulldog.

I knew that before I approach, I do some due diligence learning background information.

I knew that when a principal ruffles up my ears and then throws me into the fray, I should tread especially carefully.

I knew that yard duty is a task that requires regular scanning of the entire yard, but that when a situation came up, my focus should be solely on that situation. Plenty of scans can happen later.

I went for physio appointments in the afternoons because that is the only time they offered me. My sick leave was unaffected by these absences, however resentment was building outside my earshot.

The student, I was told belatedly, is "on the autism spectrum" which means that social interactions were difficult for him. He wanted to be on the Intermediate yard because his only and life-long friend just passed into grade 7, but he was held back in grade 6.

Neither principal or SpecEd lead see to it that the student and I have any opportunity to meet to speak, to apologize to each other, and to put this behind us.

Yikes! Thus began my daily checks for knives between my shoulder blades placed there by middle-management.

Voice:

Voice = remember to say everything on the script. My job required careful scripting so I could present the whole lesson without skipping steps or missing important details. I developed my own shorthand; my script was always in front of me. In this way, I could deliver the lesson and still keep track of which student was paying attention, was distracted, was unhappy, was angry, or was sad. Teaching 13 year olds was a privilege and a challenge; if ever there was an age group that needed an advocate, this was it. They have adult bodies, so everyone expects that they have adult emotions and brain faculty; the development of the frontal lobe and hormones waking up are a vortex of wonder and emotion.

When I spoke beyond the day to days, it was rare. Usually, this was a case where some decision based on efficiency and needs of the system were completely ignoring the human needs. Inspired by dedication and advocacy, words flowed from the end of my pen, organized into best delivery and effect, starting with inflammatory emotional statement, then giving supporting detail, and finally a call to action.

Relationships, Family, Interactions, Influences:

By the way, I highly recommend a honeymoon, in a secret location away from all, where the whispered conversations, declarations, and plans for where-do-we-go-from-heres are private, and they have time for consideration and thoughtfulness.

School Boards: one is left to wonder if people who hide

out in school board offices instead of meeting face to face with workers and parents and students aren't somehow deficient in job and people skills, and somehow creating a persona for themselves that says, "I / we don't care about anybody, staff or students." Ministry and school boards, you created a monstrously inappropriate disregard for the front line workers, who are defined as any one who has kids in front of them every day, preventing those front line workers from delivering instruction and guidance leading students to realizing their full potential.

Adult Relationships = Competition & Blame. People in my life were family, colleagues, neighbours, fellows, and all were assumed to be friends. Great pain was felt when someone in my day-to-days leashed out against me, tried to control me, distracted me from my carefully crafted action / behaviour created within my strict moral code of behaviour and responsibility and serving needs of others before / instead of serving me. Over time, my surprise and hurt became a response of determination to stick to the script of the to-do lists. Middle management everywhere, on the job, in organizations, on committees, seemed to forget that they should be facilitators rather than self serving power and control me-firsters. Competition and blame abounded, creating stress, gobbling up the time and effort that should have been dedicated to doing right by family, others in my care, and in my day-to-days.

Well, the House is Habitable, and We Are Still Speaking: Weddings are like building a house: we agree to the activity together, and end up managing to somehow still be speaking after all the compromises and mis-steps.

Health:

Ms. McGee, You Have Cancer:
Over the years, with three more surgeries, I have had a front row seat at the changes perpetuated on a system where they cut

141

front line workers like doctors, surgeons, nurses, technicians, but never bureaucrats and ministry decision makers.

Chemistry Lesson:

All this pushing me to take the oxycodone leaves me agape. This is one terrifying drug, which, according to the tv, kids find in their parent's medicine chest, and then take to a party to ingest, or to sell to other kids. The experience seemed so without concern coming from the other side of the chemical relationship.

My Dad, a bio-chemist, used to talk about the "wonders of modern medicine" and about "better living through chemistry", and, later in life, added a question mark to both of those phrases.

Now, apparently, this chemical is so commonplace that rarely is the use of it challenged or refused.

That is my wonder: I wonder how my kids' kids will grow up thinking about chemicals in our food, in our homes, in the air that we breathe, in our medicine cabinets, at our parties, in our day to day lives, or will they think about it at all?

By the way - BabyBoy developed head-to-toe eczema, which progressed to asthma and finally full blown anaphylactic shock. We were headlong into lifesaving techniques which included learning how to tracheotomize my baby with a knife, then insert something hollow into the hole with the idea that the cut will close around the tube. I had to carry anakits with me everywhere, having learned how to use them; I couldn't trust anyone with this responsibility.

I'm convinced that these extreme allergies were the fault of baby formula poison.

The Deep Dark Hole:

If meds help then this must be chemical and so the body's chemistry must be studied and corrected, something that medical mainstream know nothing about. I come to the conclusion, all on my own, that addressing past shock and trauma, both physical and emotional, is important.

Achievement, Benchmarks, Milestones:

Achievement = last completion = Milestones. There was very little satisfaction from achievement. Everything was a means to an end, and once the end result was achieved, then the list of what's next came out. And that list was endless. One completion usually found more than one task added on. Reviewing the list became an end of day and beginning of day duty. Reminders.
Having it all meant doing it all; if it is to be, it is up to me!

Parenting:

- Our BabyBoomer lives taught us to do for ourselves, learn for ourselves, rather than wait for intervention from adults and agencies who were just too overwhelmed by our sheer numbers. This independence and accountability to self is how we reached our chosen pinnacles. And this philosophy is important in the development of our kids as they achieve success and satisfaction.
- Because we BabyBoomer kids did without because of sheer supply and demand, we wanted to give our kids everything that we felt we were denied as kids. And the helicopter, over-generous, over-indulgent parent was born.
- The parenting reality is that you're on your own-own-own, MummaMelba. Focus on baby; keep away from people who make you feel bad about yourself. Protect Baby always;
- Our second child was born two years later, with only three stitches required! When the nurse brought BabyGirl to me for her first feeding, the nurse stayed to help after asking how the first baby's feeding went. She helped me

to find a comfortable way of sitting; she helped me to prop BabyGirl in my arms on my pillow, she took one look and said she'd be right back. In she came with a nipple shield; BabyGirl happily and successfully latched on and ate her fill.

I said to the nurse how wonderful she was after my previous experience, and exclaimed over the new technology of a nipple shield invented in the last two years. She snorted and said that the only reason that I wasn't offered one last time was because the nurses were too lazy to do the work of labelling and sterilizing required. Those were the only tears that I cried after that delivery.

Final thoughts: No matter the difficulties endured, at the end of it all is the wonder and joy and promise of life with baby. Keep your eye on the prize.

Keeping Your Straps Tied Tight:
Over the years of strapping our lives onto and into our car, there were many lessons learned and sights seen:

- If your first time using a diving board is a ten foot board, pulling up at the last minute will leave you flat on the surface of the water. If you survive, in the background you will hear Mum, talking to OldestJuh and OlderJuh about how they need to be careful about what they inspire me to try;
- Next time Mum told Dad to stop before dark at the next campsite, he always did so quickly and without any suggested deviations from the plan;
- When you are in the US, and walking with your Canadian family and a beautiful southern US womyn with her lovely accent and genteel manners, and when your Dad drives by as one of the two passengers in the lovely lady's husband's car, and when said-lady flags down her husband to pick her up to save her the hot humid walk

back to the motel, and when her husband drives on by, you just might hear, "No wonder he didn't pick me up! He would never expect me to get into a car with a nigger! He will have to clean the car inside and out before I'll get into it again!" "Mum, what's a n..." "Never mind, Melba! Quickly, let's go!" The first time one hears blatant racism shocks one to the core of her moral compass;

- When you are 10 and walking Times Square in New York City, with your family, after dark, through teeming throngs of people, you don't have to stop and have a conversation with every unkempt drunk who approaches your 10 year old little girl small town self. They just might not be being friendly;

- And when the door to your family's inexpensive (affordable) New York City hotel room is blowing and rattling through the night because of the wind in the corridor of the Chesterfield Hotel, it just might not be wind in the hallway (as evidenced by the number of cigarette butts in the hall outside the door);

- When you go to the glassblowing displays and find a huge room full of every flower you have ever seen, in vivid colour, looking entirely detailed and real, including goldenrod finely-attentioned with every separate floret, they just might be delicately crafted by someone like my Dad;

- When siblings, spouses, parents, children, and a dog spend twelve hours a day in a car, their metal and their mettle are tested. I now know two different spellings for metal. And I know precisely what testing mettle means;

Between the trials and demands of travel, there are sights and experiences that give you a lifelong grounding in the meaning of Joy, and dependability, and beauty, and mutuality, and singlemindedness of purpose, and what is important in life.

Happy Trails.

Keep your straps tied tight in life, including when you decide to take your own children on road trips.

Toolkit:

Tools List included: survival skills, organizational skills, quick wit, and grounding in my golden rule moral code. Continuing to study nutrition and health, mental health, and human behaviour meant that I could survive to come back to serving others another day; I was enlightening both my kids and students so they could assume their own role of self-determination.

Wisdom:

Making sense of it all - from reaction to codes to philosophies
The *2ndThird* becomes a disjointed life ... And my mantra becomes, "Works for me!"
And sometimes "This too will pass!"
Mum had always taught me that each person had something they could teach me that would be useful or helpful, no matter how badly that person treated me.
Beating a child is never ok, never an option, never to be tolerated. It changes the child and it changes you, forever, and not in a good way.
I Put Butter on my Plate Five Times yet I Still Cannot Find Any Butter for my Bread!:
Sometimes, even the best laid plans must be changed mid-stride, because it makes no sense to continue simply on the basis of the plan is the plan.

School Board and Teacher - Seven Years Later:
Years later, those maple trees are thriving, lining our horseshoe driveway, offering us shade, and reminding us to look to the bigger picture, and the final outcome.

BabyMumma ... Hitting my Stride:

Parenthood reality is this:

There are no hours of playing any flute in any lush meadow, no loving hands relieving me so I could follow doctor's strictest orders to pick up NOTHING for six weeks after the pregnancy and delivery, no empathy or sympathy, no listening ear, no contact with the others I had heretofore served and delighted, and no distracting elements from the grinding day-to-day needs of baby, and house.

When it is impossible to look back end of day and see what I have accomplished, I assumed: that is because I have accomplished nothing; or that I cannot work up to my standard with the paucity of resources and help at hand. I cannot work up to anyone else's standard when they have none.

Relationships. Why?

The blame game: when I point a finger at someone else, there are three pointing back at me.

My Years as a Union Boss:

If they can do it to one of us, they can do it to every one of us;

Solidarity is a double edged sword;

Those who demand too much of the rest of us are too often the ones who should retrain and try something more suitable to their temperament;

There are a rare few who are poorly suited, poorly trained, poorly supported, or just plain beat up by the middle managers; and

Backrooms at work and union and political associations (and everywhere) are secret, dark, smelly, and corrupted. Nothing good grows there.

Reality hits; reality bites; reality is it ...

No matter the challenges, keep your eye on the prize. Hold it in your arms, revel in the wonder and joy and promise realized in that moment.

Note on aging memory: I can remember every word of conversation from the 1960s but if you told me something yesterday, consider it in the vault ... of forgotten-ness!

Embrace aggressive, competitive, masculine and Pisces Energies to get to where I need to go.

"I always knew where was Mum, wife, sister, daughter, teacher, and Mrs. McGee, but I haven't seen Melba for years."

Conclusions: Boughs Full to Bursting

Melba's boughs are full to bursting and so she grows greater and larger boughs. She invites ideas and people to be nurtured in those boughs. And she allows people to become squatters there, too.

Though she continues to learn in this *2ndThird*, the lessons crowd each other in Melba's focus and attention, and sometimes need to be repeated and they wait, patiently or loudly, until Melba has learned them.

3rdThird - UnJobbing, Tidying Up, and Shared Wisdom

Introduction: Pause for Clarity of Thought; Decision to Continue Forward

The *3rdThird* finds Melba with boughs over-crowded and giving way, threatening the supporting trunk and roots. It is time for the kind of conscious thought that allows clear decisions for an independent future for her True Self, for finding her True Purpose, and for allowing the determination to continue in this life instead of choosing the exit ramp of illness and dis-ease.

The questions that one asks at the time of taking the exit ramp to their death bed should be asked at the beginning of each *Third*, especially at the beginning of the *3rdThird*.

Did I Live?

Did I Love?

Did I make a Difference?

The *3rdThird* is about living entirely at my own conscious choosing, freed from imposed life, from responsibilities of minute to minute parenting, jobbing, and schedule. I am finally self-affirming and self-directing. I'm still working on projects that I love, that serve my purpose, and that still follow my moral compass. I'm finding ways to serve my community.

In my father's discussion about our life as similar to the life of a tree, he described the *3rdThird* as all about pruning and eventual certain loss.

In the Pagan and Wiccan consideration, the *3rdThird* is referred to as life-as-Crone.

Now it is up to me to choose and wear the labels of the day for myself, to stand up for myself, to detail my days myself, to share the wisdom learned from my *1stThird and 2ndThird* as well as wisdom inherited from others.

The *3rdThird* is about looking forward rather than back; let the path behind remind us of its teachings; focus on the path ahead using a compass set in both our past and our today, yet readjusted and regulated by true north which is our authentic self, and then live in the moment.

Let go of the competitive, aggressive, Baby-Boomer-survival Energies of the *2ndThird*; embrace the cerebral, sensitive Energies of the *3rdThird*.

Time to find Melba again.

57 and Stuck - The Rest of the Story

57 years old and I am stuck; 6:45pm and here I sit, still at my teacher desk.

The students boarded the buses three hours ago. My colleagues went home to life and family soon after. The usual majyk that always fell easily from tip of my tongue and pen, from fingertips and forefront of my imagination, are each and all missing. And here I sit, still at my desk, munching away at reducing the piles of work, papers to grade, daybook to be filled in, and lesson plans to prep so that the students can realize an enthusiasm for both concept and learning...

I have been teaching grades 7 and 8 for 35 years, teaching in some form (Sunday school, swimming, public school, colleagues, ...) for 45 years. Yet here I sit, ground to a halt, with no idea why I am so stuck. After all this enthusiasm, and ideas, and energy in my work, after all the positive feedback from students, and their parents, and from colleagues, why am I just sitting here night after night?

There is no shortage of places and people to blame. Our federation is now a union. They are clumsy in the transition learning process and somehow have forgotten their commitment to supporting teachers in their calling to teach students, and to focus on student needs while the union watches the teachers' backs. Teachers have found themselves counting minutes, students, and prep time instead of student smiles and student light bulbs turning on.

Our administration is now out of the union, and feeling the weight of being the onsite us-versus-them gotcha person against the teachers who are their previous Federation-now-union mates. Classes and assignments are set up inequitably.

We teachers are suddenly on a slippery slope of self preservation duck-and-cover because of the target being placed on our backs, rather than focusing on ideas that will spark curiosity, and a love of learning in each child. Students and parents have heard ugly accusations and untruths about teachers, painted with a broad brush during a thrashing and slashing political battle at Ministry of Education level. They are frustrated that teachers are huddled in self preservation rather coming up with the majyk that the students need.

I am considering the R word: Retirement! As suggested, in the year of achieving my 85-factor, I have attended the union class about what to expect when expecting retirement. Just last year, when a colleague retired, I wept at the thought of my retirement. I still felt vital and capable and my students were still responding to my teaching.

This year, my class has 36 students, in a split grade 7-8 which gives me the responsibility of teaching two lessons, one grade 7 and a separate grade 8 lesson, in every period and every subject. There are eleven students identified with special needs, which means I am responsible for meeting the specified needs of each.

There are nine high-behaviours students, not all of whom have been identified, but with special needs, nevertheless.

There have been so many cuts in SpecEd that the students in my class have no SpecEd support, even though the school board is responsible for providing carefully planned individualized support. I am feeling cast adrift when I learn the other grade 7 and 8 classes have SpecEd support in their single grade class.

It is October and that means report cards and resulting interviews are looming. Great. I am anticipating angry finger-pointing conversations rather than opportunities to find a way to work together to ensure the success of the student.

My family needs my attention. We spent Thanksgiving weekend at the Heart Institute ER ensuring that this was not a return of previous problems that might require further heart surgery. Yet another member of the family was diagnosed with cancer. Our first grandchild was born. For years, I had to leave for work every day, no matter a family member's personal crisis, deferring time, attention, and decisions to when I got home from the classroom. The pull at home was great indeed and in this time there must be no deference to elsewhere.

I have seen too many people who retired badly. They were disheartened, anxious, lonely, and angry that the promised retirement freedom, travel, house renovations, and excitement were not affordable. The much-touted teacher's pension is indeed amazing, not because it is large but because it is reliably steady. All the glossy promise ads put out by the union and pension plan seem to be simply pie-in-the-sky to keep us paying into this savings plan.

When teachers retire, we leave a full-time job with benefits to a new teacher. When we face a post-retirement financial challenge such as a child's wedding or health issue, we cannot count on doing supply teaching because we are expected to move over and give over to young new teachers, even though we just did that when vacating our contract! This is the essential challenge of the Baby Boomer generation: just too many of us! Not our fault, not our doing!

So I meditate on how to retire TO something rather than only retiring FROM something.

And I found myself revisiting the Thirds of Life philosophy. When we leave the *1stThird*, we use the experience and skills gained to move into the *2ndThird* and its change of needs, activity, demands, and the excitement about moving forward. I realized this idea is the essential core of the challenge of moving into the next Third!

We move forward TO something. We do not move away FROM something. Always. The answer is in embracing what we want to do, to achieve, to succeed in the next Third. As with all things, it is all in the attitude, the effort, the gratitude!

Retirement it is!

Checking Into the Aquarius Motel

"I locked the door! So there you stay, outside, for the rest of the hour that we dictated!"

Some friends of ours had invited us to their mansion on the river for a party. Though they had space in their home to sleep a dozen couples, the party invitation list had dozens of names, many of whom came from an hour and a half away, just like us.

It was recommended that we, this year's overflow, check into a small motel, five minutes walk, or maybe ten minutes of staggering, maybe a half mile down the road from the party; The motel was: small, utilitarian, tv but no channels, AC that didn't work, fan on the table that likely doesn't work given its wiring from the 1950s, more than a little rough around the edges, clean, and almost walkable if the partying is more vigorous than legally allows driving even a short distance.

Our reservation gave us a check in time of 1pm; perfectly timed to coincide with party start time of 1pm. We arrived at 1:10pm, headed to the office for sign in, which we did in lickety-split efficient order with the older couple who owned and ran the place during the summer. They charged us about 40% more than their place warranted. They handed us a key and a room number, and told us that the cleaner is still in our room so we must wait an hour before going into our room.

Two problems:

We needed to use the bathroom after an hour and a half drive from home.

We wanted to get to the party which had already started.

We suggested that they put us into a room that was already prepared.

"No! You are already on the list under your room number!"

"Are all the other rooms full? There are two cars in the parking lot and your place looks to have a dozen rooms."

"Too bad, the list is already made up. What would I tell the others when they show up? You will not cheat your way through this!"

"Do you realize the influence of the couple who sent us here to stay?"

"Tut tut tut!" was their response.

We left the office and went to sit in our car to scope out the lay of the land. We just happened to be parked in front of our room and we could see through the open door of our room; the beds were made, the bathroom freshened and complete with clean towels laid out. The ice bucket and glasses wrapped in plastic were in place on the tv table. The cleaner was mopping the floor. Her cart was outside the door with vac and extra supplies safely stowed in preparation to move on to the next room.

We went over to the room, said a breezy "Hello!", and asked if we could toss our suitcases on the bed, go to the bathroom and get out of her way, to which she cheerily agreed, after asking us if we wanted her to stop and get out for a few minutes, telling us she was one minute from being finished. We waited the minute. I did not go to the bathroom, letting my party mate hightail it for first relief. I looked across the yard and saw the owners marching across the parking lot leaving their anger and vitriol in their wake. "Someone's coming and they don't look happy!" I called.

"You have no right to go against what we instructed; this is our property and you must do what we say. You have walked on the wet floors and now they will need to be redone. And we will need to fire the cleaner!"

"Oh no, don't do that; we simply walked in when she left. She had nothing to do with it.

We don't need the floors redone; we paid for a clean room which it is, you already have our money, the room is already cleaned. Let's leave it at that."

"Get-out-get-out-get-out!" After pushing us out, the womyn slammed and locked the door with a brisk twist of her master key. "I locked the door! So there you stay, outside, for the rest of the hour we dictated!"

... I had seen a retirement plan go bad before, when a couple decided to get a little motel in a seasonal tourist place to fund their travel plans for the off season of their year. These plans were invariably poorly planned, with no research or training, with no people skills for dealing with staff or tourists, with no positive energy reserves after retiring from a difficult career or job, with the realities of purchasing a crumbling property and business. Likely, they were short-staffed because the owners are so impossible to work for. Woe betide any poor saps who arrived to stay there.

I looked at my hand, which held our own key to the room. Our bags were already stowed in the room. Party time! Off we went to join our friends for a summer day and evening of bacchanalia, sharing the story of our experience at the Aquarius Motel.

Our host kept mum, but having known him since young childhood we knew there would be a reckoning. And they deserved it! They likely had a handsome retainer through the season so the typically huge parties would have someplace close by to offer to the overflow. Our friends are glamorous people who will not have their reputations challenged.

In another *Third* of my life, this experience might have robbed me of my party-ness, my fun-ness, my equilibrium, but even the little time that I have lived in this *3rdThird* has helped me to recognize what is my problem and what is not.

WooHoo!

Great music beating out to keep step with my heartbeats, flashing colours and lights, scents from the sea of humanity and smoke from weed, alcohol over everything, pyrotechnics display, and a crowd of similarly engaged people who are similarly affected by the vastness of sensory input.

And here I am, onstage in front of this sea of familiar faces. They beckon to me, cheer for me, invite me to dive out over them, crowd surfing as they pass me along, offering the exciting experience of just letting go. After all, they will look after me. Delicious, eyes closed, give in to others.

Leap I do! Many hands support me, moving me hither and yon, giving strong support that allows me to just give in; I make no planning for the direction or the support: I am simply allowing others to be responsible.

Then I notice: I am not a crowd surfing famous chick surrounded by adoring, and careful fans; I am not engaged in abandon. I have no idea what direction to which I am being carried or pushed. I don't even keep my eyes open, nor do I watch when and where, and ... I am completely irresponsible. I take zero responsibility for anything.

And those adoring supportive fans drop the mask of the illusion that I can completely proceed with reckless abandon, and I realize that they are the sum total of my past experiences.

My past experiences are in charge of the direction and the security of my body and my life, and my future. What if I end up somewhere I don't want to go? Perhaps outside away from the music and lights? Perhaps falling when their handstrength fails, leaving me crippled and distrusting everyone and completely unable to join into any future activity.

The secret about crowd surfing is that when you want to get down you can. Simply sit, drop your derrière, and you will surely make contact with the floor. That's the simple part. The not so simple part is that you may land on your backside, or on your feet, or on your head.

Counting on the crowd to return you to the stage feet first, pushing your body to the stage where you can stand up without a fall is not a guaranteed thing. People and experiences are fickle; they may be distracted suddenly, or they may tire of supporting you instead of seeking their own pleasures.

When I left this Light Body vision journey, I came to realize that there is always a choice: when it comes to determining where I am going in life, I can do the choosing or I can be the hapless individual who is driven by past experiences, to the good, the bad, and the ugly.

The healing journey and any day's journey, they are always my choice.

Birth

A week of distraction and challenge has passed, giving me an appreciation for the assigned topic that helped unjumble my thoughts, at least for this piece to be completed for Writing Group.

"Birth" births many concepts: birth of a baby, birth of offspring, birth of plants, birth of a season, birth of an idea, and birth of understanding. And, there are stages involved:

- Conception begins the realization of a reality from a possibility;
- Pregnancy is the development of the fetus or offspring;
- Labour is the forceful work that frees the offspring from its environment of dependency; and
- Birth is when the offspring leaves its protected environment and enters into its growth-towards-independence.

Conception of a human, a plant, or an idea has been well studied, giving scientific and emotional understanding of the how-tos and to the concept of Fertility. The offspring, season, idea, and understanding, each begin as a realization that there is a possibility. Actively bringing the production forward requires active initiation into the process; this activity is called conception. This action must find fertile ground in which to start. Fertile ground might be the earth, a womb, an open mind, or a change in surroundings, such as a change in physical environment, like weather initiating a change of understanding which coat to choose for the day.

What activity must happen for an idea to get its start? Just as a human fetus must have its beginnings from active sperm and receptive egg, an idea must come from some germane experience or thought, landing on an open fertile mind.

Pregnancy of an idea is when the spark comes to take root and develop into a conscious thought or plan.

The seed settles in and begins to change, into a new form that will bring about a new person, plant, idea, or concept. This development can only be successful if appropriate nurturing and nutrition are present. An idea that falls on a closed mind, is blocked by fear or prejudice or distraction, is destined to spontaneously abort or morph into a different idea.

Labour is as necessary to birth an idea as it is to expel the unborn child out and into the world, freeing it to begin to take on a life-force of its own. An idea must, similarly, be understood, organized, tried out, tested, reorganized into a form that reflects its true nature. Labour, indeed, but a labour of love if it is to be successful and understood.

Birth of an idea is as wondrous and awe-inspiring and fearsome as any other birth. The parent / philosopher / writer / originator of the idea must be prepared for others to influence the offspring as any parent must accept the influence of teachers, media, other people and neighbours, culture. For once born, any idea must move into its own destiny, which must be understood to be growth. Just as a parent, the writer must also be prepared for the offspring to develop into its own destiny, rather than the parent creating a strangle-hold to keep the idea as their own baby, close only to the parent.

An idea, once birthed, once spoken, belongs to the world. The writer-birther can nurture it, feed it, lend it strength and direction, but ultimately the natural order of things is for the infant idea to become a concept enriched by the influence of all.

Happy Birth day, project! Time to formalize my writing, sharing the majyk that falls from the tip of my pen. Time to develop my ReikiCommunity.

This Comment came at a Good Time …

> *"First off I want to say wonderful blog! I had a quick question that I'd like to ask if you do not mind.*
>
> *I was curious to know how you centre yourself and clear your head prior to writing. I've had a hard time clearing my thoughts in getting my ideas out. I truly do take pleasure in writing but it just seems like the first ten to fifteen minutes are wasted simply just trying to figure out how to begin. Any recommendations or hints?*
>
> *Kudos!"*

This comment came to me at a good time. I had been sucked into some kind of vacuum where there was no ink, no paper, no keyboard, and no actual work on paper. I have ideas, really brilliant ones which pop into my head and I tell myself that is the topic for the next piece of writing. Yet I don't write the topic down, and I don't belly up to the keyboard every single day; and my deadlines are looming closer and closer, one tomorrow, in fact. When I finally sit down to write, all those brilliant ideas tantalize me from just outside my reach, becoming more distant from conscious thought.

I think about writing every day. I notice things worthy of consideration every day. My curiosity is piqued every day, demanding that I thrash about and research until my head is satisfied that I have fully addressed the particular topic from every perspective every day.

My writing blogsite has 703 comments that I have not yet read. They do pop up while I am on my iPad, so I notice the first line when each notification arrives. This one caught my eye!

One of my favourite places to hide while procrastinating is a great Writer's Workshop from Hay House. It is expensive. It has many dozens of hours of presentations, each one containing a minimum of one aha and useful idea. Writers who are familiar to me and admired by me are the speakers. And they hold out the carrot that one, only one of the 900+ writers registered for the course, will be chosen to be picked up by Hay House … dream come true, right?

And Balboa, the sister publisher, has come to me ready with a publishing package to help me to move forward to realizing my lifelong dream of putting my stories out there, because "A Story Shared is a Journey Enlightened," right? Just as my blog tagline says.

After more than sixty years of picking up a pencil and watching as majyk flowed from its tip onto the blank page, I am halted. According to the gurus, I am suffering from self limiting beliefs that I am allowing to keep me from my destiny, from realizing this dream.

Here I sit, at my keyboard again, with this week's Writing Group topic crooking its finger at me, demanding my effort, conformity, and full presence in returning to the majyk. Then up pops a notification from the writing blog that starts with, "First off, I want to say wonderful blog!"

A Quest and a Gift

Dear Shaman,

Thank you for last night, on behalf of Share Circle and myself. Many questions were answered for me, I got to know a friend better, and I have found a place where I can return when I feel in need of support, protection, or guidance.

So, of course, I found my words and wrote them this morning:

Last Night's Shaman-Guided Journey ... The Morning After:

Visuals were all I got on my quest during last night's guided Journey, except for one simply worded message.

I went in with no question, no intention, and no search for affirmation or guidance. Beyond the idea that the crossroads before me may bring up ideas for consideration; beyond living in this moment with full consciousness. Though my minute to minute decisions and considerations in this moment are sure to influence and even crowd me, I am keeping a critical eye on what serves me well in this moment.

With my newly noted power animal at my side, I settled into position, physical, emotional, and spiritual, for ease and acceptance. I trusted my Shaman to guide me to a place of my own choosing, and to stand beside me with my power animal while watching my back.

Relax and notice ... The images were powerful. Tree. Ascension. Bright clear light, full of all the colours, and free of brown gooey. Hand on my totem animal's scruff. At my elbow my Shaman. Reassurance.

Then water appeared. This water-baby stepped in to swim. Glassy early-morning water on the lake before morning breezes rippled it up. Floating with mere small hand movements taking me along:

- Choppy wavy waters of larger rivers, current neither fighting me nor dragging me. Still floating with easy-action carrying me; and
- Crashing waters of seas and oceans, the waves bashing the shore, yet with no drag or threat, leaving me to choose my own path effortlessly.

Each time I stop on shore, I meet the same beings: my original Guide, and my Mum. Spirit Guide reached into flowing robes and withdrew a ball, clear, bright lighted; when I gazed into the sphere, whether glass or water bubble was a question demanded by Ego which I ignored, I could see images in the ball. They were simple images of singular things or people, and I just saw, with no judgement or evaluation or attempt to understand. There were colours and rays, formations that seemed familiar or beckoning, beings that spoke not, but who led me to an idea or thought.

Each time, after gazing into the ball, off I went into the waters again. Each time, I was offered opportunity to go into dark caves and caverns, into the centre of plants, into gatherings of beings or people, but I always observed while I stayed in the water. I stopped and shored only when I saw my Spirit Guide and my Mum, and gazed into the glass.

At one point, I asked my Guides what was happening, or what I should do, or what something meant; the answer became the simple and singular word message, *"Go and explore; go exploring."* And off I went again.

I felt completely free to choose, free from threat or harm. I became the Light and the essence of the harmony of my experience, and those who crossed my watery way.

I was called back to the circle of Questers by Shaman. Yet I persisted and returned to my Guides, both. I asked if I shouldn't continue exploring rather than leaving this Quest mere seconds after beginning.

Their answer was that this Exploration will always be there

for me, including their Guidance and including my Totem Animal, including my Shaman's protection.

This is the place where the Answers live.

Called back again by my Shaman, I descended to this Middle World once more.

I was surprised to hear that I had been Questing for more than twenty minutes, and to realize that this Womyn of Words had only one brief simple sentence spoken to her during the Quest. This was so unlike my typical and easily called-forth gush of words.

When asked if I wanted to share anything with the group, words failed me beyond the one simple worded-message received. So I waited to go last, to gather my thoughts into coherence, to not claim the Energy in the room first (as hostess, that would be incorrect). I realized that it was ok to share the message, that though the message was given to singular me, it wasn't a message of import only to me (a Story Shared is a Journey Enlightened, eh!).

Words to describe the images made their way out of my mouth, disjointed and far from carefully crafted, but vivid (to me at least). I realized the bounty that abounds in my life, realized the benevolent power of this Shaman, realized the Gratitude for my life and these Others who come to me to offer majyk both to me and to this world.

Home to an Epsom salts bath. To silence, to back-burnering the fulsomeness of what had been given and what I learned, to soaking it in until it became a part of my very essence.

Usually, I have to thrash about in an experience to make sense of it. This time it was a gentle, and protected offering laid at my feet: Blessings and Courage.

An Old Year and a New Year … Both Dear Friends and both Gifts

The best is yet to come.

As I pause on this last day of 2014, I look back following

another year with my eyes and my memory, and I look forward to the future with all its newness and promise, this time looking with my heart and all my senses. This time is typically when people make New Year's Resolutions, promises to themselves that they will do, achieve, realize, or make; all are activities that, no matter how specific, are nonetheless more smoke and mirrors than real.

I am running into a new year; the old year holds on, clutching and dragging me back.

Each year in this *3rdThird* of my life is a time of looking at each thing for a second time, a time of wisdom, because the *3rdThird* is all about realization, is all about the real. So rather than making demands and promises that extend into the next 365 days, I am looking into each moment, seeing every single one of them as its own single entity in time. This single entity of time is; it is unbounded, unpromised, unfettered, and unending. This is the opportunity to take a deep breath in, hold it for that moment, savour it, taste it, and then move into the next moment.

The present is all you ever really have.

But first, this is life itself. This present time is where I breathe, where I live, where I dream, where I share Love, where consciousness lives. This ... is.

And so, with this first breath of many, I begin to realize my own life, and acknowledge that others are realizing their own. Wishing you a Wise New Year, full of deep breaths and full of moments that take your breath away!

Hope (with a dash of Whimsy)

In this Season of Hope, when Hope seems on everyone's lips, I pause to examine Hope and where it resides in my life.

First, a definition: Hope is a feeling of expectation, belief and desire.

And some common phrases: "there was no hope", "what we all hope for", "I hope and pray", and "Not what we had hoped".

So how is hope different from expectation? There is an

element of not possible, not going to happen, but nevertheless hoped for, or the same as a miracle.

My meandering method:

So gather all round this time of year

So to share hope as well as good cheer

Though we hardly put words nor speak what we hope

in the hopes that the Universe won't simply say, "Nope!"

Children hope for a toy of their imagination

Older ones hope to score the winning run

A parent hopes for health for little one

And on the job hopes for some recognition

We hope that the rain soon and surely will come

then we hope that the storm will just finally be done

We hope to wake up from a vivid nightmare

Even pinching ourselves to assure, to dare,

That what we are living, what we cannot bear

Will evaporate with morning dew and cold air.

But real hope, bone deep hope, desperate hope arises from the depths of our soul

When we see no path but divine intervention and hope there's a God who'll pull us out of this hole.

And we cling to that hope, making promises of faith

If only we find a way through this maze.

And when dawn peeps through dark clouds of despair

We begin to have hope again and we raise

our eyes and our hearts and our hopes that we're saved.

When trite phrases are mouthed at a festival of bacchanalia,

We allow ourselves to be negative, judging others for being shallow

for placing their hopes on simple things of no ethereal value,

angry smugness born of long experience in hopes dashed.

Yet we hold deep inside us a tiny glimmer of belief in hope, in success, in Love, in the Divine

Our hope lives on, despite our anger, our hurts, and our fears come true, living and persisting in our successes (even the meagre ones), in our possessions, in our full bellies, in pulling ourselves up by our bootstraps, in our belief clinging to the idea of luck, in our persistence in the face of failure and loss, in our love, in our Wee'uns, and in our souls.

After all,

> "*Hope springs eternal in the human breast:*
> *Man never is, but always to be blest.*
> *The soul, uneasy and confined from home,*
> *Rests and expatiates in a life to come.*"

From An Essay on Man by Alexander Pope (1688-1744)

Banding

Our Family banded together for three special occasions in the last week, two birthdays and a baptism. An ole gal turned 65, and a young womyn turned 33, and a 4-month-old babe was baptized. Milestones all, each carrying its own traditional and cultural weight, demands, and expectations, which brings me to the great Joy of banding together in life's large moments.

The greatest Joy is knowing that we are all in the moment together. Somehow being together lends weight to the Joy by pausing and taking notice, and eases all weight at the same time. Smiling faces assure the one who has reached the milestone that they are supported, that we are all in this together.

No matter how hard we try to self-affirm and be independently strong, banding together reminds us that when it is a less joyous occasion, we will not have to face it alone, that there will be help, love, and time spent together there, too. Banding together affirms the simple fact that we are social animals, needing presence and also needing face-to-faces, hugs, common activity, contact and sharing … beyond screen time.

Though I have, on occasion, thought I'd like to spend some

time in total isolation as a remote cave dweller, perhaps, I yet recognize that my choice to gather together (with Loved Ones, and with others who share a common single-mindedness of purpose) is what I truly crave for special or particular occasions. By extension, we band together at Writing Group, supporting, challenging, and inspiring each other, and taking that strength to our chosen gotta-do-it activity. For us it is Writing, which feeds our soul. Then we return to the cave to be productive.

Balance of solitary and often grumpy, grouchy, and cranky cave-time with banding-together-joyful-time is what I now recognize as best for this Little-Girl from small-town-Canada.

Gathering - and a Community is Born

Writing Group is a great place to launch a piece of writing, a new idea, something different from everyone else's work. They welcome, they listen, they support, they inspire and they help me find clarity. They are the wind beneath my wings of storytelling, of allowing my visions to depart my head and land squarely on my page.

While pursuing a dream, seeking to come full circle, I wrote about Reiki and Energies in a story for Writing Group. In this piece, I wrote about Reiki from a personal point of view: Energy experiences as a child; back-burnering abilities (indeed killing some off to the point where I would have to Reiki the skill for some time before daring to accept that the ability would ever come back to non-ego-driven reliability) all in the name of social acceptance and expectation.

First one then another and another until five from the Writing Group came to me and expressed an interest in learning more about Reiki. These are the most supportive and expressive people on the planet and in my circle. My Reiki senses were tingling.

Letting an idea sit for a period of time is a method that has worked well for me, at home, at work teaching 13 year olds, and in difficult social interactions, so that is exactly what I did. The next week, at our after-Group coffee get together, someone brought up her interest again. Others overheard and joined in expressing their interest.

I had been working on a blog / website for the ReikiCommunity, grabbing an email address with the same name, wording up possible setup for the blog, planning a launch, and managing an invitation to speak to introduce Reiki at a local event; many details were swirling, and only a few alighted to meld into a possible script. I began to wonder how I would find the words to help my Writing Group friends understand Reiki from their first baby steps into this realm.

First was a go-round of emails and reply-alls about day preference, time preference, directions to the presentation location. Coordinating six schedules for six busy committed-elsewhere people is always fascinating, and a way to get to know something about each individual. Home renovations, helping family member or friend, volunteering, work, rescuing animals, and appointments. All of these demonstrated the Energies of the individuals. And our Energies began to blend even before we had found the single day so the group could be together on this journey. Though at one point I was certain that we would need to split into two groups, we finally succeeded in determining a single day and time. Adding to the auspicious regard for the occasion was the fact that it was the day after our HolyDay of Lughnasadh, and the day of the Full Moon. That's some awe-inspiring Energy.

We came together on the appointed date and time, made social chitchat, and each found a place to sit. Everyone was smiling, interacting, settling in. When I began to speak, the Energy of the collective focused immediately, wending its way in and out and through the Energies of each other, bonding us together.

We passed an evening of enlightenment, Energy, joining together, and sharing.

And it was in the spaces between all these decisions and Energies that I tingled with the realization that my Reiki Introduction was born. The ReikiCommunity was born. ReikiCommunity.ca was born. The birth of a collective, a community, or any birth really, is a thing of beauty. A first birth holds its own special presence.

Behold, a Community is Born. And a dream unfolds into reality.

Crystal - Clarity during Mental Health Week - the Autistic Mind at Work

This, by the way, is Canadian Mental Health Association's Mental Health Week, an annual national event that takes place during the first week in May, to encourage people from all walks of life to learn, talk, reflect and engage with others on all issues related to mental health.

(www.mentalhealthweek.ca)

What follows are the mental processes of someone who has several constant companions: mental health issues, clinical depression, ADHD, OCD, autism, and processing auditory information without being able to see or read it.

For the last six weeks, I have found myself back onto the conveyer belt of the medical community with hospital, scans, and appointments, and I have arrived at some conclusions which gave me clarity about how to proceed along my WellnessPath. This has led me to expand that clarity until it was crystal clear, and was sparkling as my beacon beckoning me to the healthiest direction.

So let's see how Melba's mental processes work:

First a list of "crystal'" concepts: crystal clear, lead crystal, crystal chandeliers, crystal healing / Reiki / chakras, crystals in urine, crystals from alum, building crystals, my friend's name is Crystal, crystal palace where Crystal went on vacation, making crystals from salt, sugar…

Aside: Ever notice that when you write the word crystal so

many times, you find yourself going back to look it up to make sure it is spelled correctly?

And that took me to Safari where I found Kidzworld:

http://www.kidzworld.com/article/26598-make-your-own-crystals

And now into the obsessive pursuit of something I can do or control while my head back-burners the original idea (Hmmm ... Remind me ... Oh yah, the word crystal?). The following is quoted from Kidzworld:

Aside: Not only is this something I can use for demonstration purposes, but it is something to do with the GrandKidlettes, too.

Ok, this may be another Aside ... From Kidzworld:

> *"Now, prepare yourself for some science. Crystals are so common because the word crystal refers to any matter that is arranged in an ordered form. The units that are arranged can be molecules, atoms or ions which are all much too small to see with the naked eye, but whose arrangement gives crystals their characteristic structure. There are seven categories of crystal structures which are called lattices or space lattices.*
>
> *Crystal Needles are a great introduction to crystal growing. You can have some delicate, really cool crystals going within three hours time!*
>
> *Ingredients:*
>
> *...*
>
> *Directions:*
>
> *...*

... back to my Wellness Path: Wellness is best understood by me as a three-legged stool. Those three legs are Physical

Health, Mental Health, and Spiritual Health. To be well, each of those three must be sturdy and balanced or the stool will fall over.

Off I head, focusing on the Physical world, searching out facts, ingredients, and activities that will build endurance and strength, or in this case, crystals. The way my head works is to clarify what is needed without obsessing every minute on the minute details that should help my physical health but which also distracts me away from looking to practices that will enhance Mental Health and Spiritual Health.

First leg on my Wellness stool: Physical Health world

These crystals are obviously physical because we can consider them by using the senses. The recipe is something I can control just like all my considerations regarding physical health: find the nutrient that I need, buy that ingredient, find the recipe to use that ingredient, prep, eat, clean up … See why I find myself dwelling in the Physical Health world? It's simple to understand and easy to control.

Mental Health World:

Intellectual health, though residing in the Mental Health category, is much like Physical Health, following the "use it or lose it" idea, I did my research, found ingredients, followed the recipe and used past experience in the kitchen.

However Mental Health also considers Emotional Health. This is where I must step outside myself, and watch for all my usual 'tells' for my lurking distraction issues, including clinical depression, OCD, ADHD, autism.

In this case, I put this project off till the last minute; it is now 11:30am on Writing Group day and I have only just begun, and tonight I just might not go, making excuses, citing this past month's return to the scary world of my cancer (and to my team of twenty three medical professionals who want to continue to save my life, and who want to publish everything about me and my case to help others who may have this rare cancer.

Aside: One of the medical team I "retired" because he was

acting rashly, playing the cowboy with risks to my day to day life with consequences for me to pay, arising from his interventions and procedures. Not sure if that leaves twenty two on the team or if he was the twenty fourth … See? … distraction!).

Avoidance is my biggest "tell", my typical gateway behaviour which alerts me that I am not well. How do I manage these distractions from my health considerations? I segue in through research, recipe, and demonstration. By tonight at 7pm, I shall have made myself take charge of my mental health and produce something using a medium that I find so familiar that it is just like coming home or breathing … that focus is, writing.

Spiritual Health World:

OK, so how is she going to work in Spiritual Health while addressing a mundane, yet exciting, idea like salt crystals, you might ask?

While keeping my ADHD, OCD autistic mind busy with routine activity, I find myself feeling gratitude for having been able to overcome physical and mental challenges and looking at the great large world and universe to determine my place in them. And tonight, my place is here, with you, in this writing community, where I feel like I belong, where I am transported to a place of gratitude for all of life's majyk, found even in these tiny salt crystals, even in this writing assignment, even in you and me and tonight's Writing Group.

Crystal clarity found. Balance restored.

Aside: The crystals, you will have noticed, are not here. This recipe did not work as promised. There were some tiny fine sheets on the surface that did not survive my attempt to lift them from the formative solution. Note to self: last minute is less likely to produce hoped-for outcome than is practice, and repetition which will ensure a better possibility of success!

More Mental Health exercise is required, sigh! Exercise, it's always about exercise! Back to grabbing the gusto!

Aside (further): when I dumped the bowl a couple of days later (see, procrastinator), those elusive crystals came to light, beautiful in their simplicity and determination. Sometimes, it simply takes hindsight, and time.

Wind – Lifelong Friend, Sometime Foe

Ahhhhhh! – Wind, my Wild Excellent Exhilaratingly Exciting Friend, or Devilishly Fiendish Foe?

Mmmmmm! We lean into the wind, embrace the wind, wind tugs my waist-length hair as I race the wind, I rest away from the wind, in the lee of the hill away from the wind, wind blows out the cobwebs (even in my head and my thoughts), and after all, it is an ill wind which blows no good

Delicious Wind Adventures:

- childhood experience with Hurricane Hazel, as a 4 year old in Deep River: ignoring my parents' efforts to herd their young flock to the basement, I was hiding between the screened outer door and the heavy inner door. Spectacular sights and sounds outside mesmerized me, trees pulled out by the roots like wee weeds and slammed against the wall of the house beside me, all the while completely ignoring my mother's pleas to answer her so she could find me and bring me to the relative safety of the below grade windowless basement; yes, there was a reckoning for that behaviour!
- riding my motorcycle as a 20 year old, before there were helmet laws: the whipping wind exhilarating me into feeling completely free with hair blowing behind me, in short shorts, tank top and cowboy boots to protect my feet;
- standing at the prow of boat or ship: My arms are outstretched to hug as much wind and spray as I can, revelling in the sheer volume of extra oxygen zooming from lungs through body to sparkle in my eyes;

- mid winter trek: I am snorkel-ing down into multiple full-body layers with only a slit of sight between hat-down-over-forehead and neck-warmer-up-over-nose-and-cheeks, windproof outer layer top to bottom, heading out for a walk into a frenzied wicked windy winter storm, feeling my way wielding a walking stick before me like a white cane. Now that's a favourite winter activity, day or night; Oooh; and

- Hurricane experience in Cancun: I am standing at the end of the dock, under the comma clouds, leaning into the bracing wind, while behind us the staff scurried to bring in everything, no matter the weight, which was not a secured part of the building structure. We focused on the overhead clouds and the spray off the water, exhilarated by the fury of the wind, and tried not to get pushed off the twenty foot wide railing-less dock, two hundred feet out into the wind at dock's end, a mere hour before the storm centre hit.

Windstorms whip up more than exhilaration: Uhhhhhh …

- blowing storms of wind, snow, ice, or sand, gritting off layers of skin;

- hurricanes bringing in bad air and bad water, meaning breathing in minute airborne debris, like sand and tiny critters, meaning wind whipping up the water so that large and small aggressors must come in to shore for shelter biting and stinging any who enter the water when the red flag is up banning swimming during a hurricane warning; and

- mature trees, our sheltering friends of many years, suddenly knocked over and uprooted with six foot splinters tossed against the house as though they were matchsticks, and proving to be more threatening, even damaging, than ever considered previously, and leaving a gaping hole in the yard like a missing tooth.

As a gentle wind winds about me, caresses me, I welcome my lifelong friend and revisit my many face to face conversations with Mother West Wind, and the Wind in the Willows, and with my whispering siren calling me to come out and play. Mmmmmm!

When the wicked winds huff and puff to blow me down, I spit into that wind and then dodge the returning spray! Hah!

Today I Shit My Pants - a Lesson in Grounding Self

This cannot be happening!

I follow all the rules, most of the time! I've done the research! I eat very well, better than most! I have prepped for life, laid in food and supplemental supplies, acquired knowledge, garnered strength to overcome any eventuality!

Yet here I sit, on the private toilet in my home while I am alone with my humiliation, shitty clothes in a heap at my feet, on a seat made brown with my own foul shit, with my back and legs smeared with shit and my hair wet with smearing from clothing removal.

I'm sorry, there is just no genteel way to put this horrifying experience.

Of course my mind sets to work as I sit in my own shit, waiting for the rest to be expelled. What caused this? What did I eat, breathe, take, omit from daily routine, do, not do? Why now, out of the blue, when I am feeling so well? Why now, for the first time since toileting as a child? Never during cancer years, during illness or pregnancy or endocrine challenges or on long trips with pretty poor food availability. Why now?

As I roll up my clothing to contain my humiliation so no debris trails from bathroom to laundry room, I decide that the only cleanup for myself is a shower. There just is not enough toilet paper and wet wipes in the world to clean up every nook and cranny, every crease, every strand of my hair.

And I think about a child, old enough to begin to find confidence in daily routine and body expectations, who has 'an accident' at school and who is suggested with letting her sit in shame and unpreparedness as evidence of shortcomings, suggesting it was a choice rather than a blindside. This curious, creative, willing to try, anxious to please, clever person is suddenly in the same situation as am I this day.

Only, not at home alone allowing the privacy of recovering from such a degrading indignity in a society that praises, nay demands, self control of bodily functions and body odour, and social niceties. Imagine if this happened at school, amidst snickers, admonishments, and "I can't believe she just did that in public," and ignorance born of no experience with this, and born of brainwashing-for-profits advertising for personal sweet-smelling hygiene.

After today's experience with myself, I have decided what works best for me:

- stop all supplements and meds prescribed by a health care person or even adopted by yourself after your own research;
- stop all side dietary trips into questionable foods that are chosen, likely, because they are time, cost, prep expedient;
- return to eating simple whole foods that looks like it did at place or origin;
- always carry a bag with disposable undergarments, wet wipes, clean plastic garbage bag to carry soiled clothes and another for the car seat, spare clothes during times away from home packed in purse or backpack when

under duress or during long periods in uncontrolled environments like school, work, and long trips;

- let people at daily environments like work, school, know that you may have to leave suddenly and unexpectedly and that it will require compassion, privacy from prying eyes and prurient interest, as well as require a private phone call to home for immediate pickup. That's all they need to know; there is no need to add humiliating details. Set up an emergency contact, or several, for just this kind of occasion.

Plan ahead! Always better than living in fear or question mark. It allows living life in all its glory, joy, and challenge.

Dress: Individuality or Universality

When I dress myself in the morning, before going out, it becomes an expression of individuality. The colours, the cut, the number of layers, the revealing or concealing, the flutter or sedateness, all are choices made by me as an individual. My individuality is an expression of me, is a result of my history, my experiences, my observations of how others do it. Melba is a wonder to behold, sometimes a graceful wonder, and sometimes an oxygen-grabbing crashing-through-the-undergrowth wonder, to be sure.

Other individuals make these same kinds of choices, and they make their own individual choices for their own very good reasons. Different colours, cuts, and flutter-presence or flutter-absence.

Some individual choices in the first world are made so that we standout, screaming "Look at me!", and "Can you see that I am bigger / better / richer / more artistic / smarter / wiser / greater party animal?" This is not the individuality that I am talking about; this is egotistical selfishness born of loss or denial, or of having one's power or Energy stolen or bullied away. This greedy individuality is a bid to bully the individuality away from others, to steal Energy, power, and control away from others, which IS the philosophy and the psychology of bullying, and it is the aggressive, competitive, Baby Boomer, Pisces Energies of these last millennia.

Individuality abounds here on this plane:
Melba is not Robert;
Robert is not a basil plant;
A basil plant is not a redwood tree;
A redwood tree is not a bat;
A bat is not a raven;
A raven is not a dolphin; and
A dolphin is not a vein of silver in the ground.

Everything and everyone is an individual, with their own recognizable traits and abilities, similar to others in their individual species, but individual within the species, too.

And here is the lesson that I learned from today's Meditation: Individuality is Universality.

Our individuality is a result of our history and our experiences and our physical makeup and our genetics, is an expression of what sets us apart.

That same individuality becomes a universal expectation: Every one and every thing is individually recognizable; and that individuality is behind the universality of expectation where we can expect every silver mine to have its own traits; every dolphin, every raven, every bat, every redwood tree, every basil plant, every person is an individual.

Our individuality IS our universality.

The Greatest Gift

The definition of "gift" all depends on whom you ask.

Certainly, gift has one meaning for a child the week before Christmas or their birthday. Gift means something else to one who waits desperately needing some particular thing, such as a heart for a transplant for a loved one, or a way to stretch desperately low funds to cover food and shelter for children dependent on you for their health and protection. Advertising at this time of year, as we wait for Santa to come, seems to define gift as an expensive, sometimes mindless, thing that helps us meet the obligation of gift giving so we are able to check that person off the To-Buy-For list, something that, perhaps, will make up for our inattentiveness and transgressions of the past year.

Other concepts of gift include a gift bestowed on one as a special ability to be used in this world; a service voluntarily given to another; an invitation; a smile in passing; a helping hand or a kind word in a low moment; insight and clarity in moments of confusion; music, art, and creative endeavours shared; and harmony.

In this week before the HolyDays, we pause and have a long look at the concept of gift. We ask our children to tell us what gift they might like Santa to bring. We might even ask other adults around us what gift they would like. And we might even get bogged down, distracted by the sparkle and allure of some item or of some lifestyle, in the search for finding the "Oh wow!" gift.

For me, the greatest of presents is presence: when someone spends time with me, when we gather together, when someone reaches out, when someone invites me, and when someone notices me.

This Season is a time to avoid the trite, the rote, the expected, and the demanded. Love is figuring out what will be the greatest gift in the heart of the Loved One to whom we are giving the gift.

Grateful for You …

Hi my Friend and Fellow Traveller,

Yes, I realize that you left me a message a couple of days ago. Thank you.

I have just finished the fist day of a meditation series. Today's meditation was about Gratitude, and I could hardly wait to finish and then to write to you…

Thank you, Friend. I am Grateful:

- for you;
- for your broad shoulders that have allowed me to follow the tangled path of the emotions of the rant and to vent and ventilate that emotion until it is blown away, thereby releasing me; and
- for the opportunities you bring to me to examine then release then blow away to reveal the Light that is Gratitude and Grace.

My hope is that you are standing strong and tall in your own Grace never being burdened by carrying your own or my heaviness, or any burden, yours or others.

Light and Love.

Namaste, Happy Trails until our Paths cross again.

Holidays or HolyDays

When I was a child, vacation and holiday were synonymous. The Family would be together; no one left home to go to work or school; there were special preparations, meals, and activities; everyone was happily relaxed away from routine demands, and distractions of our usual days.

When I was older, I noticed that some people said vacation and some said holidays and I began to wonder. Though equally applied in common speech, each word had a different root: vacate and holy.

Religion was something I took in, with blind faith, from my parents. Though they had differing specifics in their views, they held Christianity, equally, as their religion. As with all topics in this household of a mathematician and a scientist, we had an open and free sharing of ideas at the dinner table and any time in our home. Sometimes answers were given; sometimes a story of questing answers was told; sometimes questions to make me think were the response. Sometimes we simply agreed to disagree, which is to say that the topic was still open but would be taken up after a time of "back burner-ing".

Along with that came an understanding about what Holy meant to me: an observance having to do with religious teachings of family and church.

In my *2ndThird*, I was so busy with keeping body and soul, kids and home, bills and paycheque together, that I mused and examined daunting ideas in those free moments available, usually just before the sweet blessing of five or six hours of sleep after reviewing my todo list for next day. Which is to say, unless it impacted kids, family, and job for next day, it could await answers until "some day".

Because I was a teacher, the furor over whether or not to allow religion in schools or workplace became part of our day-to-days on the job. Then, the powers-that-be decided that, if not all religions were recognized at work and at school, then no religion should be recognized at work and at school. And then the silly rules followed: no Christmas tree, no stars, no manger scenes, no Christmas concert or party, became no gift exchange, no menorah, no HolyDay greetings, and no mention of values, all of which entered into conscious thought.

The world became dry and cold.

Every religious sect forgot that they, too, each, had instigated their own hunts, trials, and killings over the centuries, all in the name of their own holy leadership.

Yet, in the dusty old rule books, Judeo Christian roots are still the basis of the School Act, in classrooms, in schools, in governments, and in court rooms.

I knew denying all personal expression in not only the workplace but also in community was, well, just wrong somehow. The practice was simply the latest in the history of reviling and persecuting other religions whose outward symbols were different, but whose basic principles were the same as every other one. Then, cultural slurs and public aggression against all "others" began to creep into the norm of daily activity and speech. The squabbling had begun, this time amongst adults.

I began to wonder where the holy went: no golden rule, no ten commandments, and no freedom to practice one's own religion in one's own way at one's own community gathering place.

Now that I am in my *3rdThird* I have more than those *2ndThird* brief moments to contemplate, to examine my precepts and also to examine my unconsciously and subconsciously programmed, pre-determined fallback responses.

Today, the HolyDay emails are rife with denigrating other religions, demanding that everyone "take back Christmas", all the while denying Hanukkah - Jewish; and Rohats Bodhi Day - Buddhist; and Yule - Wiccan, and Zarathosht Diso (Death of Prophet Zarathushtra) - Zoroastrian, leaving only Christmas - Christian in the public purview.

Some Christians are offended when I say Happy HolyDays to them, their unhappy outburst surpassed only when I say Happy Yule to them. And yet these same people demand and claim freedom of religion and speech, and the right to congregate in lawful religious assembly for themselves.

Each person's right to their HolyDay is sacrosanct. Whether we display a five or a six pointed star, a cross or a menorah, tell stories of Baby Jesus, or Santa Claus, or The Old Man from the Forest, or the Universe, or Siddhartha Gautama, what matters most is that we share, with each other, happy and celebratory greetings, and blessings for the future. Each of us determines our own religion, develops a moral compass upon which we can depend and to which we desperately turn when making sense of impossible-to-survive situations.

Our culture, here in Canada, is to allow time off work to observe our HolyDay, and to share the gratitudes and blessings of that HolyDay with everyone around us, as long as your HolyDay is on an official list somewhere.

Now, when someone says "Merry Christmas" to me, I pause and smile with the blessing of them sharing their great Joy with me, and simply say "Merry Christmas and Happy HolyDay" back to them. Shared Love and Joy is the Blessing of this and every HolyDay.

How can I Possibly Make Sense of This?

I am standing here in a church that is at once familiar yet unfamiliar, with people familiar yet not familiar, focused on an event that is beyond unfamiliar, trying to make sense of it.

Crash!

"You!"

Click click!

Bang! Bang bang! Bang!

Eyes filled with sights of bits and pieces dripping from the family breakfast table.

Air hanging with the smells of toast, gun-smoke, and gore.

Ears still ringing with breakfast routine family at the table, but now realizing those sounds, gone forever, are replaced with horrific details.

The scene has evolved from a peaceful three-generation family breakfast, who wants what for breakfast, what the day's schedule looks like for each individual, what's on tap for supper and evening. All was so familiar, predictable, gentle, and mutually supportive, until the unimaginable.

When all turns silent, the young children are whimpering quietly, their mother lies on the floor wounded (attempted murder), grandfather lies mortally wounded (murdered), father lies mortally wounded (suicide), grandmother calls 911 in complete shock, "Yes, police, ambulances, quick!"

Whom would you cradle first? Your husband? Daughter? Distraught young grandchildren? You would have to rise above the fog of your own symptoms of medical shock to even make the 911 call. Imagine a scene you would never allow the children to see on a TV hanging in suspended animation in front of them.

Why sets in. Moving forward is halted beyond any consideration.

The community abounds with stories:

- of a difficult and fearful split, father goes his way and children with mother, and
- of a mother's fear for her children because of their father's emotional state and things he says.
- And then other suppositions surface:
- of a discharge from military job.
- of a recent court ruling about child support from father who no longer has a job, and must pay more than most make in a month before he can ever hope to buy a piece of bread to feed himself or find a warm place to put his head down each night.

Now here we stand. Where does anyone go from here?

We go through the traditional motions of a funeral, proceeding on numb acquiescence to a religious routine followed throughout a lifetime: bible readings, hymns, eulogy, and then sermon for this friend-since-childhood who served the community, supported his family, and was loved by all who knew him.

Why and what-now hang over us. Until the priest tells a story of a call he received from the grandmother, who is now a widow, while he was struggling with this sermon. He tells us that he received a call away from his desk, and his prayers for guidance. The call was to say, "I am very sorry to call you with such sad news, Father. He has died of his self-inflicted wounds. And Father, I ask something more of you: please, Father, pray for this young man and for his family, for they, too, have lost someone dear." The priest went on to say that if this womyn who has lost so much was calling to ask on behalf of the person who had taken so much from her, then this was the lesson of the sermon.

We can only move forward when we have compassion for all, when we pray for everyone, and when we pray together for a way through this.

And me? I'm just a person who had, and whose family had, close ties with this grandfather and his family since young childhood. What can I do:

- have a look at military dismissal in Canada after a time of service. What should debriefing look like? How about medical and emotional and spiritual support for our service men and womyn during and after their service is finished;
- have a look at what any young family can do when their means to support their family is taken away or lost;
- have a real look at child support and spousal support ordered by the court and where that support will come from; and
- have a look at our social and support network system, and ensure sufficient personnel with sufficient training to offer real support, and enough time and expertise to actually make the compassionate difference they took the job to make.

We have much to do...

Night Time

Mum always said, "Nothing good happens after 11pm." I had, much earlier, heard her tell this wisdom to my older brothers, and then the lesson, in turn, was told to me. In my typical fashion, I wanted clarification, answers to my quest for detail, understanding, and minute consideration so that I, also in my typical fashion, could determine if this was just another nonsensical attempt to save me from myself and my lifelong pell-mell questing, or if there was some merit in this advice that made it worth heeding …

Looking back on that message from Mum, having delivered the same message to my own kids in their early teens, I now fully understand what "Nothing good ever happens after 11pm" means.

My questing years brought up considerations:

There were songs on my pre-teen, teen, and later radio ages, that say: "the night time is the right time to be with the one you love"; "night life ain't no good life but it's my life."

Paganism celebrates by dancing naked under the Full Moon, perhaps with the night-time faeries .

Entire stories and sonnets and songs are written about the joy and wonder of sunsets and full moons and night-time assignations.

Trysts are planned for night-time.

Parties that continued late into the night went at such pell-mell break-neck speed that one would suddenly look up and wonder why we were driving drunk or toked up, to Montreal or New York from small-town Ontario, then realize it is because the clubs, restaurants, and bars there stayed open, and we could continue until we ran out of steam and money. Then we would drive home, put in a righteous day before partying again into the night or falling onto any flat surface, asleep before our heads hit horizontal.

I think that what Mum was trying to tell me, was trying to convince me, was hoping for, was that my YeeHaw and WahHoo nighttime activities were still way-way into the future so that she could sleep at night. She was likely fervently praying that my typical questing would not take me into those dark and risky places where a ten year old's lack of experience could not possibly be called upon to successfully guide me away from the distracting pathways of under-cover-of-darkness delights, from simply under-cover delights, from absolutely-no-covers-at-all delights, or from under-the-moon delights. She had always hoped that, somehow, I would not quest my way into yet another escapade that might, this time, completely derail me from my purpose in life, from the purpose she had chosen for me as a child, or from the one she was helping me to explore and decide on my own for my older self.

Mum would say that skinned knees, silliness, and fights could be recovered, but birthing babies, disease, broken hearts, destroyed reputation in our small town's regard, lost nerve, lost self-determination, and broken body, were much less recoverable.

So when I wake up in the night, unable to sleep, with a swirl in my head about some deep issue, I return to a lifetime of words, lyrics, and rhymes, going deep into the nighttime, to rediscover what my questings had brought to my bag of tricks, so I could return to more peaceful, more joyous, more YeeHaw and WooHoo, and more satisfying nighttime activities rather than lying while spinning my wheels about some nameless fear or concern.

Because the night time, Is the right time, for ... so many things!

Seeds – Planting for the New Year

Today is Lunar New Year, Chinese New Year, Thursday, and Writing Group. And while I focus on the year ahead, and take in our position in our weather, or seasonal, year looking at where this year's turning of the wheel will take us, I see "seed" pop up in many places.

Any New Year brings me to what lies ahead, and finding my way through the challenges, and aiming for particular goals I wish to achieve. This inevitably brings me to making lists, seeking ToDo achievements, and taking action in the desired direction. Sometimes this focus seems arrogant in its expectation; sometimes it seems wise!

Though my jumping off point is with my favourite seed catalogue and my impending order for seeds and plants, as I *see'd* my summer garden taking shape (ok, I envisioned my summer kitchen garden), I find my way to delving into the Universal truths.

Many aspects crowd into my thoughts. It struck me: we are planting seeds all year long.

When we do our NowILayMe meditations in the hour before sleep, we plant seeds into our brain so that our subconscious brain can help us. This concept was reinforced by Wayne Dyer's conversation on PBS when he said these seeds of positive intention, planted into the brain before sleep, guide us subconsciously through the next day to make it so, taking us to Happyness and satisfaction. Too often, for me, I take that just-before-sleep time to review ToDo lists, look back over my day, and beat myself up for things I did not do or did not do well, vowing to make amends and make myself do better next time, thus planting a negative seed and crippling my ability to succeed, and move in a positive direction.

When we have a conversation or an interaction with others, we plant seeds with every word and every gesture. How we behave, how we speak, what we say, how we initiate, how we listen and watch, all sow a garden of relationship plants, some unwanted weeds, some prickly destructive growths, and some lush nourishing plants.

A parent or teacher plants seeds into the gardens of children's minds. Some conscious recognition of this is required to avoid any negative direction leading the child to an unsatisfying, or destructive path. "Do as I say not as I do," comes to mind as a classic negative direction.

We are teaching the children not only the facts of Math or History or how to make their school lunch lessons, but we are also teaching attitudes, choices, and methods for dealing with the world around them and their lifetime.

Focus on planting robust, healthy seeds in a supportive soil, tending the garden with nourishment, time, and love, seeding the future with bright promise.

With difficulty, I cede the point that Karma will look after the negative and destructive seeds sown, bringing its own lessons. Meanwhile, we look upward and forward, planting seeds into the fertile soil of our minds. Now, back to the seed catalogue. Hmmmm, what kind of tomatoes did I plant last year? Where's that list?

Letter

And there it sits. I wondered when this might happen, and now here it is.

Tucked in back, in the mailbox sits a letter. Last time we spoke, there was such a maelstrom of words, emotions, and hurt that came tumbling out from both our mouths until they gained momentum from pent up shut-ups, hold-backs, and turned into outpourings of emotional pus-oozing release.

You know, my professional work and title ought to stand for something, ought to guarantee something, ought to dictate words, actions, unemotional measured responses, and ought to ensure enough dispassion to hear beyond the momentous words of others. On the job, I can rightly claim that feedback from others indicated that I had achieved that professional regard in my job-related interactions.

"But", and there is that word left hanging in the midst of this consideration, when a fellow traveller on this plane approached me with friendly request (which I heard as offerings of sharing our paths in friendship), I agreed to help where I could, to offer mutual Fun-ness, to lighten the load of day-to-days, to confide and receive confidences, to share what-works-for-mes, and to spend time together in fun pursuits to take us away from our overarching burdens.

We chuckled our way through the frightening, over lunches, while learning from each other methods of cooking, crafting, and home-keeping, and during research into alternative medicine answers to our dilemmas.

It never occurred to me that the sharing of burdening-loads

was seen as unbalanced, was anything but equal sharing in both directions, with no need to measure the equal-ness of efforts.

However, when someone sees the relationship as tilted in one direction, in this competitive keeping-up culture, an unbalanced relationship weighs heavily on the one who feels like they are not, can not keep up their end. Before you know it, perceived duty and obligation turn ugly, turn into responses that give one pause for thought, turn into hints that all is not well in the other person and in the relationship.

The cancer starts doing the talking.

A dig, a public reminder of things given, a marginalization of the other in social situations, an inability to follow through on promises given and activities proffered, and careless treatment of the other coming up more and more often.

Then old hurts and unresolved issues from each other's long-pasts rose up, taking each one back into a past that should have been resolved in that moment a long long time ago, unleashing even a professionally guarded tongue, even a friendly tongue, which now has turned into a sharp and vicious reminder of times from the far past that still sting like a bee and cut like a knife.

The interactions which occurred, followed into days, and then resulted in a request for some time apart, felt icky. No matter the professional terms like un-balanced, overriding hurts and fear, panic attack, and anxiety, when it's personal, reason is crippled into survival. The trouble and difficulty are that the survival sought is not the result of this particular occurrence but rather is from some terrifying event from the far past.

Over time, overtures were offered, sparking responses that spoke of illness-caused and implied blame. That is to say, a seeking of an opportunity to clear the air, or to change the friendship into another more healthy form was not accepted by the other of the pair. And then, in the normal day-to-day activities, we bump into each other at mutually appreciated events. And still, the prickliness continues.

And now, here sits this letter. After all this time. Here in my mailbox.

Maybe I'll open it, because letting it sit is agony and unhealthy, turning it into an elephant in the room, in all the rooms of day to day life.

Maybe I'll be pleasantly surprised to hear that the other person feels as I do, bereft at the loss of friendship and fun-sharing, feeling ashamed at my behaviour, wishing there was some way to majykally bring our friendship back with no further un-anaesthetized surgical digging into the causes and the faults and gaps.

Maybe they had a few things they needed to say, and wanted to make sure that they had an uninterrupted opportunity to vent, to catchup their unspoken hurts and claims against me. Maybe that would unleash in me a need to pick the scabs off a few hurts of my own.

What I think that I truly need is to return to a place of gratitude for time with this fellow glorious creature of the Universe and their enlightenments, which I still carry with me. And a return to the days of splendid friendship.

I rush home, unopened letter in hand, to my desk to pen a simple note to the other person.

"Thank you, FunAmie:

For your friendship that gave strength and confidence,

for the happy times that made us laugh,

for the lessons learned,

for the strength gained from knowing you."

Simple, to the point, positive, true-self based.

The dilemma: open the letter first or send my note first? Or perhaps just let the elephant be?

Hello avoidance my old friend ... Should I open the letter? Should I send my note? Should I let it be?

Masks: the Alice Effect

Which Mask will I don tonight?

Halloween is just past, and the decision about choosing a mask arose. I thought i'd like to wear this one. So I asked someone, and they said this one. Another opinion sought brought me to this one. And then further, this one … So I chose this one. Really? This one? Is this how I wanted to define myself tonight?

All my life I have followed Wonderland Alice's philosophy:

"Alice come up out of there!"

"First tell me who I am and, if I like that person, I shall come out and play with you!"

Always taking cues from others around me, always affirming myself by being what others expected me to be. Sort of a: "Tell me the rules of the game, and I'll tell you whether I will play. If I have zero chance of winning, what's the use in playing any competitive game?"

Over the course of my 2.16 *Thirds* of life, I have worn many masks, played many games, donned many uniforms, learned many recital routines, played many roles, walked and lived as others told me to do. Now, here I am in the middle of defining my *3rdThird*, and my place in it.

Coincidentally, I have started a meditation series on the topic of becoming what I believe. Today, I learned that we are what we believe. We shape our identities around what we feel to be true about ourselves. Sometimes we don't even clearly know what our beliefs are, because many are hidden and unconscious. Beliefs we hold about ourselves may be either mild or passionate, but they all still contribute to who we are. Our meditation brings us greater clarity about how our beliefs form our identities, because to truly understand ourselves, we need to examine our beliefs closely in the light of our awareness.

I made a list of my identities. Labels and masks having been applied to Melba: I am ...

Daughter, Sister, Friend, Mother, Grammum, Auntie, GrandAuntie,

Teacher, EnergyWorker, ReikiMaster, ReikiCommunity founder and director, Writer, StoryTeller, Advocate, Activist, Organizer, a Sensitive, crafter, artist, builder, piano-player, mixed-media-artist, prima-ballet-dancer-scouted-by-National Ballet-at-10, majorette/baton-twirler, swimmer, white-pine-climber, synchro-swimmer, tennis-player, car-mechanic, knitter, crocheter, embroiderer, macramé-ist, cook, Brownie, Girl-Guide, CGIT, actor, set-designer, life-guard, swim-instructor-and-examiner, Beach-supervisor, dishwasher-at-Jasper-Park-Lodge, Curly-Cone-worker, university-res-fellow, New-Age-nutritionist, anticancer-warrior, survivor-of-evil-challenges, successful-student (managing to give just enough effort to my studies to achieve my typically high grades just high enough so I could go forward with my plans for what I considered success along my chosen path), teacher, figure-skater, skier, swimmer, camper, horseback-rider, climber, volunteer, prefect, res -fellow, corresponder and pen-pal, following my passions of reading and writing and music, dancing every chance I got, filling my days with laughter and achieving goals and serving others, re-inventer-of-self, redefiner-of-rules, bargainer, thinker, researcher, student-of-life-and-how-things-work, Wiccan, Spiritual-being, WellnessSeeker, Workhorse ...

Now in my *3rdThird*, I not only choose which uniform to wear, but I have developed my own mask and my own clothing; "carefully casual" is what I like to call my relaxed and comfortable-in-my-own-skin self. It is no longer a choice of playing by the rules of any other, but of being faithful to my True Self, and acknowledging my Ego Self and my Higher Self with Gratitude for all their lessons.

I am... Melba.

Care to join me? Bring your own True Self and we will find some music and a dance that we can enjoy together, neither leading, neither following, just together.

Not That Long Ago

Not that long ago, I was a rollicking, frolicking, gangly, freckled, braided, and red-headed girl, busily and happily keeping up with my three brothers, and even leading in my share of times.

Not that long ago, I wore many masks.

Not that long ago, I jumped at every chance to travel, to check out the view from somewhere else, to experience what people who lived there experienced, to learn the truth of the "pussycat pussycat where have you been" nursery rhyme, realizing that one doesn't waste effort and time in doing things typically done at home when there is a banquet of new ideas and vistas and ways of doing things at every turn while traveling – geographically, visually, mentally, emotionally, and spiritually.

Not that long ago, I was starting and enjoying family, and building the home that I always dreamed, while continuing and extending the family of my childhood.

Not that long ago, I was a teacher of 13 year olds, offering side doors and back doors to learning so that the students who were not able to go through the usual front door could still successfully learn; and listening to the students and the parents to understand how, together, we could overcome impediments to the student's learning then help them to realize they are capable and successful.

Not that long ago, I lifted my nose from the grindstone and entered into the larger arenas around me; to find out how things really worked; to unlock the mysteries of government, union, confederation, church, and community both large and small.

Not that long ago, I found myself thrust into the frightening arena of a health challenge that had killed my mother.

Not that long ago, I found myself suffering in the clutches of an employment regime that was a system which had lost its way to achieving its mandate to help kids learn, (instead it focused on and allowed some of their own to 'rise up the ladder of success' - which meant serving their own selfish ends, and on beating up a successful worker with meaningless and distracting abuse just because the middle manager's position allowed them to do so).

Not that long ago, I found myself choosing to retire from a world, and a life, that I had built, that brought me much satisfaction born of finding the answer to how to serve others, and to help them to succeed.

Not that long ago, I reacquainted myself with myself, with finding Melba, with living in the moment, with sharing light and laughter, with continuing to serve others, but now without losing myself in the process.

Not that long ago, I had realized that I had passed through the *1stThird*, and then the *2ndThird* of my life, and was now firmly planted in my *3rdThird* of life.

Not that long ago, I was invited into and engaged in new arenas, experiences, friendships, and collegialities.

Today, right now, I am fully engaged in my *3rdThird*, examining and defining and engaging and embracing today, to ensure the achievement of this moment's success born of happy-ness that is vital at every age.

Passenger

I am but a passenger in this vessel of flesh and blood.
Sometimes we imagine that we are the driver making all the decisions.
Sometimes we think that we are committed to ride out the latest route with no choice, Like a prisoner, consignee, or trapped with no escape but the final one.

I used to take my ride for granted.

I rode hard, made bigger and bigger demands on myself, and I
ignored warning lights and messages from my ride, from others.

My ride has been like a roller coaster, with all the high highs, and
all the low lows.
With all the sudden stops,
the jerky turns,
the feeling of imminently being thrown into the air, or losing my
stomach contents.
With all the wild and exciting rides.
With all the satisfaction gratification rides.
YeeHaw!

And now I pause, and notice that I am
not so high,
not so fast,
not so quick to meet demands,
unable to ignore messages about my tenure as a passenger on
this ride.

I certainly am still a passenger on this ride,
but my vehicle reminds me often that my tenure as passenger is
coming to an end, and that I must take the wheel for this *3rdThird*
of my life
if I am to avoid being ejected or suddenly grinding to a stop, once
and forever.
Steady on...

Struggle for Power

> *"A trapped emotion we have found is literally a ball
> of energy ... And these will lodge anywhere in the
> body and disrupt the normal energy field of the
> body."* Dr. Bradley Nelson

A German New Medicine reference:

> cancer (and disease) is a result of shock or trauma which has not been dealt with. Rather, it is a festering which will continue to cause damage until it is brought to the light of day, understood, forgiven, and let go.

After last night's blowout, this morning is about learning the lesson so we do not need to go through that ever again. My ego self wants me to catalogue the events.

Some people in my life have marginalized me, taken advantage of me, beaten me verbally, emotionally, or physically, while controlling or manipulating me into submission.

Those people have not taken the time to get to know me, to appreciate me, or to acknowledge my presence.

That is their problem and burden to carry, not mine.

My reaction is my responsibility, be it enlightening or burdening me.

When I choose to go into duck and cover survival mode until the beating has finished, until the other person has lost their strength to continue, they think that I have assumed the weight of their burden. They even go so far as to make it clear to me what I have done wrong, how I have earned and deserved this abuse.

I and they must expect that each person has a responsibility to either assume their own burden or put it down.

The healthiest thing for all is to acknowledge that there is some burden, to offer a hand on the shoulder as an "I'm here" kind of support, to grant the other person time and space to come to understand their burden and then to set the burden down, and then arrive at the next step in their journey.

A temper tantrum is ugly at any age. It is a panic attack, a desperate grasping at one's own survival. It has nothing to do with the person alongside. It is an ugly ghost arising again from an experience or emotion of long ago.

Both the panicked and the panic-observer must understand that this is not a time for competition, not a time for a fight.

Acknowledge the other person's dis-ease, and offer support (though there may linger too much emotion for this offer to be heard). Separate until emotions, and dark ego are in check.

I forgive, but I also learn the lesson. I won't hate you, but I'll never get close enough for you to hurt me again. I can't let my forgiveness become foolishness.

When back together again:

-   recognize that it happened;
-   verbalize and acknowledge the experience so no one is left hanging in ugly dark ego land;
-   apologize for any ugliness;
-   determine a safe word or sign to use if or when it comes up again;
-   make statements about the value of the relationship; and
-   offer promises around not doing that again, and around doing it better.

To skip any step keeps the sails from fully capturing the wind and the relationship is likely to run aground in the inevitable stormy seas.

I have no responsibility for what happened to me as a child.

I have complete responsibility for what I do about it now.

Step Lively

On this single day, I was stung by a bee while pulling down over-running grapevines, and a hummingbird flitted through perspectives in my spiritual class. What can this mean? What steps should I take?

Outside in the early morning early August sunshine, watering what is left of my gardens after a hot, humid, lethargy-producing summer, I was liberally spraying all my favourites in the hopes that they would forgive me my lapse in attentive applications of loving and watery Energy. Hanging potted plants have the worst time maintaining their cheery colours and optimum water level on their own. They get it from all sides, literally, fighting to survive despite blistering sun's rays, heat, humidity, and evaporation. My meagre attention to their needs can't possibly keep the plants from wilting when only a fraction of the plant's challenges are making me completely limp!

As I tour my garden, I turn first to an herb garden on the front step, surrounding my favourite Adirondack perch (brought home from someone's cast off pile the night before a garbage day), where a corner under the overhang provides relief from early sun's rays and where I'm completely protected from afternoon's relentless sun.

Beyond the steps is a wild garden. We established creeping thyme, peonies, purple smoke bush, phlox, irises, burning bush, daffies, tulips, hostas, and crocus all to bring colour to spring and early summer and winking at us when we leave or come back home.

The bulbs were purchased at work to support students' need to sell those bulbs, to make money to offset the cost of their annual class trip. Each year I would order $25 worth of bulbs from the first student to ask me, bringing the bulbs home and planting them willy-nilly. Over time, I had ordered quite an assortment of less expensive bulbs so I moved on the the $25 per bulb exotic varieties.

Our cat had prowled and protected our gardens during her eighteen year tenure with us. The summer after our cat died, I'd arrive home to find my dug-up half eaten bulbs lying on the walkway, taunting me. Some welcome home! I tried replanting what was left, after-all, there was only one wee bite out of the bulb, but never was that plan successful. I tried leaving the bulb on the walkway for the next day's meal, but apparently chipmunks don't do leftovers. I tried tossing it into the foliage a hundred feet from the gardens. No dice! I felt like the chipmunks were taking it personal by targeting my garden instead of the rest of the hundred acres. Over time, the chipmunks finally moved on, having decimated all expensive bulbs and many of the other bulbs. I did notice that there were some bulbs that were never eaten. These became our lastingly reliable early popups of colour, winking at me in collaboration against the small stripey wild friends.

We introduced indigenous Black-eyed Susans, daisies, burdock, Queen Anne's lace, wild fern, Scots thistle, lambs quarters, milk weed, mullein, all of which took over where the chipmunks' work left off, filling corners and broad sweeps with such natural abundance. Still there was no sign of any chipmunks and their munchings.

And in moved some new squatters, like wild grape vines and cedar seedlings.

I can pretty much gauge my state of mind by just how wild has become this wild garden. And this summer it was wilder than ever!

In the front yard is a huge spreading crabapple tree, claiming the entire area and surviving mockery when this newlywed brought the sapling home and chose middle of front yard placement. Our beautiful crabapple tree survived a half dozen woodpecker summers until we learned the value of wind chimes hanging in the tree branches. It provided our table with crabapples for crabapple jelly, pickled crabapples, and apple cider vinegar.

First comes buds, then scent, then humming bees at work among dozens of cubic metres of blossoms.

Bambi is not our friend here in the country; the deer are not awwww-cute, because they literally eat the low hanging fruit the day before the apples have enough blush to make my jelly pink; they leave the stepladder-harvest to us forcing a much greater effort on our part. After their crabapple harvest, they move onto other highly valued plants of our human intention. Not "awwww-cute", indeed.

The northwest garage end of the house is shaded by huge

trees, hardwoods freed to soar into the sky beyond overarching cedars and grapevines which had been lost during the 1998 ice storm when the weight of all that ice on the grape vines pulled down tall willowy cedars who were doubly disadvantaged by their ice-catching, year-round foliage. After the lilies-of-the-valley make their sweetly scented appearance, this shady garden area is left to find its own way. Probably a better place for the hostas than the morning sunny garden.

The other end of the house became a repository for family-ancestor lilac bushes that grew wild around the home place after it burned down in 1958 while the family was away on their first-ever and last-ever family drive and picnic day. Bursting forth lilac blossoms, and scent under bedroom windows waft toward us as we drift into sleep once the dew releases the smile-inducing perfume.

Back of the house is the southwest side of what was, for many years, a chocolate brown bungalow. Strong sun is best place for our kitchen garden. Sandy soil full of tiny shells with six generations of manure from the farm on top is where we plant our kitchen garden of salad fixings, and preserves ingredients. This is where the deer move after apple season is done, where the garter snakes grow to an inch in diameter and who sun on the cubic foot rocks cornering the fourth generation logs of the raised beds making the produce easier for us to tend, and easier for the deer to munch.

The lawn at the back is really hay instead of costly grass seed. When we built the house, we found hay more likely to thrive in sandy soil.

Clearly, our job in the country is to be smarter than the critters and interlopers.

During a summer such as this, the grapes greedily climb over top of everything, blocking out sun from reaching photosynthesizing leaves of domesticated plants, and galloping across the soil to claim every drop of water in the earth. It might be different if they produced any usable grapes, giving us grape jam, or grape juice, but no such luck. Even the inch thick vines produce no discernible fruit. My quest to determining a use for these ubiquitous plants found me allowing their incorporation here and there, and now they override all.

Just the day that I decided to step up my efforts to encourage and support my hard-won gardens, I was stung by a bee busily working amongst the vines!

Scratch out stinger, Reiki the two centimetre, white, swelling pocket that featured a red dot in middle, all of which was throbbing from the bee's application of attention seeking behaviour. Finish hacking the grapevines so visitors could make their way to front door, and so other tender and more desirable plants could gain some foothold in the week that the grapes will require to return in full force. Inside, I had a better look at the sting site, applied apple cider vinegar, then lavender essential oil (the workhorse of any essential oil first aid kit). Voila! Half an hour later it was like nothing ever happened.

Once back inside, I found myself with some hours, having just finished my meditation cycle, so thought I'd catch up with 274 emails. Out popped a webinar for sensitive souls. The lesson started with Grounding, why it is important (not getting things done), how to tell when you need to ground more often (not getting things done), and then a hummingbird flitted by, both here at home and, as well, at the webinar studio.

My Shaman Guru taught me that critters come into my life to teach me something, to lend me strength and notice.

And I went running for my animal totem volume and my two usual sites:

http://www.fourwinds10.net/siterun_data/government/native_american/news.php?q=1240169532

http://www.spirit-animals.com,

and *Animal Speak* by Ted Andrews.

Lessons that we learn from deer, chipmunks, snakes, bees, hummingbirds...

Deer: Compassion, peace, intellect, caring, kindness, subtlety, grace, femininity, gentleness, innocence, and seller of adventure;

Chipmunks: trust, something good is on its way to me, balance within the circle;

Snakes: Impulsive, shrewdness, rebirth, transformation, initiation, and wisdom;

Bees: Organized, industrial, productive, wise, community-based, celebration, fertility, defensiveness, obsessive nature, and enjoyment of life;

Hummingbirds: Messenger, timelessness, healing, and warrior.

Step lively, Melba. Get to work. Go for it. Be productive. Finish. Accomplish. Step it up, Melba!

So, What's a Jump List?

After watching a movie about a bucket list, I took stock. Having survived, beaten, stood victorious: over cancer; over threatening health crises; over looming financial insecurity; over bullies in my world; over whisper campaigns; and over threatening nose-to-nose challenges from various bull-moose types, I thought that this *3rdThird* would be a good time to make a celebratory and congratulatory bucket list of my own. What a good time to ensure that I got everything done on that list, before time ran out, was cut off. Such a daunting thing to plan against the clock, to get things done before … death.

A disorganized disjointed list of all the things that I never got to do, and always thought I wanted to do before I die, fell onto the page.

My Bucket List:

Travel to Scotland, Australia and New Zealand, Southern Hemisphere, swim or at least dip my toes into every ocean and sea, make a million dollars, write a best selling book, give speaking engagements, start a school, build my dream house, have wondrous love-imbued family get-togethers often, dance, swim, cycle, garden, belong to clubs, be of service ...

Broad general ideas came out of the end of my pen, ideas that lacked detail, energy, will, just a negative-feeling list of things that I never got to do.

Then I realized that I was still in survival mode, seeing myself as a struggling victim rather than a gloriously vivacious recipient of so many one-day-at-a-times stretching out before me, with all their promises and duties and pleasures and satisfactions.

Rather than call this my Bucket List, the idea of a Jump List leapt into my mind! What would I jump off the chair to do with these many many days beckoning me forward?

The Plan: Melba's Jump List
Places to Go, Things to See, Thinks to Think:

Help/Give...
Volunteer for the Joy of helping another

Travel:

North; South; East; West;
Drive, walk, cycle, swim, ride, sail, fly;
Cycle: ride a motorcycle again, regularly bicycle;
Swim: diverse venues; dive / snorkel;
Sail: skim the waves;
Fly;

Walk with the Faeries under overarching trees;
East: Visit family; Bus / Drive and Ferry tour of the Canadian Maritimes: south shore of New Brunswick, past Hopewell rocks at low tide; southwest in Nova Scotia along Bay of Fundy continuing northeast to Cabot Trail; visit family in Nova Scotia; ferry to Newfoundland then tour

coast; ferry to Prince Edward Island to tour island then drive the Confederation Bridge back to New Brunswick; north to tour Gaspé then south shore of St. Lawrence River; cross River to north shore then north to Tadoussac; follow north shore to home;

Rail: tour west across Canada, through Rockies by daylight then Ferry to Victoria. Drive tour the island;

Drive west coast US; Navajo historical location tours;
Ship: tour through Panama Canal; Tour west coast of North America, Central America, South America; Tour Great Lakes; Tour Mediterranean; and South Pacific.

Classes:

Reiki Classes at Stonehenge/Glastonbury, England with William Lee Rand;
Scottish Gaelic;
Quilting; and
Fine lace making.

Achieve:

Grace;
Gratitude;
Peace;
Joy in all things; and
Debt-free living.

Experience / Revel in...

Love;

Happyness. An old movie teaches that there are
six Happinesses which we seek during our lifetime.
They are:

Gratitude;
Health; Celebrate that I am alive;
Spirit; Virtue;
Wealth; Writing, Blogging;
Peaceful Death in my Old Age; and
Determine the 6th Happiness for Myself;
Be Melba; Expectation; Longevity;
Satisfaction.

And then the bottom fell out of our financial world.
When I retired, I brought with me

- my gold-plated Pension, "the best in the world"
- my retirement gratuity which was negotiated legally and
  securely waiting for me;
- all the brain washing advertising bombarding us until we
  BabyBoomers found ourselves believing by sheer force of
  insidious repetition and energy of proclamation, such as:
- what we would do with all our spare time;
- what glorious and lavish places we wanted to see simply
  because any educated person must have this place on
  their bucket list;
- how it was our time to get everything we wanted after a
  lifetime of dedicating ourselves to needs of home, children,
  family, and job; and
- we deserved the very best after our lifetime of dedication
  and servitude;

- a plan to sell the land for which we had taken responsibility these many years; and
- foolishly, trust in the too-good-to-be-true prattlings of the Zoomer generation who had committed to the brainwashing so that we would fall into place ensuring the future of Zoomers without keeping our eye on our own future; after all, the Zoomers had smiled their perfect-teeth smiles and said, "Trust me," so we did trust them, even the greedy ones.

So much of our promised and planned future fell away when we began to attempt access to the Promises:

- that gold-plated pension plan is only gold-plated because of its security. It will come to me forever, hopefully, but it is modest in size. Oh, that's why they told me that I was asking too many questions and that I should just trust them;
- that retirement gratuity was toggled by the employer after the agreement was signed, with a scratch out on the document and only their initials, but not mine, beside the correction, and then without a mention to me, the cheque was sent to my bank for deposit missing 10% of the agreed amount meaning that I could not afford to pay off my debt;
- that we did indeed have plenty of spare time to do things ... that did not cost anything;
- that we could not afford a $15000 trip, or even a $5000 trip or most of the trips advertised to us monthly in our glossy pension plan magazine;
- that our kids would continue to need our financial support;
- that our kids, meanwhile, would also be socially engineered, but in a direction unique to their own age group;

- that our opportunity to make some money (for sudden expenses like funeral, wedding, repairs to house, new reliable car) by supply teaching is lost because we should move over for the next generation of new teachers (who continue to be graduated by universities who are interested only in being paid for registrations rather than fulfilling their promise of training which would enable and ensure that their graduates to get a job) when I already gave up my full time pay cheque and benefits for a new teacher at my retirement;
- that the Municipality, Province and Conservation Authority would cause us to pay out seven digit dollars for us to jump through their hoops before we would be able to sell even one lot or realize even one dollar for sale of our land;
- that the Greedy sect of Zoomers would cause a crash that rattled the world and the value of our biggest investment (our property) and they would continue to gouge us all through government bailouts, through insisting that we continue to pay usual payments for now sub-prime mortgages, through firing workers while continuing to offer gigantic salaries to those at the top of the heap, through putting up rates for water and electricity so they could give themselves salary hikes....

So, the Jump List changed again, dropping expensive activities.

The challenge became one of realization, of changing mindset through mindfulness, and practicing Gratitude every day for what we did have.

The Jump List (Final Redux):
Places to Go, Things to See, Thinks to Think:

Help / Give:
Volunteer for the simple Joy of helping another.

Share:

My home, my Love, my bounty, all that I have to offer.

Travel:

North, East, South, West -look to the four corners of the Earth, and every corner of the Universe in search of Wisdom, Love, Gratitude.

Learn and Teach:

Share in the bounty of the Knowledge that we find everywhere we go and right right under our feet, above our heads, within our heart.

Achieve:

Peace and Calm within, Understanding within self and outside ourselves, great Joy that arises from every task well done, and simple pleasures Recognized in every moment.

Live every day to the full extent of possibility and then some, reaching and stretching and embracing. Live within my means without succumbing to advertising, brainwashing, or appeal.

Make a Difference that serves others.

Jump List settled. My cup runneth over.

The Table

Our table is just a table, wood, clawed feet clutching wooden spheres, interesting wood-grained geometric design on top, typical warm brown wood-coloured stain.

While recently excavating our dining room table out-from-under, I found more than just the deferred-put-away items.

Yes, there were:

- the last of the groceries;
- a wooden bowl of stones from my summer series of tours down east, including Les Isles de la Madeleine, Prince Edward Island, Cabot Trail, Gaspésie;

- nine bags of items to go to a better home through the Salvation Army Thrift Store;
- coats left to dry after use during our recent rainy day;
- the last of the summer centrepiece and the beginnings of the fall display;
- paper, pencil, iPad, charts, tables and writings from various projects;
- a hand-made gift for Grammum from last GrandKidlette visit; and
- bits or pieces we turned the rest of the house upside down looking for, but had not yet found.

And there was more.

This table has been as much the heart of the home as has been the hob or the hearth. Memories flooded in, covering the table which has been:

- where our family gathered together at day's end, to eat supper, to discuss the latest news and activities, to make plans, to consider each other, and to ponder the great large ideas of the world;
- where the extended family has come to celebrate occasions. When our number surpassed the sixteen who could sit together round the big table, we took out the leaves and the table became the buffet serving table;
- where, after Dad died, my brothers and I and our families tore apart ninety years of family albums, each taking what they considered a particularly poignant photo, with promises to scan and send to the others.
- If someone was thirsty or hungry, they got up and prepared a round for everyone. We played piano and sang Dad's favourite hymns. We read the prayers and readings that Dad had chosen for his funeral. We told the stories, the ones that still make us laugh or weep until tears rolled down cheeks, washing away feelings

of loss and reminding us that we are left with memories and experiences aplenty. It was a much more soothing celebration of Dad, Mum and the larger family than a stiff arms-length church ceremony;

- where the kids piled and organized what they wanted to take away to school or to camp;
- where we still sort out piles of things during organizational bouts of catching up to ourselves;
- where family babies drummed, banged, scraped, and left marks on the table and joy in our hearts while they matched the rhythm of a tune only they were hearing;
- where crafted items were carefully prepared and wrapped for the intended recipient;
- where minor surgeries were performed by a caring family member;
- where we served our traditional as well as our newfound food favourites; and
- where we retire to the circle for discussion, for laughter, for mutuality and closeness.

This table has been our centre, where family and friends have turned for stability and affirmation and love and sharing and trust.

Missy Porkypine

Today, my path was crossed. A porcupine was hit and killed, coming to her final rest fifteen feet from our gate.

Our three GrandKidlettes came to stay with us for some days while the heavy lifting of their family's impending move takes place, leaving one home for another, leaving the security of one set of walls for another, leaving one school neighbourhood for another.

The GrandKidlettes are oft-time residents at our home, each with their own bed, linens, sleep buddies, drink bottles, toothbrushes and some clothes that Grammum has picked up along her travels. They each have a treasure box into which go bits and pieces that had a message only they could hear, bits of nature, their moonstone or sunstone necklace, their lithium Quartz Crystal that delivers calm and peace on a day when neither is present, their angel wing locket, and their claddagh, to name a few. This weekend, this place will be their stability during the upheaval of a move. At ages of 2, 5 and 8 years, they needed a spot away from the scene of heavy lifting.

When they arrived, they noticed the porcupine "sleeping" on the road at our gate. In the midst of a beautiful summer's day which was filled with the Joy that comes with the wonder and laughter of children, with the clock ticking for three ventures on the calendar each with opportunity to do something, that calls to me, with people I love, the GrandKidlettes and Grandad and Grammum went to the porcupine.

Porcupine looked as though in peaceful sleep on her back with one paw on chest.

There was little blood and physical trauma at shoulder impact site. Black tire skids along the road. Roadway strewn with white toothpicks. Long teeth so brown they looked like strips of ebony-dyed leather. Long, sharp tree-climbing claws on black padded feet. Little ears. Brown-black fur on grey skin, with some long white quills sticking out from the fur.

We talked about whether we might be looking at an herbivore, or a carnivore. About how we could look up at night and find the dark lump in the tree boughs that were really "porkypines", and whether we would be able to see them in summer when the tree limbs were obscured by leaves.

MissyMoon, the five-year-old, decided we should name the porcupine MissyPorkypine. The brothers had no objection. Grammum was relieved that she would not need to part quills to examine genitalia to determine gender which would be a whole other discussion.

Once named, MissyPorkypine became personified. We talked about how yesterday she was running and playing, carefully, with other porkypines, searching out food and places to drink (we decided that the spring at the old cow well was likely the best spot, but that the ditches could work well, too). Now, today, here she lies alone on the road, with so many quills spewed along twenty five feet of roadway.

We wondered what would happen to her body, whether other creatures like turkey vultures and crows would feast on her for supper, adding her to their food chain; whether all the flies on and around her would hatch-out babies, called maggots, who would also eat their fill; or whether we should get a shovel and bury her deep, robbing the rest of the food chain of their chance at life.

We honoured MissyPorkypine, thanking her for her place in the beauty of nature and of life and of death as with all living things, plant, animal, human, large, and minuscule.

We moved her body to roadside for a day of feasting for the food chain; we harvested quills from the road because we lacked the will to pull them from her hide. We talked about how we could put the quills to good use in a way that would remind us of this experience that would live in the treasure box of of our hearts rather than the wooden boxes in our bedrooms.

We decided that if MissyPorkypine was still there tomorrow morning, we would bury her with our thanks for the lessons and the quills that she gave us.

We spent the day with our iPads, searching for pictures of porcupines in nature, practicing how to pronounce the name correctly, drawing pictures of MissyPorkypine.

We searched for meaning we could draw from the teachings of a much appreciated Shaman friend and looked up porcupine totem: spirit-animals.com

> *"You are being reminded that the criticism of others often has nothing to do with you personally and everything to do with their own personal walk in life. Let it go."*

Thank you, Missy Porkypine!

Finding Myself

Finding myself has many meanings:

- being true to myself;
- finding and holding, as a beacon, my authentic self;
- following my own dreams;
- remembering that every action results in a reaction from the gal looking back at me from the mirror. What action will satisfy that gal, or will allow me to affirm myself; and
- seeking affirmation from outside myself creates a series of fickle masters, leaving one with an ever-changing landscape of opinions and demands and leaving one with no real affirmation at all

Hmmmmmmmm! ... thinking ...

3rdThird: Themes, Lessons Learned, and Wisdom

In the life of a tree, the *3rdThird* is the pruning time for the tree. In our own *Thirds*, this equates to losing our teeth, hair, eyesight, hearing, jobs, regard of others, satisfaction from a job well done, reputation, losing our place because we must move over for others to take our place.

Our *3rdThird* is also refered to as our years as Crone. This label satisfies me because it has an element of wisdom born of experience, and sharing that wisdom, and being valued for our wisdom.

Hats and Labels:

I have no intention of ever wearing a hat or a label again. I shall simply be myself, doing what is right, what I am called or driven to do. No matter the task, I shall be Melba. Now to stand in the hard light of day, in the hard image in the mirror, with a critical eye, and determine which of those hats were ones that I chose and which were imposed by others and must be let go.

Alice Effect:

The Alice Effect in this *3rdThird* became one of a decision to go down the hole, and then follow the experience, to the lesson learned, to understanding Melba and her value in and of herself.

Self:

Self? "Who is Melba, what is she?" My childhood friend's father, a psychiatrist and an eccentric, would sing that phrase from some song only he knew whenever I arrived at their home to visit my friend. I politely smiled as though accepting his recognition of my presence. Looking back now, I realize that this is the time to dive into that thought. I know who I have been; now I learn who I am today, and at the beginning of each new day going forward.

Note to 4 year old myself from grown up self:

Always bring bright clear Light into my life.

I am still myself, still a good girl, still have a right to be heard, still have my sparkle, still innocent, and still have the rights to my own body and my own pleasures.

I am still a gift from the Universe to this World.

I am still a bright shining Light.

When something happens, tell someone. If they don't listen, keep telling until someone listens and helps you.

When someone else does something to you, that's on them and their karma. You have complete control over your response, your life's path, living your authentic life.

Selfish? The airlines tell us that we must put on our own oxygen mask before looking after others; lifeguards are taught that one drowning is a tragedy, and two drownings is a worse case. If I am not to be thrown under the bus, lost from my quest to help others, I must look to my self and my needs first, for the first time in my life. Cancer has taught me four times that these miracles will not continue unless I look to my physical, mental, intellectual, and spiritual health for myself.

Happyness:

Happyness is Joy, and bliss, and contentment. It is rebirth, and sharing, and giving. It is freedom. It is more than simply smiling at a new dress kind of happiness.

Individuality:

Working to fit in; Happy to stand out.
Satisfying ego, higher self, true self; each serves its own purpose, all are necessary to be me.

Education:

Education will come from being a self-observer, and this education will be self-directed. As opportunities and health, tasks, and desires come up, I will study them minutely, using the knowledge to successfully find Melba, and be Melba.

Busyness, Work, Job, Career:

Work as Unjobbing is the springboard in the *3rdThird*. Gone are peeing, eating, chatting, serving self only when determined by a bell ringing through my day, robbing me of satisfaction in the moment after a natural conclusion to the activity. No longer will I be "On the Job". I may work, I may seek paid work or employment, I will certainly put considerable effort into tasks chosen, but never again Jobbing for this simple-truth small-town-girl, who has been around more than one block, some more than once.

When I reached 50, I was told that I should move over and hand my Job to the next generation of teacher who was more energetic than I, who had more bills to pay, who was just starting out and should be given the chance to do so.

Striking were the thoughts that this smelled like my whole life as a Baby Boomer, during which I had to move over, and to share my school desk, get out of the way for others, and not be Selfish.

My energy on the Job and in my life was boundless, tapping into personal energy reserves in service to others, inspiring others who told me that I was a master teacher and should be teaching others how to do what I do by becoming an Associate Teacher for student teachers going through teachers college, and a mentor for new teachers at our school.

My over-arching debt was gigantic, having given my kids an education in life skills and in experiences including those which cost money and in post-secondary education and in supporting milestones like weddings. Shelling out was for my kids and for my eventual retirement.

If someone wants me to get out of their way, they must demonstrate to me how their need is greater than mine, whether in line at the grocery checkout or in taking on my job.

Voice:

Voice means finding my own voice, my true self in day-to-days. I don't have to speak all-the-time. I need to listen to myself and to others, and then simply act. Voice should be saved for time of need, rather than being a constant filling-the-air-around-me activity.

Relationships, Family, Interactions, Influences:

Relationships begin with my relationship with myself. Then that will dictate my activity with others which will lead to friendships as shared activity, love, and compassion. Otherwise, time spent with others is simply collegial, mutual task completion which should be polite and positive, but without any expectation beyond happy and satisfying efficiency.

Relationships will be rebuilt real.

Be who you are and say what you feel - because those who mind don't matter, and those who matter don't mind.

Writing Group fascinates and encourages me. My blog is underway.

Hay House Writers Workshop finds me and inspires me and spurs me on to the growing-up of my writing.

Health:

Laughter really is the best medicine.

When going to the doctor, I have come to some conclusions that work for me:

- Go to a compassionate, though likely, over-worked MD medical doctor, prepped with a full list of complaints and questions, hand them their own copy of the list so they can speak from the list and therefore avoid skipping any in the mere eight minutes that they have been allowed to listen;
- Listen to what they say, writing notes or taping, compare it with your own research and your experience with your body. Decide if their idea shakes hands with your own knowledge and expectation;
- Go to compassionate alternative holistic health care professionals with the list and do the same; and
- Make a conscious sentient choice for yourself about what advice you will or will not take, being compassionate with yourself, meeting your own needs.

Achievement, Benchmarks, Milestones:

Achievement is a simple matter of task completion. Celebration is had. Smiles are shared. Outright laughter is de-rigour. Life is seen as good.

I am moving forward to realizing two dreams:

- formalize my writing, and put it out there into the Universe, and share my story in the hopes of enlightening the journey of others; and
- reacquaint myself with Spirit and Reiki and start a local Reiki school so others can heal.

Parenting:

In the *3rdThird*, we parents must finalize (if we haven't already done this) the act of stepping back, allowing our kids to become adult individuals in their own right. They will still bite off more than anyone can chew, still fall and skin their knee, still turn to us for help. But, it is essential that we wait until they turn to us; yes, this is true, but when their pride or their level of being overwhelmed is an impediment to their rising again, we parents must recognize that are still parents, wise parents. If we intervene, it must be more a matter of lovingly and gently offering a hand up, offering an idea of what works for me, rather than taking over. We raised our kids to be proudly independent; now is the time to remember to encourage that same strength.

Toolkit:

Tools List is simplified to *Love* and *Compassion* and *Wit*. *Sense of Humour*, and "*Sparkling on Command*" make all better, easier, and more successful. Living in the moment now becomes my mantra. All else has no effect on my moment which is my life.

Wisdom: Making Sense of It All - from Reaction to Codes to Philosophies

I am reviewing my Life in Thirds, making sense of it all, offering myself *Forgiveness* for caving to demands of the *FUD* (fear, uncertainty and doubt), of fast paced society, of speaking when commanded rather than listening to what was going on above and beyond the fray. I am offering *Compassion* to my younger self for all *She* has not only survived, but for all she has turned from dirt to gold for others around me.

Find your *Truth, Self,* and *Voice.*

Chin up: the *3rdThird* is just as bright and colourful as the others.

Crone or croney were words that held much emotion. I pictured white hair, crankiness, judgementalism, blamer, control freak, sitting in a rocking chair while watching the world go by and being generally disgruntled. Then I retired and found myself in the *3rdThird*, as a Crone. Suddenly, I had no one to report to other than myself. And I came to realize that I had lost my self in the demands of the *2ndThird*. I knew where was Ms. McGee, Mum, wife, sister / daughter / cousin / aunt / family member, colleague, volunteer, but I hadn't seen Melba in years. And I had no idea who she was without all the adjectives, labels, hats, and masks.

I had arrived at a brave new world, and this world was entirely up to me. Just as in the previous two *Thirds*, this Crone stage required thought, planning, decision and learning if it was to become something other than a period of being cast off since I could no longer contribute paycheque, direction, or hard work.

The pruning in *3rdThird* is letting go of all that no longer serves me.

Womyn are *Angels*, and when someone breaks our wings, we continue to fly, on broomsticks. We're flexible like that.

Just because they didn't give me all that I needed, doesn't mean that they didn't give all they had to give.

When *Cancer* does the talking, recognize it, carefully ascertain underlying need that caused cancer, and then release it with gratitude for lesson learned.

Writing:

So, what *Enlightenment* do I have to offer from this Writing assignment?

- regiment and regulate myself;
- begin with the end in mind, not the big giant overwhelming end, but the end of this story, of this challenge met, of this response to someone who took the time to compliment me and my work, of meeting this small deadline and then on to the big gigantic deadline;
- decide to stand up and be counted by my dream. Could I live with myself if I did not realize my dream because of a lethal loss of accountability;
- notice something, and go to the keyboard straight away, with all of the energy and enthusiasm, turning idea into words, using every bit of commitment, flourish, and command of language and emotion that I possess to enlighten both myself and the reader;
- the keyboard is my muse, along with the majyk that falls onto the page; and
- just do it, do it right, do it right now. Do it so even the harshest critic (myself) will have no choice but to say, "Nailed it!"

Hope:

The very fact that we have the word "future" in our vocabulary gives me hope. The trick, I feel, is in living today's moment in its own fullness. That way of living gives me hope for the future. I cling to that hope, sometimes desperately, sometimes confidently but always with hope. To do otherwise would be to give up, leaving all hope lost.

Some quotes that give me hope;

Mum: "The harder I work, the luckier I get;"

Thomas Edison: "I have not failed. I've just found 10,000 ways that won't work."

Alex Haley: "In every conceivable way, the *Family* is our link to our past, bridge to our future."

When bad things happen, tell yourself:

- that this has happened to others, and will happen to others;
- that you are still lovable and capable; and
- that this, too, will pass.

That, as of this moment, this is all behind you, adding to your capacity for empathy, compassion, understanding, and joyous celebration of yourself.

You are loved.

Despite all the head shaking the medical community has done each time I fell so ill, I am insisting on claiming every second, minute, hour, year and chuckling laugh of my *3rdThird*.

After that, I will invent the *4thThird*!

Such is the *3rdThird* within this treatment of life's *Thirds*.

... With gratitude, with *Happyness*, with *Energy* and enthusiasm, with *Sharing*:

May your journey be enlightened.

Conclusions: Pause to Clarify Thoughts; Decisions to Take the Exit Ramp or to Continue on this Plane

Highly organized people like Melba are driven by a desire to be of service to others by hearing their dreams, and by helping them to remove impediments and so to realize those dreams.

We are dream catchers, facilitators, and roadblock busters. We don't fix; we don't carry their burden; we simply walk alongside them and encourage them to set down their own burden.

We clarify our thoughts. Our own impediment is other people's roadblocks, their fears and their jealousy which distracts both them and us.

We need to set down our own burdens first. And then we can decide whether to continue on this plane or to take the exit ramp.

4thThird - Letting Go
(and Just Being Me)

So Here I Am

So, here I am, and where is this? What are my tasks, roles, expectations, duties, dreams, jump-list items ...?

I have been through all the allotted phases:

1stThird, *Maid, Child*, student, sparkler;

2ndThird, *Mother, Wife, Teacher*, paycheque earner, keeper of appointments and meet-er of expectations, time and paycheque stretcher; and

3rdThird, wise *Crone*, reinventer of self, dream maker, chaser and catcher.

Plan for the *4thThird*:

- *Happyness*;
- Peaceful death in old age:

Already have I nailed the old age part.

Likely, this is it; this is the Third where I shall depart to the other side;

- Maintain physical, emotional, spiritual health so I can outlive my clothes:

Eat real food and only when hungry;
Laugh, share laughter and *Hugs* often, and every day;
Keep a lively conversation with *Spirit*, and live by my *Moral Code*;

- Be a contributing member of the community or circle:

So I don't outlive my usefulness;
Sparkle on my own command: the warmth of my sparkle is the warmth that draws others to my campfire on long dark lonely cold nights;

- Choose the labels I shall wear:

Be self directing by only listening to myself, and by wearing the positive labels that I choose. Or, just reach in the closet, grab what comes to hand, and that is my label for today, but better make sure to have sorted out that closet long before to rid myself of unwanted or untrue labels;
Live consciously every day with positive affirmation of self in mind;

- Be frugal in things and rich in Love and Joy:
Share all that I have;

- Make way for all the happy memories:

Lose all the unhappy memories by making peace with them and the people involved in them, by offering first apology and then forgiveness and THEN LET IT GO! and
Live the cerebral, peaceful, and collaborative energy.

The Art of the Drift

Drift drifted into my line of sight this week, drifting through my thoughts, drifting back through my experiences in life, making me a drifter in my present day-to-days, causing me to to be adrift from duty and from connection with others. Like drifting clouds passing quietly overhead, my attention has drifted with those clouds, to memories and experiences from the past.

I was taught to "sparkle on command" from a young age, and I embraced that outlet for my ADHD and my autistic thinking.

Whether commanded by my parents ("Melba, play us your latest piece on the piano.");

- or commanded by my teacher ("Melba, make your presentation, with your usual vim and vigour and tremendous ability.");
- or commanded by friends ("Melba, you organize the next party because you are the only one who gets it done right.");
- or commanded by myself ("OK now Melba, just do it, do it right, do it right now.");

I was fully committed to success-oriented linear thinking. I mean, why drift away from a winning formula, right?

From time to time, I encountered drifters who were the complete opposite of me, who drifted into my life, who appeared completely adrift from the laws and duties that governed me, and brought me success. They appeared content and even happy; they measured on the plus side their own success; they were relaxed; they mocked me, and admonished me for being so uptight; and they turned to me when they wanted something done on time and done right.

Though I envied and relished the drifter lifestyle, and the apparent ease with those issues that called me to action and caused me consternation, and the drifter's ability to just let go of expectation and the drive to succeed in someone else's definition of success,

I just could not let go of my inner sense of accomplishment, of a job well done, of keeping up with the expectations of self and of others, of being successful at being a people pleaser. And I had diligently, with great effort, with much sacrifice of my own self and desires, achieved a lifestyle where I had what I had set out to get, where I had like-minded people around me, where that little clamouring siren's voice in the background of my mind was silenced thus allowing me to revel in my hard-won success.

But sometimes I wish, oft-times I wish, more and more times I wished that the little voice had its way with me:

- letting me relax and be spontaneous and just drift into whatever came along, and
- helping me to silence the mocking of others and of that little voice in the back of my own mind.

I could do that. I could be adrift. I could manage whatever came along. I could fit that into my chosen lifestyle. I could let go of unpleasant and demanding situations that no other would take on.

But then, wasn't I simply adjusting and applying my OCD competitive energy to achieve the goal of drifting, by planning it, organizing it, achieving it, patting myself on the back for my success in reaching this much touted state of the drift?

And yet...

A piece of driftwood is a thing of beauty. It has achieved a smooth surface from drifting through waves, wind, and sand. All edges and corners have become rounded curves. Its life and experience is evidenced in its present form; all those demanding elements having wrought a beauty that would not be possible without first going through those demanding elements.

Perhaps my arrival at the drifter lifestyle, in this *4thThird* of my life:

- is experienced in withdrawing from experiences that simply bash and break me up in waves that are too aggressive and abusive; and
- is experienced in entering into waters and winds and sands of continuing life allowing me to achieve my *Grace* as evidenced by my rounded and gently curved thinking.

Silence all little and big voices … I am engaged in the practice of drifting … Mmmmm, the lapping waves and the blowing winds … Wh…wh…wh…wh…wh.

New Perspective

Here I sit, in this comfy old rocker with just the right squeak, a shot of aged sipping whiskey in my hand warming my insides with each sip, looking out from this rustic established structure with the proven-secure roof over my head.

And I am gazing, then staring, then sensing, then taking in all that is before me.

The scent of wood surrounds me: new wood, old wood, treated wood, raw wood, damp wood, waxed wood, wood smoke; chair, stool, and table beside me, walls behind me, porch roof above me, railings in front of me, steps leading to gate beyond me. Beautiful wood that was well chosen and has known loving care for a long long time.

The colours meander their way into my consciousness, made more obvious in their rain splattered condition.

The wood varies from new wood sandy brown in the rails replaced recently, to established-wood-ebony of the rocker, to old wood weather-greyed as it stood guard silently sheltering any and all from what pours down from the skies.

Beyond the gate is a lane leading over a gentle rise and out of sight, its slate colour claiming its grounding solid presence.

Blackened stone dust lines the lane,

Canadian Shield granite colours create the stone fence piled alongside the lane over the time of generations, placed there to delineate the field where animals must remain, to be stored for future use in footings and foundations, to protect the plough from work-halting breakage caused by these same rocks if they remain in the fields where they popped up from the earth's ever-shifting depths.

To the left of the lane, beyond the stone fence, is the old gold colour of recently harvested crop. Looks like straw stubble left behind to be turned back into the earth to replenish some of what the grain took to grow its life-giving crop of oats and wheat.

And on the right, the last of the season's hay still struggling green after the final cut, where Holstein dairy cattle graze on the fall's final still-lingering fresh feast, with white hens and red rooster strutting and voicing their presence.

Beyond the usual solid mature cedar growth fencing the nearby fields, there are fields that have already been turned over for the winter, scenting the air with newly turned rich dark brown soil.

The taste of the whiskey is reminiscent of the family whiskey barrel where it spent its childhood and maturing years. Oven baked biscuits with freshly churned butter at my elbow taste like home.

Squeak, squeak, squeak ... back and forth I rock, as one with understanding the rhythm of these surroundings, and yet new to them.

My shaded two-seater swing is absent from this yard. As is the old hand pump that has produced most excellent water in abundance for family generations until it didn't during my watch on the family farm. My family's gardens are relocated to odd and unfamiliar locations, with most of their bounty long gone onto table, and into jar or freezer for winter's mealtime delights.

My hands have the evidence of a long life, serving in productive work, holding gentle onto a wee one snuggled into my neck or at my breast, holding back an animal that is ten times my weight, lifting giant pots of breakfast, lunch and dinner, brushing away the tears of a loved one, knitting love into sweaters, scarves, and toques, sewing quilts to guard my family against winter's chill. But now my hands are pale pink, with no calluses or tan, still sporting scars of life lived in activity, no fresh tears or cuts, clean neat nails that once needed attention after each day's chores.

My jeans are faded and fitting to my form, my familiar sweater starting to lose those stitches I placed there long ago. My brown leather shoes are comfortable and scuffed and fit my stool-rested feet just as if they are a second skin.

Why I am here in familiar, yet strange surroundings is just beyond my reach.

Until the womyn of the house comes out to sit, and chatter with me. From her appearance and her familiar manner of speaking with me and her gentle love, I realize that this is someone I know, someone who knows me, my history, and my real self. Someone who can answer my questions about where, why, how, when, and who. She calls me Grammum and invites me inside, beckoned by the aroma of favourite foods, warm welcome, and love. In plain sight on the side board is our family bible with all its contained family history, in the breakfront are the Bunnykins dishes from which all the family children have learned to eat, on the table is my favourite teacup that I purchased at Carp Fair instead of going on that ride all those years ago.

I have come home again, at once new and yet tantalizingly familiar.

No longer do I spend entire empty-hearted mind-numbing days sitting alone in the hall that is lined with all the other aged and unfamiliar inmates, who have the same questioning look on their faces that I surely do.

Here is the same table, the same home, the same family that have sustained me during my, apparently, long long life and where I shall spend this *4thThird* of my life.

The Older I Get

The older I get, the more I appreciate being home doing absolutely nothing.

Nothing needs doing.

Nothing to do.

I have achieved nirvana. My world is inside me, inside my heart, inside my head, inside my body.

Having completed the three Thirds of my Life, means that I have:

- spent the *1stThird* growing and learning;
- spent the *2ndThird* dancing as fast as I can while keeping body and soul and community and job together; and
- spent the *3rdThird* finding myself for myself whilst serving others, and realizing those last lifelong dreams.

Here I am, in the *4thThird*, at home within myself, within my home, within my family. I am doing absolutely nothing beyond the day-to-days, reminiscing, feeling the Love, the Light, the fulsomeness and wholeness of this plane. I simply am.

When I Die

I have spent my life trying to Live Well, and defining what that means.

Today, a Truth came to me, an epiphany, the understanding that not only do I want to live well, but I want to die well, too.

What does living well and dying well mean? Today's meanderings follow:

My conclusions about living well boil down to several understandings.

By all accounts, living in this moment is a truth, and it is one that resonates for me.

Live life on my own terms. I define what I am here to do, with the help of lessons from my Mum and all of this world's mothers, family, loved ones, and from all of my life's teachers.

To be of service to others was an aha moment for me when, as a seven year old freckled braided redhead, I was sitting in a Sunday School lesson about the Golden Rule. I bring my service to others, and my willingness to advocate on their behalf, freely offered, with love in my determination to do the work or task well, looking myself in the eye beginning and end of each day, self-affirmingly, introspectively, in a clear light, pondering what each of those mean. Is my service clear of ego, free of my own needs (including free of my will - free of my need to serve)? Is it about others or is it about me? Is it making a small corner of the Universe somehow better? Is it seen by the others as intrusive (perhaps they are not ready or don't want it)?

Dying well is, similarly, about dying on my own terms.

I will determine if I am meant to take this proffered Exit Ramp. Life offers us many forks in our path; some of those forks lead us to death and departure from this plane. This, to me, means asking, "Have I finished what my sacred contract tells me is my purpose for being here?" "Am I escaping or am I choosing to move into the next plane?" "Have I actually fulfilled my sacred contract?"

Dying well is about choosing how and when to die. Will I let life be ripped from me, kicking and screaming, railing against death? Or will I give into heroic actions of the medical community to save my life? Or will I allow myself to be called back by loved ones just because they feel that is what is expected of them? Or will I go, satisfied with my efforts, with an understanding that I will meet up with my loved ones on the other side? Will my loved ones understand that I am not gone, that they can still feel my love and can still have conversations with me?

I decided that I will orchestrate my death instead of only making a Will, Power of Attorney, Executor assignment, and Living Will efforts (though, yes, I will do all of these, as well). Rather I will choose my time and place, choose how traumatic it will be for my loved ones, not put the decision onto them.

How will I die well?

In a place that feels like home, not a sterile institution with noisy distracting clatter and beeps, surrounded by strangers. I shall die *at home*, which is to say surrounded by loved and loving ones.

I will continue to do activities that bring me Joy. Even to the last minute, I shall be cooking, researching new information, outside and feeling nature and all its elements' embrace, surrounded by others living well, too.

And when the minute comes for me to go, I shall ask loved ones around me to open a bottle of wine, drink and toast each other, and life, and this moment, past, and future.

No frantic call to 911, distracting us all from this moment. Unless, of course, it is an accident, and then, yes please stop my bleeding, start my breathing, restart my heart, set my bones, get the surgery that will cut out whatever cancer or stabbing item that needs to be taken out, but only IF it will bring me back to living well!

References that inspired me:
Do Not Stand At My Grave And Weep
by Mary Elizabeth Frye

> *Do not stand at my grave and weep*
> *I am not there. ...*

Remember
by Christina Rossetti

> *Remember me when I am gone away, ...*
> *... Better by far you should forget and smile*
> *Than that you should remember and be sad.*

A Silent Tear
(Gaynar Llewellyn)

> *Just close your eyes and you will see*
> *All the memories that you have of me ...*

Do Not Go Gentle Into That Good Night
by Dylan Thomas
Do not go gentle into that good night, ...
... Rage, Rage Against the Dying of the Light ...

Also written by Dylan Thomas:
"I hold a beast, an angel, and a madman in me, and my enquiry is as to their working, and my problem is their subjugation and victory, downthrow and upheaval, and my effort is their self-expression".

Music to Play for Me:
Amazing Grace - bagpipe version - John Newton
Magic Carpet Ride - Steppenwolf
Crazy on Me - Heart
Paradise by the Dashboard Lights - Meat Loaf
Swan Lake - Tchaikovsky
Sylvia Ballet (*Sylvia, ou La Nymphe de Diane*) - Merante and Delibes
Church in the Wildwood - Pitts
Hotel California - Eagles
Hallelujah - Leonard Cohen

4thThird: Themes, Lessons Learned, and Wisdom

I return to the basics of life: gratitude, compassion, love, peace, calm, wit, laughter, and mirth.

When I die, I want to die well, to die satisfied that I have used up all the gas in my tank, to die happily ready to go to the other side where I shall join all the others of my life who will tell me their side of all these stories.

Won't we just laugh and laugh, together.

About the Author

My Writing to Publishing Path
by Melba McGee
At Writer's Discussion Group, November 15, 2016

I stand before you to tell you about how I got this far, how I find myself at the brink of publishing my first book called 4/3, by Melba McGee.

I have been writing ever since I can remember. The first time I got my hands on a pencil, it entranced me; I picked the pencil up and held the tip to paper and *majyk* came out. I knew that I wasn't supposed to have access, but I just had to have a pencil and its *majyk*. To call it magic reduces it to a trick; *Majyk* denotes the full measure of awe and inspiration.

"Oh no, where's Melba?! There is scribbling all over the wallpaper here in the hall by the phone!"

Of course there is WRITING (NOT scribbling) by the phone! Everyone in the family writes while they are on the phone. Sometimes they write on a writing-pad, sometimes on a piece of paper, sometimes in a notebook. But they always write at some point while by the phone.

I realized that the phone must somehow be connected to the *majyk*, so I made a beeline from the pencil finding place to the phone place. I ignored the distraction of the voice demanding a "Number, please" over and over again. Without this code number, I just hoped that the majyk would still come across the phone line to me.

Sure enough, I was right and I wrote. My writing looked like the lines and pages of writing in my storybooks. And I proudly remembered to add pictures, just like in books. You know, if they had asked me, I would have been happy to read my majyk to them, telling them about who was in the majyk and what they were doing. Just like when they read to me at bedtime.

My three year old self felt decidedly left out when they read to me from their books, but they would not allow me to share my own majyk from the phone wall. I cried and clutched when they took down the 'ruined' wallpaper and replaced it with admonishments to never write there again. They would not let me keep my majyk that was so cold-heartedly ripped from the writing place by the phone, saying something about poisonous glue. Hmph!

Over the next months, I would have to hunt high and low to find a pencil and some paper. My favourite paper was brown paper grocery bags. Again with all the fuss because there was some soaking from garbage into the paper onto the furniture and linens. By that time I was desperate! You cannot just find the majyk and give it up just because everyone is hollering and angry.

Some months later, on my birthday, I received my own pencil, eraser, and diary. The pencil was yellow and my Dad used his pocket knife to make a fine tip. The eraser was pink and did not smudge. The diary had ballet dancers on it.

And then the inevitable lessons:

1. ONLY write in the diary, NEVER anywhere else.
2. Hold the pencil this way. Oh, I see you already understand that. Use the eraser to remove mistakes.
    (Mistakes, how could there ever be mistakes in majyk?!).
3. This is how to write your name. These are the letters of the alphabet. You can use your diary to practice writing your letters.
    (But this slows me down! I just want to get to the majyk part! And I don't want to waste my pages writing other

236

people's majyk. I am learning to read so I can see for myself any time I feel like other people's majyk.

But, my diary was reserved for my very own majyk!)

That story from my childhood tells why I write. I write because I must write, I need to write, to put it all on paper before the majyk evaporates, crowded out by other people's majyk. From that point, my writing path is history.

And now, who is Melba McGee.

Like Melba in this book, I am

- a child of the Universe, a fellow traveller, an Energy worker,
- a freckled redheaded free-spirited sprite,
- hyperactive and go-go-go all the time,
- darting to and fro with hair on fire and taking up all the oxygen in the room all too often,
- the product of small town Ontario and Quebec life and now living on a rural property amidst nature,
- a member of an amazing Family of two parents, three brothers, a husband, two kids, and three grandkids with whom I can share anything, who tolerate my idiosyncrasies and ground me by holding my hand whenever I have spun off the earth.

Married, retired from teaching grade 7 and 8 after 35 years in the public school system, and now living in the *3rdThird*, I am making sense of what I saw and felt by shining Light on the life of any Baby Boomer. The experiences shared in this book have some small kernel of truth, having happened in one form or another all around all of us.

I am a channel for the message that dictates that we live a meaningful life first by making sense of everything we saw, by recognizing our own Truth, by knowing who we are, and then by being of service.

CPSIA information can be obtained
at www.ICGtesting.com
Printed in the USA
LVOW11*0142180917

549077LV00006B/104/P